THE
LANGUAGE
OF THE DEAD

THE
LANGUAGE
OF THE DEAD

A WORLD WAR II MYSTERY

STEPHEN KELLY

PEGASUS CRIME
NEW YORK LONDON

THE LANGUAGE OF THE DEAD

Pegasus Books Ltd
148 West 37th Street, 13th Floor
New York, NY 10018

First Pegasus Books paperback edition July 2016
First Pegasus Books cloth edition April 2015

Interior design by Maria Fernandez

ISBN: 978-1-68177-148-9

10 9 8 7 6 5 4 3 2

Printed in the United States of America
Distributed by W. W. Norton & Company, Inc.

For the three people I love the most—Cindy,
Anna and Lauren—and for my late parents,
Edythe and Omer Kelly.

THE
LANGUAGE
OF THE DEAD

PART ONE

A Witch's Death

ONE

—⁓—

ON A LATE JULY DAY IN 1940, A BUTTERFLY, AN ADONIS BLUE, landed on a sprig of honeysuckle in a meadow above the village of Quimby, in Hampshire, and began to suck the blossom dry. Peter Wilkins noted the presence of the creature but did not move.

I must, he thought.

The words bloomed in his mind like wings opening. The boys were in the tree. Crows cawed from the branches of a dead sycamore farther down Manscome Hill. Peter gazed past the old tree toward the village.

In that same moment, Will Blackwell moved up the hill from Quimby along the ancient path that bordered the wood. The day was hot, the sun bright, and Will moved slowly under the weight of the pitchfork and scythe he rested on his right shoulder. He came to the old sycamore in which the crows roosted; for two weeks the crows

3

had been speaking to him, and the message he'd heard in their harsh cawing had troubled him. He knew the crows as carrion eaters, lickers of bones. As he passed beneath the tree, the crows dipped their heads in Will's direction and shot invective at his breast, like arrows.

Up the hill, Peter moved. Startled, the blue butterfly parted its wings and fled.

—⁜—

David Wallace sat in The Fallen Diva, his hand around a pint of local bitter.

Forty minutes earlier, he'd nipped out from the nick for what he'd told colleagues was an early supper. In fact, the detective sergeant had eaten nothing but had downed two pints of ale in less than fifteen minutes and now was on a third. He'd done his drinking at a table in a corner and spoken to no one, to decrease the chance of someone recognizing him. He felt light in the head, certainly, though not what he would call drunk. It was time, though, that he returned to work.

A young woman entered the pub and sat alone at a table near his, away from the window. The woman had pale skin, green eyes, and auburn hair and was nicely plump, busty. She wore a simple moss-green serge suit and black high heels. Wallace thought she might be waiting for someone; he watched her for a moment from his hiding place in the corner. She threw glances about the room—nervously, he thought—as if she hoped she wasn't being conspicuous. She turned in Wallace's direction and their eyes met. He smiled; she looked quickly away. He thought of approaching her but decided against it. He'd been gone from the nick too long already and faced nearly a fifteen-minute walk back; he counted on the walk to sober him up a notch. The girl was attractive enough, but with the war nearly a year old now, Winchester was full of lonely women looking for a tumble.

He rose and headed for the door. As he passed the woman's table, he caught her eye. To his surprise, she smiled. He touched the brim of his hat. He glanced at her left hand and was relieved to see that she wore no wedding band. He did not want to cuckold some poor sod in uniform.

Now, though, he had to hurry. His drinking had begun to scare him recently and he'd entertained glimpses of himself sinking to the bottom of a bottle. He stepped through the door into a warm, clear evening, feeling pleasantly elevated. Twenty minutes later, as he mounted the steps to the nick, he assured himself that he was in perfect command of his senses.

He headed for his desk, where he intended to spend the last few hours of his shift attending to paperwork. He believed he needn't worry overly much about anyone noticing his mild drunkenness, given that the only person who seemed able to unfailingly catch him out was Lamb, who had gone home for the day. In recent weeks, Wallace occasionally had detected in the Chief Inspector's expression toward him a strange combination of exasperation and empathy. He was convinced that Lamb *knew*. And yet Lamb had said nothing—issued no advice, warnings, or ultimatums. In the end, Lamb's silence had spooked more than reassured Wallace.

The phone on his desk rang, which made him jump. *Calm yourself.* He picked up the receiver. The voice on the line was that of Evers, the man on duty at the front desk.

"Have a call here I think you should take, Sarge."

Bloody hell. Wallace didn't want a call. He wanted to finish his paperwork and go home. He had a bottle of gin there. He planned to fall asleep listening to the wireless.

"Put him through," Wallace said.

"This is Constable Harris, in Quimby," a voice said.

"Go ahead, Harris."

"Well, sir, it's complicated."

Bloody hell. Here we go. "What do you mean, 'complicated,' Harris?"

"Well, sir, we have a body. A dead man."

"Hold on a second," Wallace said. "Did you say *Quimby*?"

"Yes, sir—Quimby. It's just west of—"

"I *know* where it is, Harris, thank you. Hold the line while I scare up a pencil."

Wallace found a pencil and a sheet of paper among the piles on his desk and tried to clear his head of rubbish. *A dead man in Quimby.* He must call Lamb, obviously, but would endeavor to get to the scene ahead of the Chief Inspector to take care of the preliminaries, so by the time Lamb arrived everything would be in order. He sighed and was disturbed to find that his breath smelled obviously of beer.

"Go on, Harris," he said. "I'm listening."

———

Slightly more than a mile east of Quimby, Emily Fordham pulled her bicycle off the road near the village of Lipscombe, in which she lived with her mother. She laid her bike in the lush grass at the side of the road and found a comfortable place in which to sit and study Peter's sketch anew.

She understood well enough from the sketch, and the photograph that Peter had enclosed with it, that Peter remained troubled by what had happened to Thomas the previous summer. Thomas's brief disappearance had upset them all. But that had been a year ago and, in any case, Thomas had returned. Peter knew that. But one could never tell with Peter, really.

She studied the sketch for several minutes but still could not divine what seemed to be its larger message. *A spider devouring a butterfly.* Was she *supposed* to understand its meaning? Frustrated, she folded the drawing and put it in her pocket. She would decide what to do about it later. She had to consider the idea that Peter might have sent her the sketch merely to get her attention. She knew that Peter loved her, in his way, though he didn't understand love—couldn't understand how love was different from friendship. She would ask to see Lord Pembroke about the matter. He would know the best way in which to approach Peter. She didn't want to hurt Peter's feelings.

For the past five mornings she'd awakened feeling sick and gone to the loo to retch. Although she'd flushed it away, she worried that the smell had lingered and that her mother would detect it and divine the truth. She could not let her mother know that she was carrying Charles's baby.

She had not yet even told Charles about the child. She didn't want to burden him with another worry. Instead, she prayed each day for his safe return from the skies. On some days, the Germans were forcing his squadron aloft two and even three times. She hated the Germans and their stupid war. And yet, were it not for the war, she never would have met Charles.

She decided that she shouldn't worry overly much about Peter. Peter, and all he represented, had become fragments of her past.

She cared now only for the future, for Charles and the baby growing within her.

TWO

—⚬—

DETECTIVE CHIEF INSPECTOR THOMAS LAMB SAT DOWN WITH HIS wife, Marjorie, to a tea consisting of weak coffee, two poached eggs each, and dry toast. Although they had a half-full tin of marmalade in the larder, they were rationing it—one day with and one without. Today was a "dry" day. Lamb raised his coffee to his wife.

"Cheers," he said, smiling. He had begun raising his cup and offering "cheers" at their evening meal three or four days earlier, as a kind of joke in defiance of the war's scarcities. Slightly more than ten months had passed since the war had begun and, in that time, nearly everything of any worth had shrunken and diminished—food, laughter, comfort, security. But even as he said it, Lamb wondered if Marjorie was becoming tired of his little attempt at levity. Even irony had begun to wear a bit thin as the war dragged on; the too-obvious joshing seemed to contain a whiff of defeat, of whistling in the dark.

Marjorie raised her cup and smiled slightly. "Cheers," she said.

Lamb had close-cropped brown hair that was graying prematurely at the temples and a generous smile that softened a buried intensity that shone in his eyes. He wanted a fag but long ago had stopped smoking at the table because the smoke bedeviled his wife. It drifted into her nostrils and made her sneeze and into her eyes and made them water. And the smell of the bloody things permeated everything. Lamb reckoned he did not own a single tie, shirt, coat, or pair of trousers that did not reek of cigarettes. A week earlier, he'd decided that he would give the damned things up. They were ruining his lungs and threatening to send him to an early grave.

As of yet, though, he'd had little success in quitting. He still smoked more than a packet a day—and that even as fags had become a matter of patriotism. One should not hoard boots, blankets, or food; all were needed on the front lines. The same was true of petrol. Now the government was making noise about bloody fags. Still and all, Lamb knew from his service in the first war the importance of cigarettes and liquor to frontline soldiers. Rum and fags allowed the average man to keep on despite the hellishness. Two days earlier he'd bought a tin of butterscotch drops and was attempting to train himself to pop one into his mouth each time he wanted a cigarette. Now, as he finished his coffee, he fished the tin from his pocket and denied himself what he really wanted.

He unfolded the evening edition of the *Hampshire Mail* with slight trepidation. Evenings, he normally checked the day's turf results, except on those days when he felt certain that he'd lost. That morning he'd put two pounds on a horse called Winter's Tail in the fourth race at Paulsgrove, in Portsmouth, and almost immediately a bad feeling about the bet had surged through him. Such instinctual feelings came to him now and again, he didn't know from where, and often too bloody late, he thought. He found that he couldn't quite bring himself to check the race result. He *knew* he'd lost. Two bloody quid down the drain. He and Marjorie couldn't afford it—not really. Although he didn't believe in luck, necessarily, he couldn't help feeling that his luck was running poorly at the moment.

He turned instead to the usual spate of grim war news. Less than a month earlier, the Germans had defeated France and backed the British Expeditionary Force against the Channel, at Dunkirk. Then the Germans had stopped, an uncharacteristic pause that had allowed the British to evacuate more than three hundred thousand men from France. Still, the British Army was a broken one. Then, three weeks earlier, the Germans had begun bombing southern England almost daily. The reason for this bombardment was the planned German invasion of Britain from France. If the Germans could gain control of the skies above the Channel, they then would send men and arms across to invade—to crush Britain in the same way they'd crushed France and most of the rest of Western Europe.

On four of the past eight nights, the Luftwaffe had attacked the Blenheim aircraft factory—which made bombers and lay about twenty-five miles to the southeast—though without much success. Neither side had quite yet figured out how to effectively maneuver airplanes in the dark and so the German bombers often missed the mark, and sometimes widely. Around the bomber factory they'd seemed to have blown up as much farmland and pasture as legitimate targets of war. This was partly due to the fact that the German fighters, the Messerschmitts, which escorted and protected the stodgy bombers, lacked the fuel capacity to stick around for the show once the German armada hit Britain. So they would turn and leave the bombers exposed as sitting ducks to the much faster British fighters, the Spitfires and Hurricanes. Consequently, more than a few German bombers each night turned for home and dropped their payloads willy-nilly, on all and sundry. The press had taken to calling this "tipping and running."

A month earlier, the Lambs' eighteen-year-old daughter, Vera, had taken a job in the village of Quimby as its only full-time air-raid warden and civil-defense employee. With the German bombers arriving daily, even the tiniest hamlets along the coast had begun to maintain some manner of full-time civil defense presence. Quimby lay along the route the German raiders normally followed across the Channel from France to the port city of Southampton, which also had become a principal German target. Lamb and Marjorie worried that the village could become a prime target on which frightened, failed, or merely confused German pilots might unload their payloads before scarpering back to France.

Lamb closed the paper. He knew that Marjorie had read about the previous night's bombing in Bristol and that the story likely had called up in her the same anxieties as it had in him. Even so, neither spoke of it; they'd already exhausted the subject of what they called "Vera's decision."

The telephone in the front hall rang. Lamb went into the hall and picked up the receiver.

"Lamb."

It was Wallace. "Got a body, guv; an old man, past seventy. Pretty brutal, sounds like. Someone ran a pitchfork through his neck."

"Where is it?"

Wallace hesitated a hitch. He knew about Vera Lamb's civil defense posting. "Quimby. The body was found on a hill above the village."

The news surprised Lamb. Here he'd been worried about stray Germans unloading their bombs on Quimby. He hadn't counted on a bloody maniac with a pitchfork roaming the place.

"Who called it in?"

"Local bobby. I've rung Harding and the doctor and rounded up Larkin and am heading there now."

"Do we know the old man's name?"

"William Blackwell. A farmhand. The bobby says he's pretty certain the pitchfork belonged to Blackwell himself. A farmer named Abbott had hired the old man to trim a hedgerow along the edge of his property. Blackwell lived with his niece in the village proper, apparently, and when he failed to show for his tea, the niece went looking for him and sought out Abbott, who took her to the hedge, where they found the old man. Abbott tried to remove the pitchfork from the old man's neck, after which the niece went to pieces."

"All right, David. We'll have to move the body out of there before it gets too bloody dark. I'll see you there in forty minutes or so."

"There's something else, guv. Whoever killed the old man also carved a cross into his forehead, then ran a scythe through his chest."

Bleeding hell, Lamb thought. "A cross?" he asked. "Was this man Blackwell religious, do we know?"

"Not that I know—though, according to the bobby, some in the village considered him to be a witch."

"A witch?"

"Yes, sir. So the bobby says."

"But aren't witches female?"

"I don't know, sir. Maybe the old boy was one of these witches who used a pitchfork rather than a broom." As soon as he said it, Wallace realized that the joke had not come off as he'd hoped. He counseled himself not to overdo things. He believed that Lamb had not detected any hint of the fact that, less than an hour earlier, he'd been sitting in a pub feeling elevated.

Lamb returned to the table. "I'm afraid I have to go out," he said to Marjorie. "Someone has killed an old man near Quimby." He emphasized the *near*.

Years before, Marjorie had grown used to Lamb having to leave the house at odd hours. "What happened?" she asked.

Lamb always tried to spare Marjorie the gory details of the murders he investigated. "The usual thing, I'm afraid," he said. "He probably quarreled with somebody."

"All right," Marjorie said. "If you see Vera, give her my love. And try not to stay too late." She rose, kissed Lamb's cheek, then began to clear the dishes from the table.

Lamb picked up the *Mail*, grabbed his hat, and went to his aging black Wolseley, which he parked in the lane in front of the house. He was one of the few men of his rank who drove his own car. He preferred it that way: driving himself allowed him more freedom of movement. A month earlier, though, his Wolseley had developed the habit of failing to start faithfully; sometimes he had to give the bloody thing seven or eight cranks before it turned over. He wasn't sure what the problem was—he didn't understand motorcars. But he hadn't found the time to turn the thing in to be checked. In truth, he was afraid they'd take the old car from him and he didn't want to lose it. He'd grown comfortable with it, despite its eccentricities. He understood that the entire business—becoming attached to a bloody car—was asinine. But there it was.

He settled behind the wheel and lit a cigarette. Given that he was about to go look at an old man with a pitchfork rammed through his throat and a scythe in his chest, a butterscotch wouldn't do. And he decided that he'd had enough of his own cowardice—he opened the paper to the turf results, where he discovered that his instincts had failed him: Winter's Tail had won the fourth race at Paulsgrove. Rather than being two quid lighter, he was four richer.

He pushed the starter and the ancient Wolseley sputtered to life on the first try.

He smiled slightly and thought, *Lucky indeed.*

THREE

—◦◦◦—

LAMB PULLED THE WOLSELEY TO A STOP IN FRONT OF WILL BLACKWELL'S stone cottage in Quimby. Several other dark motorcars belonging to the Hampshire police were parked by the cottage, as was the large, dark blue Buick saloon that belonged to the police surgeon, Anthony Winston-Sheed, and the van in which Blackwell's body would be transported to the hospital in Winchester.

A dozen or so villagers milled in groups by the cottage, talking quietly. Lamb felt their gaze turn toward him as he emerged from his car. He knew Quimby to be a former mill town in which many of the older residents still looked upon the police as mere extensions of the mill owners, though the owners had abandoned the place more than forty years earlier. He looked for Vera among the knots of people but did not see her.

A trio of small children—ragamuffins in torn clothing—sprinted past him, nearly bowling him over, then vanished in the twilight up a footpath near the small centuries-old stone bridge that lay at the center of the village. The bridge conveyed Quimby's High Street across Mills Run, which tumbled into the village from the top of Manscome Hill.

A bobby approached Lamb at a trot. "Inspector Lamb?" the man asked. He stopped and saluted. He was fit-looking and fresh-faced, not more than twenty-two or so. Prime cannon fodder, Lamb thought—he couldn't help it. The bobby's face was flush.

"Constable Harris, sir. Sergeant Wallace asked me to meet you."

Harris made a gesture in the direction of Blackwell's house. "This is the deceased's cottage, sir," he continued. "His niece, Lydia Blackwell, is inside. They've lived here together for many years. Miss Blackwell is rather taken out, I'm afraid, as she has seen the deceased's body. She is lying down at the moment, on the order of Mr. Winston-Sheed, who looked in on her on his way to examine the deceased. Sergeant Wallace has instructed several uniformed constables to stand by the house and let no one in other than yourself and other officials of the law. He has asked me to guide you to the scene of the crime. I'm afraid it's up the hill a bit." He hesitated again, then said: "Unless, of course, you'd rather talk to Miss Blackwell first."

Harris's brisk thoroughness impressed Lamb, though he found Harris's reference to Will Blackwell as "the deceased" irritating. He wondered if Harris always spoke as if he were giving evidence at an inquest.

"No, no," he said. "Lead on, please, Harris."

Harris saluted again and gestured toward the path by the bridge. "Right this way, sir."

As Lamb turned toward the hill, he heard Vera call him. "Dad!"

He turned to see her approaching along the High Street from the western end of the village, where she kept her daily vigil in the Quimby Parish Council hall, watching for any sign of a German invasion. She was dressed in the denim overalls and soft service cap the government issued to members of the Local Defense Volunteers.

A young man dressed in dark slacks and a bone-colored sweater kept pace with Vera. His right arm was missing from the elbow down and the right sleeve of his shirt was pinned back at the shoulder. He appeared to be no more than twenty. Lamb wondered if he had lost his arm at Dunkirk—though Dunkirk had only just happened.

Vera embraced her father briefly and kissed his cheek. They hadn't seen each other in more than a week, when Vera had spent most of a Sunday with Marjorie and Lamb at home in Winchester.

"Hello, Vera," he said, smiling. He missed her presence around the house. Even so, he kept his tone businesslike, so as not to embarrass her. "Your mother sends her love."

Vera smiled back. "Love to mother," she said. She was a slender girl, with a youthful face, though Lamb had long believed that she possessed what people sometimes called an "old soul"—a seriousness of purpose and wisdom beyond her years. She had big, bright brown eyes and smiled often and was capable of great stubbornness in defense of ideas and people she respected or loved. She glanced toward Blackwell's cottage. "It's terrible what's happened," she said.

"Yes," Lamb said. "Did you know him?"

"Not really. I heard, though, that he was just a quiet old man."

"He was a bit more than that," said the young man. He was slender and, Lamb thought, quite handsome, with luxuriant black hair that was a bit longer than normal and dark eyes that seemed fired with emotion.

"Dad, this is Arthur Lear," Vera said. "He and his father have a farm near the village." Vera smiled at Arthur Lear in a way that left Lamb feeling unsettled.

Arthur extended his lone hand—his left—and smiled. "Pleased to meet you, sir," he said.

"The pleasure's mine," Lamb said, shaking Arthur's hand.

"Well, we should let you go, Dad," Vera said. "I'm sure you're busy and we don't want to get in the way. We only heard an hour or so ago."

Seeing her father had left Vera feeling more conflicted than she'd guessed it would. She might have come without Arthur—kept him a secret. She probably should have done. Her feelings about him had begun to change recently, and she'd begun to worry if she'd done the right thing in allowing herself to become so quickly involved with him.

"Well, I'm glad you came," Lamb said. "If I have time, I'll stop by your billet."

She smiled. "No need, Dad. You've got a lot to do and I'm fine."

Lamb wondered if Vera planned on going back to her billet with Arthur Lear. "All right," he said. He wanted to kiss her on the fore-head—but that, too, would embarrass her. "I'll give your love to your mother." He turned toward Arthur. Arthur certainly had his eye on Vera, he decided. He felt bad that the boy had lost his arm, but he also understood how a lost arm might play to Arthur's advantage.

Vera nodded farewell to her father, then she and Arthur went back down the High Street toward her billet. As he watched her go, Lamb felt that Vera had moved to a point in her life in which she was all but out of his reach. Strangely, he hadn't seen that moment coming, as he should have.

He turned to Harris. "Let's go, Constable," he said.

—⁓—

Lamb and Harris moved up Manscome Hill through an area bordered on their left by meadows and hedges and on their right by a small wood.

The twilight air had grown cool and redolent of the fragrances of wildflowers and windblown grasses. Bees and butterflies busied themselves in the meadows, and the first bats appeared. Small birds occasionally darted from thickets to alight on sagging fences. The sun had eased its way down to a point just beneath the tops of the highest trees of the wood to their right, slanting shadows across the footpath.

They soon passed a gate through which the path branched off and led to George Abbott's farmhouse. Their passing frightened a flock of fat sheep that scuttled, bleating, off the path into a meadow.

"You were the first called to the scene?" Lamb asked Harris.

"Yes, sir. The body was discovered by Miss Blackwell and Mr. Abbott; seems Miss Blackwell missed her uncle when he failed to show for his tea. The deceased was, according to his niece, a man of singular habits who never missed his tea. So when he failed to show after Miss Blackwell had finished her own tea, she began to worry and came up the hill to fetch Mr. Abbott, who had hired the deceased to trim the hedges along one of his fields."

"So they went in search of Mr. Blackwell together, then?" Lamb asked.

"Yes, sir. According to Miss Blackwell, Mr. Abbott went directly to the spot. Afterward, they called me from the pub—I live in Moresham—then went to Miss Blackwell's cottage, where I met them. That was about half past six. When I arrived, Miss Blackwell was still very much in a state. They led me to the scene, after which I told Mr. Abbott to wait at his house. I escorted Miss Blackwell back to her cottage. I then telephoned the constabulary and spoke to Sergeant Wallace."

They passed beneath a massive, long-dead sycamore near a small wooden bridge that conveyed the path across Mills Run. From here, the creek moved into, through, and out the opposite side of the wood to their right, where it once had powered a grain mill, which had lain abandoned now for nearly fifty years and fallen into ruin.

Once they were across the footbridge, Harris led Lamb off the path into the meadow on their left, where they began a gentle, sloping climb of about a hundred meters to the place where Will Blackwell's body lay. Several people stood in a rough circle around the old man's body. One of these was Wallace, who approached Lamb.

"Evening, sir," he said, touching the brim of his fedora. As usual, Wallace was dressed in a smart-looking dark suit. He wore a yellow silk tie and an expensive-looking pair of black patent leather shoes, which had become stained with mud.

"What have we got?" Lamb asked.

"A complicated scene, I'm afraid. We've photographed the body and the immediate surrounding area. We're trying to get the out-of-door matters cleared up before it gets dark."

The doctor, Winston-Sheed, was kneeling next to the body, while Cyril Larkin, the forensics man, stood by. Lamb exchanged nods of greeting with them, then turned his attention to the body.

Will Blackwell's arms were flung away from his body, as if in a gesture of ecstatic welcome, and his legs spread wide. The position of the old man's limbs put Lamb in mind of a child lying in the snow making angels. The leftmost tine of a rusting pitchfork with a worn, weathered handle was thrust into the center of his neck while a scythe with a curved blade of roughly twenty inches long—also partly rusted—protruded from his chest. A copious amount of blood had pooled in the dry grass around the body, and the old man's eye sockets were full of fleshy pulp.

"Best guess at the moment is that he's been dead about six or seven hours," Winston-Sheed said. "It appears he put up no fight. My guess is that he was first knocked unconscious, probably from behind. The killer then thrust the scythe and the pitchfork into him. Given the amount of blood around the head and neck, I'd say the pitchfork came first; the lack of blood from the chest argues that he was dead when the killer drove the scythe in there. Still, either one would have killed him outright; the second would have been unnecessary if the killer's goal merely was to send Mr. Blackwell to the hereafter. Both implements are buried very deep, which would suggest that the old man was on his back and not resisting when the thrusts were made."

Winston-Sheed stood and pulled a tarnished silver cigarette case from the pocket of his waistcoat. "At some point the killer carved a cross into his forehead, also post-mortem," he continued. "It's possible the cross was inscribed with the tip of the scythe. As for his eyes, they appear to have been pecked out. Crows, probably. I shouldn't wonder that when we take a look at this mess in the light of morning, we shall see their unpleasant little footprints in the ground around the body. In fact, the little blighters have stuck around for the show."

Winston-Sheed nodded in the direction of the dead sycamore, a hundred meters down the hill. Eight or nine silent crows roosted in the tree's crooked branches. Lamb thought that they seemed to be waiting for the human interlopers to leave so they could resume their feast. They reminded him of the rats that scurried through the trenches on the Somme and over the rotting bodies lying in no man's land—opportunists attuned to death. One of the birds suddenly took off from the tree and made its way across the meadow, as if it realized that Lamb was scrutinizing it and was guilty.

Winston-Sheed offered Lamb a cigarette from his silver case. "Thanks, but no," Lamb said. The pain of refusal was nearly physical. Reluctantly, he dug into the pocket of his jacket, found the tin of butterscotches, and popped one into his mouth.

Lamb stared at the body for a moment, rolling the candy in his mouth. The killer seemed to have posed the old man, he thought. "It all seems too bloody obvious somehow, doesn't it?" he said finally, as much to himself as to Winston-Sheed. "Too dressed up."

Winston-Sheed lit a cigarette. He was a tall, slender man of about forty. His father was some sort of titled someone—Lamb was not sure who, or from where. His appearance, speech, and manner bespoke the casual elegance of a born aristocrat, though he was not averse to dirtying himself at a crime scene and was tireless in the work he did on behalf of the constabulary. Winston-Sheed exhaled and looked at the sky, which was growing darker. In Quimby and all over England, the blackout soon would fall. That meant all outdoor lights extinguished, all windows shuttered or curtained, and no torches. Even fags were discouraged, for fear that their glow might give the German bombers a target.

Winston-Sheed looked at his cigarette with affection. "I sincerely hope this doesn't bring the Stukas down on us," he said. "It's rather too uncivilized to think that we should go without a fag now and again just to avoid attracting a few bombs." He took a long drag of the cigarette, which made Lamb jealous. "There is rather a baroque viciousness to the thing, certainly," the doctor said, returning to the matter at hand.

"Given the depth of the wounds, the killer must have been a man, yes?" Lamb asked.

"I should think so," Winston-Sheed said. "Either that or a very strong and vicious woman."

Lamb examined Blackwell's clothes, digging into the pockets of his trousers and jacket, but found them empty save for a scrap of paper upon which someone—presumably Blackwell—had written, in a shaky hand: *in the nut.* He held the note out so that Wallace and Winston-Sheed could read it. "What do you make of this?" he asked.

"Damned if I know," Wallace said. "Perhaps something to do with gathering nuts? They do that sort of thing hereabouts, I would imagine. Gathering nuts and berries and the like."

"Perhaps," Lamb said absently. He pulled a billfold from his pocket and placed the note within it. He looked at the sky; they had perhaps an hour of decent light in which to work. They would have to accomplish what they could for the moment and save the rest for tomorrow.

"Have you done all you need to do for now?" he asked Winston-Sheed.

"For now, yes," the doctor said.

Lamb stepped away from the body. "All right, then, Mr. Larkin—your turn," he said to the forensics man. "We'll have to move quickly."

Larkin was a tall, reed-thin young man whose dark suits didn't fit him properly; his trouser legs and the sleeves of his jacket always appeared to be several inches too short for his limbs. He wore heavy-framed glasses with thick lenses that invariably slid down his nose. When Lamb had first met Larkin, he'd thought *The bloody forensics man can't see!* But he'd discovered that Larkin possessed a kind of lanky, wiry energy and a good mind.

Larkin had come to the constabulary two months earlier, after Hampshire's longtime forensics man, Harold Llewellyn, had joined the RAF as a medical officer. Lamb had liked and trusted Llewellyn and had been sorry to lose him. But he also knew that Llewellyn was to be only the first of many solid, skilled men the war would vacuum up. First, the experienced, able-bodied men would go off to battle, to be replaced by the less experienced and able. Then, if the thing dragged on long enough, even these replacements would be taken up, to be replaced by—who? He could see a time coming when solving domestic crimes, even murder, might get pushed so far down the list of priorities that it ceased to matter.

Worse for Lamb even than the loss of Llewellyn, though, was the departure into the Army of DI Richard Walters, his primary lieutenant and good friend. He and Dick Walters had come of age together in the Hampshire Constabulary. Two months earlier, as the Germans were on the verge of defeating France, Walters had quit the police in a surge of patriotism and entered the Army as a captain of military intelligence. Lamb admired Walters's spirit and partly shared it. But he was not about to leave Marjorie and Vera for a foreign field. He'd done his bit the first time round. Police Superintendent Anthony Harding had not yet replaced Walters, though the super had told Lamb less than a week earlier that a transfer was due in soon from up north.

Larkin stepped forward, pushing his glasses up the bridge of his nose. He looked at Lamb and smiled, clearly pleased to be on the case. "It's not every day we get a case like this one," he said with genuine enthusiasm.

"No," Lamb replied. "It certainly isn't."

As he spoke, the murder of crows roosting in the distant sycamore arose as one with a squawk and disappeared into the wood.

FOUR

—✺—

THE PROCESSION CARRYING WILL BLACKWELL'S BODY MOVED slowly down Manscome Hill, along the old footpath.

Larkin had collected the murder weapons, though yanking them from the old man's body had required that he and Wallace work in tandem. They'd bundled the body into a canvas bag and put it on a stretcher. Four uniformed constables carried the stretcher down the hill, accompanied by the others. A knife-gash of light remained on the western horizon and the stars had become visible. Despite the blackout, Winston-Sheed led the way with a torch, its beam dancing along the path, the bright red tip of the cigarette between his lips keeping to the same rhythm.

Lamb halted the group when it reached the gate through which the path veered in a spur toward George Abbott's house. He instructed Winston-Sheed to go ahead with the body and Harris to inform Blackwell's niece that he would be down to speak with her shortly.

Lamb and Wallace moved through the gate and down the path toward Abbott's house, which nestled among a stand of oaks just beyond the meadow. The same flock of fat sheep that Lamb and Harris had frightened on their march up the hill earlier that evening noisily trotted away again, their white bodies partly dissolved in the gloom, giving them the character of clouds moving across a dark sky.

"What was the gist of what he told you when you interviewed him initially?" Lamb asked Wallace of Abbott. When Wallace had first arrived on the scene, he'd conducted brief interviews with Abbott and Will Blackwell's niece, Lydia.

"He hired the old man regularly for such work—or so he said," Wallace said. "Made a point, in fact, of saying as how he didn't really have to give Blackwell any work—that half of it could just as well have waited or gone undone. But he knew Blackwell hadn't much else. He made it sound as if he were Blackwell's benefactor."

Wallace nimbly hopped a pile of sheep droppings, saving his shoe and the cuff of his pants from being soiled. He'd been sober for more than two hours and felt free and clear for the moment.

"Abbott said the niece came to his door in the middle of his tea and told him that the old man had not returned for his," Wallace continued. "Apparently the old fellow was as reliable as a clock when it came to his meals. So Abbott led the way up the hill to the hedge and the two of them found him there. The niece went to pieces, according to Abbott. He tried to restrain her but she broke free of his grasp. He said he tried to remove the pitchfork and the scythe in an effort to calm her. When he couldn't get them free, he thought better of touching anything—realized that he should leave well enough alone. Or so he told me. He managed to calm the girl and persuade her to walk back to the village with him. I had Larkin take his prints, which he grumbled about. He has the aspect of an embittered old country arsehole. But I got the impression he's no fool."

They were nearly to the house.

"What about the niece?" Lamb asked.

"When the doc arrived, he had a look at her and gave her a sedative—though I think it was a bit of placebo. Salt tablets, perhaps. In any case, they seem to have done the trick in that she began to calm down once she swallowed them."

"What was her story?"

"The same as Abbott's. She began to worry when old Mr. Blackwell didn't come home and so went to fetch Abbott. The two of them went up the hill to find Blackwell and she saw her uncle's body and the state it was in. As I was interviewing her, she began to cry—fell right apart—so I let it be for the moment."

Here was the one thing in which Wallace feared he might have bollixed things before Lamb arrived. He'd gone soft when he shouldn't have. He turned to Lamb. "She seemed so upset that I thought it unlikely that she was going to give up much more of use at that point."

Lamb would have preferred that Wallace had gotten as much as possible from the niece at the outset, before she'd had time to solidify her story. But he let the mistake go.

They reached the door of Abbott's house. A young PC whom Lamb didn't recognize answered Wallace's rap on the door.

"I take it our man hasn't flown the coop?" Wallace said to the constable.

"Not a chance, Sarge. He's in the kitchen, drinking tea. He offered me a cup, but I declined." The constable smiled at Wallace. "Didn't want him to get the impression that I was in the mood to be friendly, like."

"Very good, Pearson," Wallace said. "You can return to the village now."

"Yes, sir," Pearson said. He headed toward the gate, sending the sheep bounding away again.

Abbott appeared in the parlor as Wallace and Lamb stepped inside. Wallace introduced Lamb to Abbott. "We'd like to ask you a few more questions," Wallace told Abbott.

Abbott grunted; his big toes protruded through identical holes in his dirty green wool socks. "Can't sleep anyway," he said, as if the matter of his interrogation was up to him. "Not after seeing Will like that."

Abbott was short, stocky, squared off at the shoulders. Despite his age—Lamb guessed that he was in his early sixties—he exuded an impression of physical strength. His manner, the way in which he stood, as if prepared to take a punch, put Lamb in mind of a boxer. Abbott had a head of thick, tousled, unwashed gray hair, deep-set dark eyes, and graying stubble on his chin. He held a cup of tea in his hand and a cigarette in his lips. Once again, Lamb reached for his tin of butterscotch.

Abbott turned and headed back into his small kitchen, which was dominated by a round wooden table at its center. An open bottle of whiskey sat on the table. Lamb could see no hint of a feminine presence in Abbott's life, and yet he could see how Abbott might hold sway over an apparently lonely and isolated spinster such as Lydia Blackwell.

Abbott sat at the table and poured some whiskey into his tea. He held the bottle aloft and waggled it in the direction of Lamb and Wallace.

"Care for a nip?" he asked. Wallace eyed the bottle. He would have loved a drink.

"Sergeant," Lamb said and nodded at the tea. Wallace snatched Abbott's tea from the table and poured it into the sink. He then snatched away the bottle.

"My bloody tea!" Abbott protested.

Lamb cast a cold gaze at the farmer. "I'd prefer that you remain sober while I question you, Mr. Abbott," he said.

"It ain't right of you to take my tea."

Lamb ignored him and sat down. Wallace wiped his hands on a towel by the sink and also sat at the table.

"How long have you known Will Blackwell?" Lamb asked Abbott.

Abbott ground out the cigarette he had been smoking in a small ceramic bowl that was full of ground-out cigarettes. He pulled another from a pack on the table, placed it between his lips and, squinting, lit it with a match he struck against the bottom of his shoe. He was stalling before answering—an act, Lamb knew, that was designed to show that he would not be intimidated, even if they could take his tea from him.

"All my life—like I told your man there when he questioned me earlier," Abbott said, nodding in Wallace's direction.

"Were you friendly with him?"

"Aye—as much as a man could be a friend to Will."

"What do you mean?"

"Well, Will kept to himself mostly. Didn't fancy people much, did he?"

"You hired Will to trim your hedge today?"

"Aye."

"And when did he head out to the job?"

"I saw him coming up the hill from his cottage at about half past eleven. But I didn't keep an eye on him now, did I? Wasn't my brother's keeper. Just told him what needed done and he'd do it in his own time."

"And Will brought his own tools to the job?"

Abbott blew smoke at the ceiling. "Aye."

"And he used those tools on this job for which you hired him?"

"Aye, them were Will's tools." He grunted. "Can I have my tea if I put nothing in it save milk and sugar?"

Lamb nodded at Wallace. "Get him some tea, please, Sergeant," he said. He turned back to Abbott. "When Miss Blackwell came to your door, you led her directly to the body, is that right?" he asked.

"Aye."

"How did you know that Will would be there?"

"Well, I sent him there myself, didn't I? Hired him to trim that very hedge."

"But wouldn't he ordinarily have finished that job hours earlier? What made you believe he would still be there at nearly six o'clock in the evening?"

"Well, I didn't know. I guessed, didn't I? Used the common sense God gave me. I thought that maybe his heart had failed him—that the exertion of the cutting might have done him in. So I went to the hedge. And when I seen them crows rise from him, I knew the truth."

Wallace put a cup of tea in front of Abbott.

"Would you have liked to have seen Will die a natural death up there, Mr. Abbott?" Lamb asked. "You just said that you thought the work might kill him. And yet you sent him up there. Were you hoping he would die?"

Lamb was fishing. He expected Abbott to protest. Instead the farmer narrowed his eyes and asked, "What are you getting at?"

Lamb ignored the question. "So you saw Will only once today, when he was heading up the hill?"

"As I said." He hunched closer to the table and encircled his cup of tea with his arms.

"You didn't go up the hill to check on him—to check on his work—during the day?"

"I'd no reason to. Will could take care of himself."

"What is your relationship with Miss Blackwell?"

Abbott stared at his cup. "I have no relationship with the woman."

"No?" Lamb asked. "You being a single man and she a single woman? And she living right down the hill? Nothing has ever passed between you? You've never looked on Miss Blackwell and thought to yourself, 'I could use a bit of that'? And then one thing leads to another, as it naturally would?"

"No!" Abbott said in a tone that suggested that the question insulted him. "I've never laid a finger on the woman. Never had no cause nor desire to."

"Oh, come now, Mr. Abbott," Wallace interjected. "Nobody would blame you if you had. A younger, available woman and a lonely soul, such as yourself? Maybe she fancied you as well, eh? Maybe she offered herself to you? Any man in your position would say aye to that. As the inspector said, it's only natural now, isn't it?"

"I told you—I never touched her!" Abbott said. Although Abbott's eyes were full of fire, Lamb sensed that Abbott was attempting to bring his anger under control, perhaps worried that it made him appear defensive and guilty. Smoldering, Abbott drew in a lung full of smoke, then exhaled it.

"Had you and Mr. Blackwell quarreled over anything recently?" Lamb asked.

"No," Abbott said. He stared at the table.

"How much did you pay Will for these jobs for which you hired him?"

"Two bob or thereabouts. Sometimes more, sometimes less, depending on the job."

"And how often did you hire him?"

"Whenever I needed the odd job done. A few times a month."

"Did you hire Will for all of these odd jobs because you owed him something? A debt, perhaps?"

"Well, Will didn't have anything else, did he?" Abbott said. "He'd gotten too old to work as he used to. Nobody in the bloody village hired him for anything anymore. None of them gave a damn for Will. Had I not hired him, he would have had nothing."

"And why is that?"

Abbott hesitated—then laughed. "You mean to say, then, that you don't know?"

"Why don't you fill me in?" Lamb said.

"Well, it's common knowledge that some in the village thought Will to be a witch."

"What do you mean by that?" Lamb asked. "A witch?"

"Just as I said. A witch. You know—one of them that rides around on brooms and make potions out of toads' ears?" He slapped the table and laughed. "Toil, toil, bubble and boil, eh?"

"I haven't the time for your jokes, Mr. Abbott," Lamb said. "In fact, I've half a mind to take you in right now and charge you with Will Blackwell's murder."

Wallace tried to hide his surprise. Abbott appeared shocked.

"What are you on about?" Abbott asked. "I told you I never killed Will! I only tried to help him."

"I've no doubt we'll find your fingerprints on the murder weapons," Lamb said.

"Here!" Abbott said. "I tried to pull them out of Will. I was only trying to calm Lydia! When she seen her uncle, she went into hysterics."

"So you say. But I find that story far too convenient, Mr. Abbott."

"I say it again—I had nothing to do with Will's murder!"

Lamb thumped the table with his fist. "Then answer my bloody questions!" he said. He allowed the silence that followed to linger for a few seconds. He looked at Abbott and said, "Now tell me what you mean when you say people thought Will to be a witch."

Abbott's voice was quiet. "Well, he'd seen the Black Shuck, hadn't he? The black dog. When he were ten. And once that happened, his sister suddenly died and no one knew why."

"The Black Shuck?" Lamb asked.

"Aye," Abbott said. "The hell hound. The dog that appears to those who have allowed the devil into their souls."

"And where did Will see this dog, according to the story?"

"Here on the hill."

"Other than to have seen this dog, did Mr. Blackwell do anything else that would have made people believe him a witch?" Lamb asked. "Were there rumors that he cast spells or got up to mischief?"

"There were always rumors about Will," Abbott said. "When some of the autumn wheat came in bad last year, some blamed him for that. Said he'd run toads over the crop in the night."

"Toads?"

"Yeah. Said he'd harnessed them like a team of horses and run them over the crops, as did the witches of older days."

"Did you believe that Will practiced witchcraft, Mr. Abbott?" Lamb asked.

"No. I never put no stock in that mumbo-jumbo. But if you want to know about it, you can ask the bloody lord of the manor himself, can't you? Lord Pembroke. He wrote a whole bloody book about it, didn't he? Ghostly legends of Hampshire and the like. Strange subject for a lord, I say. Has Will's story in it. Will never liked the fact that his story was dredged up again, I can tell you. And while you're at it, you can track down that mute boy Pembroke has living with him—though you'd need some magic for certain to get anything out of him."

"Which mute boy?" Lamb asked.

"The one who lives on Lord Pembroke's estate; spends his time drawing insects and the like. He used to walk over from the estate and spend time with Will. He would sit and watch Will work and make his drawings and that. Will didn't seem to mind. But there are those about who said that Will was training the boy to take his place, as if he were Will's apprentice, like."

"How old is this boy?" Lamb asked.

Abbott shrugged. "Hard to tell. Fourteen, maybe fifteen. Maybe more. He don't talk. Won't even so much as look at me. He just wanders over here from the estate and makes his insect drawings. He avoided everybody save Will."

"Do you know this boy's name?"

Abbott shrugged again. "No. Like I said, he don't talk."

"Where were you this afternoon between noon and two?" Lamb asked.

"About the farm, working. Cutting hay, mostly."

"Can anyone vouch for your whereabouts?"

"I saw no one."

"Very well, then, Mr. Abbott," Lamb said. "We may have further questions, so I advise you not to leave the area."

Abbott did not look up from his tea. "Where would I go in any case?" he said.

FIVE

—⚏—

LAMB AND WALLACE SAW THEMSELVES OUT. FOR THE FOURTH TIME
that evening, the sheep by the gate scattered. Lamb lit a cigarette.

"What about the Stukas?" Wallace joked.

"Sod the bloody Stukas."

As they moved down Manscome Hill in the dark, Lamb gazed
over the moonlit meadows. He easily picked out details in the
landscape—hillocks, trees, shrubs, a ramshackle shed by a gate,
another ghostly flock of sheep grazing on a far hill. Although
he'd grown up in south London, the natural beauty and apparent
peacefulness of the countryside always had attracted him. As a
boy, he'd harbored a notion of the country as "simple," though
since coming to Hampshire more than twenty years earlier he'd
learned that the country villages—and country folk—often were
nothing of the sort.

Wallace longed to finish and to get back to Winchester before the pubs closed. "What do you make of this witchcraft business?" he asked Lamb, partly to get his mind off drink.

"I think it's possible that someone wants us to believe the whole thing's wrapped up in black magic."

"What about Abbott?"

"He might easily have done it."

"Him and the niece, then? The two of them getting up to something and needing the old boy out of the way?"

"It's possible."

It was past nine when they reached the village. Winston-Sheed had departed with Blackwell's body, and the people who'd gathered in front of Blackwell's cottage earlier had gone home—though the three children who'd sprinted past Lamb earlier that evening had returned and were loitering near the house. They appeared poised to run again, but when Lamb called to them they froze.

The oldest, a boy who had no shoes, appeared to be nine or ten. The other two were girls. Their arms and legs were dark with filth. The youngest looked to be about three. She clutched in her tiny fist a stick with a pointed end. As Lamb squatted to speak to them, they remained rooted, their eyes wary. Lamb wondered what they were up to, out at such a late hour with no one looking after them.

He smiled. "Here now," he said. "What are you lot on about at this time of night?"

None of them spoke.

"I hope it's nothing I wouldn't want to know about," Lamb said.

The children continued to stare at him for perhaps ten seconds before the boy spoke. "We was waiting for the witch to come home," he said.

"Well, I'm afraid you're out of luck," Lamb said. "There are no witches around here and never have been."

"Old Will's a witch," the boy said.

"I'm afraid that's not true," Lamb said. "Will was no witch. I'm from the police, you know, and I've done an investigation of the matter and concluded that Will was nothing of the kind. So there are no witches." He wondered what good any of this was doing.

Lamb held out his hand to the youngest girl and softly said to her, "I'll take that stick, love. That's nothing for a pretty little girl like you to be carrying around."

The girl tossed the stick in Lamb's direction. He picked it up and handed it to Wallace.

"Now then," he said to the group. "Where do you belong?"

The boy pointed toward the path beyond the stone bridge, which led to the mill ruins.

"Well, time for you to be off home now," Lamb said. "Time for bed."

He wondered what awaited them at home—likely nothing as wholesome as a proper putting-to-bed. If the Blitzkrieg reached England, little ones such as these would be consumed like so much underbrush in a forest fire, he thought.

The boy broke into a run, heading in the direction of the path. The girls followed. Lamb watched them cross the bridge and disappear.

Harris met Lamb and Wallace at the front door of Blackwell's cottage. "No one has gone in or come out," Harris said. "Miss Blackwell is still awake."

"Thank you, Harris," Lamb said. "Please stay until we're finished with Miss Blackwell. Then I think you can call it a night."

A large black car crossed the stone bridge and pulled to a stop near the cottage. Lamb and Wallace recognized the saloon as police Superintendent Anthony Harding's.

"A bit late for the old man, isn't it?" Wallace asked.

Lamb sighed. "I don't think it's ever too late for him." He turned to Harris. "Wait here, please, Constable."

Harding stepped from the rear seat of the car with a man Lamb recognized immediately, although he had not seen the man—nor had he wanted to—in more than twenty years. The sight of Harry Rivers so stunned Lamb that he literally stopped. He immediately understood what was happening—Harry Rivers was to be Dick Walters's replacement.

"Good evening, gentlemen," Harding said. "It sounds as if we've rather a mess here."

"Nothing we can't handle, sir," Wallace said.

Harding glanced at Wallace; the super considered Wallace a good detective, though volatile and potentially unreliable; Wallace secretly loathed Harding as pompous. Lamb, though, trusted and respected Harding's blunt honesty.

Harry Rivers moved next to Harding, who was unaware of the past that Rivers and Lamb shared. "This is DI Harry Rivers," Harding said. "He'll be replacing Dick Walters, at least for the time being. He comes to us from Warwickshire, where, as we're all aware, the Germans aren't dropping as many bloody bombs." Harding nodded at Lamb and Wallace. "DCI Tom Lamb and DS David Wallace."

Wallace offered Rivers his hand. "Rivers," he said. "Welcome aboard."

"Thanks," Rivers said, shaking Wallace's hand.

Rivers turned to face Lamb. "Lieutenant," he said. "It's been a long time."

"Yes," Lamb said. "Quite a long time, Harry."

"You two know each other, then?" Harding asked, looking from Lamb to Rivers, genuinely surprised.

"Second Somme," Rivers said. "Fourth London. DCI Lamb was my direct commanding officer." Rivers smiled slightly, a smile lacking warmth. "He was Second Lieutenant Lamb then. I was Sergeant Rivers."

"Old comrades, then," Harding said, bringing his hands together, pleased. "All the better."

The four men stood close together for a couple of seconds in silence. Wallace sensed Lamb's discomfort.

"Rivers arrived a few hours ago," Harding said. "Given that we have a bit of a juicy situation here, I thought it best that he jump right in. Old man with a pitchfork in his neck, then?"

"That and a bit more," Lamb said.

"And there's a possible witchcraft angle of some kind?"

"Well, there's some talk that the dead man was known in the village to be a witch or warlock or something of the kind."

"What's the bloody difference?" Harding asked.

"I don't know," Lamb said. "It might turn out to be nothing."

"A ruse, then? Well, let's not let it distract us overly much. In the meantime, the three of you can get to work on it together from the start line."

Lamb thought of asking Harding if Rivers wouldn't be more useful clearing up Walters's backlog. But that would sound puny and calculating. He didn't want to work with Rivers and doubted that Rivers wanted to work with him. His last impression of Harry Rivers had been of how thoroughly Rivers had loathed him, though he knew Rivers's hate to have been misplaced, a kind of war casualty rooted in genuine grief, and guilt. For that reason, Lamb hadn't entirely begrudged Rivers his antipathy. But when the war had finished, Lamb had been glad to rid himself of it and of Harry Rivers. He'd joined the Hampshire police, married Marjorie, and got on with his life.

"Very well, then, I'll leave the three of you to it," Harding said. "We'll meet tomorrow at the nick, eight A.M. You can fill me in then." He rose slightly on his toes. "Rivers has taken rooms for the moment in Winchester. I'm expecting that one of you can give him a lift back."

"I can give DI Rivers a lift," Lamb said. He glanced at Rivers, who seemed not to react to his offer, which would sequester them alone in a car for the half-hour drive back to Winchester.

"Splendid," Harding said. He climbed into the back seat of the saloon and left.

Lamb turned toward the door of Will Blackwell's cottage with Wallace and Harry Rivers in tow. He rummaged in his pocket for the butterscotch tin.

—⚬—

Earlier, Harris had given Wallace a brief history of the relationship Will Blackwell had shared with his niece, Lydia, and Wallace had delivered the same history to Lamb as they'd descended Manscome Hill. Lydia had come to live with her uncle thirty years earlier, at the age of eight, after her mother, who was Will's sister, had died. She worked as a seamstress for a small factory in a village north of Southampton that made woolen coats and had done so for as long as anyone could remember. She seemed to have no men in her life beside her uncle and, like her uncle, generally kept to herself.

Before they entered the cottage, Wallace delivered to Rivers a brief summary of Abbott's and Lydia Blackwell's story of finding Blackwell's body, along with the fact that Abbott denied sharing any close relationship to Lydia. Rivers found the story dubious.

The detectives removed their hats as they entered Will Blackwell's cottage. The cottage's ground floor consisted of a small rectangular space that was divided into a mudroom, kitchen, and sitting room. Cut-up dark woolen blankets shrouded the windows. Lydia sat in a green upholstered chair, near a cold fireplace, in the sitting room. She clutched a robin's-egg-blue handkerchief embroidered with yellow lace.

Lamb noticed in the kitchen a round table surrounded by four wooden chairs. "Fetch us some chairs, please, Constable," he said to Harris.

While Harris got the chairs, Lamb approached Lydia. Her face was flushed and her fingers skeletal, the skin stretched tight over them. One of the pins she used to keep up her brown hair had come loose so that a strand slightly obscured her right eye. Lamb wondered what sort of relationship she'd had with her uncle—an old bachelor sharing a cottage in a remote village with a younger female relative.

Harris placed three chairs from the kitchen near the hearth. Lamb introduced himself, Wallace, and Rivers, and asked Lydia Blackwell's permission to sit in her parlor. He sensed that few people bothered to ask Lydia Blackwell's permission for anything.

"Yes," Lydia said. "Yes, sir." She straightened in her chair.

The policemen sat before her; Rivers sat next to Lamb, a move Lamb thought deliberate. Wallace removed a small notebook and pencil from the pocket of his jacket, flipped open the book, and laid it on his knee.

"First, let me say that I am sorry about your uncle," Lamb said.

Lydia sniffed. "Yes," she said. "Will were a good man."

"Constable Harris tells me that you arrived home from work this evening and found Will gone."

"Yes. Will never misses his tea. I usually get home from my job a little after five and wash up the dishes."

"And where is Will, usually, when you arrive home from work?"

"Sitting here in front of the fire," she said. She gestured to the wooden chair that faced the hearth. "Smoking his pipe."

"He never went out after his tea—say for an evening constitutional?" Rivers interjected.

"No," Lydia said. "He waits for me to wash up the tea things, then to cook my own meal. Then he sits with me while I eat."

Lamb noticed that Lydia continued to speak of her uncle as if he were alive. If this was an act to convince him of her grief and devastation, it was a sophisticated one, he thought.

"And did you talk while you ate?" Lamb asked. Rivers glanced quickly and queerly at Lamb, as if he thought the question irrelevant.

"Yes."

"What about?"

"He usually tells me about his day, though sometimes he likes to talk to me about his birds."

"His birds?"

"Yes, sir. Will believes that he can talk to birds and they to him. He can entice a songbird, a sparrow, like, to eat right out of his hand."

Lamb decided to leave alone for the moment the subject of Will Blackwell's alleged ability to communicate with birds. He could see, though, how such beliefs and behaviors might have led some of the least-educated souls of Quimby to believe Will a witch.

"Had Will spoken to you in recent days or weeks about something that might have been weighing on his mind?" Lamb asked.

"No, sir."

"How about a dispute he might have been having with someone? Had he a row or an argument?"

"No. Will didn't spend much time with other people."

"So Will hadn't had a disagreement with Mr. Abbott recently?"

The question seemed to surprise Lydia. "No," she said quickly. "Will didn't have no disputes with people."

"But everyone has disputes with people, Miss Blackwell," Rivers interjected.

Lydia looked at Rivers with something like wariness in her eyes. Lamb worried that Rivers's bluntness might cause Lydia to fold up her wings. Apparently, Rivers hadn't changed much since the war.

"Will didn't," she said to Rivers. "He stayed away from people."

"Except for yourself and Mr. Abbott, of course," Rivers said. He didn't bother to hide the sarcasm in his tone.

Lydia glanced at the floor. "Yes."

Lamb leaned forward in his chair and rested his hands between his knees. "How did your uncle treat you, Miss Blackwell?" he asked. "Did he treat you well?"

"How did he treat me, sir?" she asked.

"Yes. Was he kind to you? Did he have a temper? You told us that you washed up his tea things every day, even though you had yourself just returned from a full day's work. If you weren't prompt in this, might Will have become angry with you?"

"Washing up is one of the jobs I do to earn my keep," she said, as if the answer to Lamb's question was self-evident.

"So when Will failed to return for his tea, you went to Mr. Abbott, is that correct?" Lamb asked.

"Yes. I knew that Will was to trim some hedges for him."

She recited for them the narrative of her fetching Abbott and the two of them heading up the hill to the hedge to find Will. Her story fit with Abbott's. Lamb found it interesting that Lydia exhibited no strong emotion as she described breaking down upon seeing her uncle's mutilated body. Perhaps she had cried herself out for the moment. Perhaps, too, her earlier tears hadn't been genuine.

"Did Mr. Abbott attempt to remove the tools from your uncle's body?" Lamb asked.

Lydia wrung the handkerchief. "Yes, he did, sir." She looked at Lamb. "For my sake," she added woodenly. "I was just so shocked, you see."

"How would you describe your relationship with Mr. Abbott?"

Lydia sat up straighter and smoothed her dress over her legs. Wallace and Rivers exchanged quick, knowing glances. "My relationship, sir?" Lydia asked.

"Yes," Lamb said. "Did the two of you know each other well? Had you ever taken tea with him, perhaps? Or danced with him? Did he ever write you a letter or give you a gift? Did you fancy him? Did he fancy you?"

Lydia looked askance. "No, sir—nothing like that."

Now Wallace piped in. "So Mr. Abbott never made any advances toward you, Miss Blackwell? Never tried to have his way with you?"

Lydia smoothed her dress again—roughly this time—and looked directly at Wallace. Her eyes flared, indignant. "No, sir," she said. "*Nothing* like that. Mr. Abbott has always been a gentleman to me."

Her expression hardened, and Lamb sensed for the first time that she was afraid.

"Several people have mentioned to us that some in the village believed Will to be a witch," Lamb said. "That he'd once seen a black dog on the hill and that he'd since been mixed up in some way with the black arts."

"Those are *lies*, sir," Lydia said, looking directly at Lamb. "Will was no witch. Those are hateful people who think that way."

Lamb withdrew from his pocket the note he'd found on Blackwell's body and showed it to Lydia. "Does this look like Will's handwriting?"

Lydia looked at the note: *in the nut.* "Yes. That's Will's writing."

"I found this note in the pocket of your uncle's jacket," Lamb said. "Do you have any idea what it might mean?"

Lydia shook her head. "No, sir."

"Mr. Abbott told us of a boy who sometimes visited Will—a boy from Lord Pembroke's manor who can't speak," Lamb said. "Do you know this boy?"

"Yes, sir. That is Peter."

"Can you tell me anything about Peter? How long has Will known him?"

"He draws things—bugs and that. He likes to watch Will work. But he's soft in the head; he don't speak."

"Do you know if Will was supposed to see Peter today?"

"Peter just shows up, like."

"Do you know if Will had any disagreements with Peter, especially recently?"

"I don't know, sir."

"Does Peter strike you as a strong boy—someone who could overpower Will if he'd a mind to?"

"Yes, sir. He's skinny—lanky, like—but tall."

"Have you ever seen Peter get angry?"

Lydia mulled the question. "Just the once. I looked out the window and he was in the front there, stomping around. Will was out there and I think Will might have said something to make Peter mad."

"Did you ask your uncle what he might have done to make Peter angry?"

"No, sir. It weren't my business."

"When was this?"

"Last summer."

Lamb was dying for a fag. He and the other two still had to make at least a cursory search of Blackwell's house, inside and out. Tomorrow they could return and make a more thorough exploration of the place.

"I realize that this has been a trying day for you, Miss Blackwell," he said. "But I'm afraid we have one more duty we must perform before we leave. Perhaps I can have Constable Harris make you a cup of tea?"

Rivers shifted in his seat, as if uncomfortable and wanting to make his discomfort obvious. Again, he briefly looked at Lamb quizzically. He wondered why Lamb was treating the niece with such solicitousness. Instinctually, he felt certain that she was involved with her uncle's murder.

Lydia shook her head. "No—no, thank you."

"Very well," Lamb said. "Sergeant Wallace and DI Rivers are going to search upstairs. They shouldn't be too long. If I could just prevail upon you to wait here a bit longer, then we can all go to bed. Constable Harris will sit with you."

"Where will you be, sir?" She couldn't quite hide the wariness in her eyes.

"Outside," Lamb said without elucidating. "I'll also be back shortly."

Wallace fetched Harris from his post outside the door. Harris removed his hat and sat in the chair that Wallace had occupied. Lydia sat with her hands between her knees, staring into the cold hearth. She sniffled.

Lamb, Wallace, and Rivers went into the front yard, where they could speak without Lydia hearing them. "You two see to upstairs and I'll have a look around outside," Lamb said.

"She's lying about Abbott," Rivers said.

"Maybe," Lamb said.

"No maybe about it. She practically jumped out of her chair when you asked about him."

"We'll see," Lamb said.

Rivers and Wallace climbed a narrow, switchback staircase that led to a small landing on the second floor. The landing gave on to a short, narrow hall lit by a single bulb in the ceiling. Off the hall were two rooms, one to the right and one at the end.

Wallace opened the door to the room on the right and shined his torch into it. It contained a small single bed upon which sat a wicker basket full of freshly washed women's clothes—dresses, petticoats, and stockings. He found a switch on the wall and turned on the light, another bare bulb in the ceiling. The bed was neatly made, with a yellow blanket pulled over, then tucked beneath a single pillow. A narrow space existed between the foot of the bed and the wall opposite the door, and on this wall was a single window shrouded with a dark green wool blanket. Above the bed was a painting of red flowers arranged in a white vase. Near the foot of the bed, against the wall, was a bureau. On the bureau lay several combs and brushes; above the bureau a mirror was positioned on the wall.

"Looks as if this is the niece's room," Wallace said.

"Right," Rivers said. "You have a look round and I'll take the old man's room."

Wallace searched Lydia Blackwell's tiny bedroom thoroughly but found nothing interesting save a diary. He flipped through its pages but found they contained only notations of the weather and meals and an occasional passage describing a walk Lydia had taken in or around Quimby. He found no impassioned confessions of love, lust, anger, remorse, guilt, or the desire for revenge; no explication of fantasies and dreams, triumphs, or heartbreaks; nothing dear and intimate—not a single letter or photograph; not even a flower— pressed between the pages. As he closed the diary, he felt pity for Lydia Blackwell.

In Will's room, Rivers found a narrow bed against the left wall, next to a closet, and a squat wooden bureau against the right wall. The room's whitewashed plastered walls were bare of ornament, and the top of the bureau contained only a razor and shaving cup. The mirror above the bureau was cracked and missing a portion of its bottom left corner. The shallow closet contained several shirts, jackets, and trousers hanging from a wooden rod. Rivers went through the pockets of the clothes but found nothing save a few pence. He looked beneath Will's bed but found only a layer of dust and a few cobwebs.

In the bureau he found three shirts, four pairs of socks, and two pairs of old black trousers with holes in the knees. Beneath the trousers he found a framed photograph of a young woman and a small drawstring pouch made of blue felt. The photo clearly had been shot in a studio. The woman was posed on a chair, by a small table on which stood a vase brimming with large roses. He guessed, given the clothing the woman wore, that the photograph had been taken near the turn of the century. Rivers opened the pouch and found that it contained a heart-shaped gold locket on a gold chain. He opened the locket and found in it a photograph of a young man standing by the sea that he guessed was Will Blackwell. The man was tall and slender. He wore a dark suit, a bowler hat, and a broad smile.

He put the locket into his pocket and picked up the photograph. He found Wallace awaiting him in the hall.

"Anything useful?" Rivers asked.

"Nothing, save a diary," Wallace said. "Though it had nothing in it. Just odds and bits about the weather and so on. Rather sad, actually."

Rivers showed Wallace the photo and the locket.

"Mementos of happier days, then?" Wallace asked.

"Apparently. What do *you* think, then, Sergeant—about Abbott and the niece?"

Wallace agreed with Rivers that Lydia Blackwell seemed to be lying about her relationship with Abbott. But he didn't want to undercut Lamb.

"I don't know," he said.

Rivers smiled crookedly and clasped a hand on Wallace's shoulder, which surprised Wallace. "Loyalty, eh. That's good. Still, you have to be careful with who you're loyal to. Don't want to back the wrong horse."

Wallace glanced at Rivers's hand on his shoulder. He wasn't exactly sure what Rivers meant except that he seemed to be referring to Lamb. Wallace wondered what had transpired between them.

"I'm comfortable with my bet," Wallace said.

Rivers widened his oblique smile a notch, but said nothing.

Lamb made a circuit of the house but found nothing save a small toolshed in the back. He tried the door but found the interior utterly dark and without a light; he decided to leave it for tomorrow. He returned to the cottage to find Wallace and Rivers descending the stairs. The trio rendezvoused in the kitchen and shared what they'd found, which, aside from the old photos, amounted to nothing.

They returned to the chairs in the sitting room.

"We won't trouble you but for a few moments more, Miss Blackwell," Lamb said. "Just a few more questions and then we'll be on our way."

He showed Lydia the framed photo Rivers had taken from Will's room. "What can you tell me about this photograph?" he asked.

"That is Claire, Will's late wife."

Lamb was surprised to hear that Will had been married. Everything he'd heard and seen suggested that the old man always had been a bachelor.

"When did Will's wife die?"

"Many years ago, sir. Before I was born. They had been married less than two years when she died."

"And Will never remarried?"

"No, sir."

"Did your uncle leave a will?"

Lydia's eyes widened. "No, sir," she said. "Will never would have done that."

"Do you know, then, what will become of his property—this cottage, for instance, and anything else he might have owned or put away?"

Lydia twisted the handkerchief. "I suppose it will come to me, sir."

Lamb stood. "Constable Harris will look in on you tomorrow morning to see if you require anything," he said. "We also will return tomorrow and do a more thorough search of the house for evidence. I'm sorry for the inconvenience, but hopefully we won't be in your way for too long."

Lydia nodded her assent and wiped her nose.

Outside the cottage, the faint sound of air-raid sirens some distance to the east impinged on the quiet. Lamb and Wallace had become used to distant sirens and understood that they had nothing to fear—at least for the moment—from such a far-off warning.

"It's the bomber factory again, then, would you say?" Wallace said to Lamb.

"Probably," Lamb said.

Lamb had considered saying something to Wallace about his performance that evening—praising it while, at the same time, hinting that he knew of Wallace's drinking and was watching the situation. But at the moment this seemed to him not worth the trouble.

"Do we need to get under bloody cover?" Rivers asked. He looked at the sky. As had Lamb, Rivers had learned in the first war never to take a warning of danger for granted. Those who did normally ended up with their stupid, bleeding heads blown off.

"Not until the ground begins to shake," Wallace said. He was joking—a joke Rivers didn't seem to get. A bombing was nothing to joke about, of course, and, at first, almost no one had joked about the Germans. But most people did so now, at least occasionally. Oddly, at times joking seemed the only sane thing to do under the circumstances.

"Yeah," Rivers said, eyeing Wallace with a hint of mistrust. "I see."

"Nothing to worry about," Wallace added. "If they do decide to come here, you'll know."

Lamb turned to Harris.

"Can you get me a copy of a book the title of which is something along the lines of *Ghostly Legends of Hampshire*?" Lamb asked. "It was written by Lord Pembroke, apparently. Do you know it?"

"Yes, sir. I think I know where I can get my hands on a copy."

"Good man."

Lamb, Wallace, and Rivers walked to Lamb's Wolseley.

"I'll arrange to conduct a search of the house tomorrow morning," Lamb said. "After that's done, we'll begin a proper canvassing of the village."

"What about Abbott?" Rivers asked.

"I haven't forgotten about him," Lamb said.

"He and the niece are up to something."

"All right, then," Lamb said, ignoring Rivers's protestation. "We'll see you tomorrow, David."

"Yes, sir."

Wallace was certain that he'd made it through the evening without Lamb catching on to him. Even so, he had cut it very close—*too close*—and decided that he must watch himself more carefully in the future.

SIX

—⟋∞⟍—

PETER WILKINS SAT IN THE DECREPIT SUMMERHOUSE LEAFING THROUGH *Walton's Field Guide to Butterflies*, the kerosene lamp burning beside him.

Adonis Blue, Brown Hairstreak, Duke of Burgundy, Scarce Copper, Sooty Copper, Brown Argus, Chalkhill Blue, Purple Hairstreak . . . Hesperiidae, Lycaenidae, Nymphalidae, Papilionidae, Pieridae . . . Skippers, Hairstreaks, Dukes, Emperors, Admirals, Browns, Swallowtails.

Cole Porter's "You're the Top" spun on the wind-up Victrola. Its repetitive refrain soothed Peter.

You're the top!

You're the Coliseum.

You're the top!

You're the Louvre Museum.

But the other words, the words in his mind, intruded: *I must!* He stood quickly, popping up like a jack-in-the-box, then sat again, agitated.

White Letter Hairstreak, Scotch Argus, Queen of Spain Fritillary, Mountain Ringlet, Red Admiral, Small Heath.

Lord Pembroke had given him the Victrola and many records, but he did not like the other records. Lord Pembroke had given him *Walton's Field Guide to Butterflies.*

You're the top!
You're an arrow collar.
You're the top!
You're a Coolidge dollar.

Now was the peak time of butterflies—the time of emerging and seeking. The estate was vast but he knew it intimately, every inch. He caught the butterflies in a net and pinned them to boards. When they crumbled, he replaced them. And he made drawings, like the drawings in *Walton's Field Guide to Butterflies.* Sometimes, too, he drew beetles, grasshoppers, bees, wasps, and spiders. He killed them with poison, then sketched their dead bodies. But he liked butterflies best.

You're a Waldorf salad! (He liked that one because it made him laugh, though tonight he didn't laugh.)

The lamp cast its light on the book in the shape of a circle, *a hole.* The boys were in a hole.

Hermit, Wall Brown, Apollo. . . .

He stood. *I must!*

You're the boats that glide
On the sleepy Zuider Zee,
You're an old Dutch master,
You're Lady Astor,
You're broccoli!

He'd seen the crows eat Will's eyes.

The words surged within his mind, like a wave that was not really something so singular as a wave at all, but the merest edge of an ocean, of all the oceans in the world.

At that same moment, Emily Fordham sat at the desk in her bedroom and thought of what she must write to Lord Pembroke.

She wanted to be fair to Peter. But she understood that she could not put stock in anything Peter had tried to communicate to her. The spider and the rest of it probably was nonsense. Still, Peter's recent behavior had concerned her enough that, two days earlier, she'd written to Donald. Peter's flights of fancy—his fears and aspirations and dreams—were so unlike those of a normal boy.

She wished that Donald were there. He would know what to do. Donald had been Thomas's leader on the estate the previous summer, when Thomas had run away. Donald had been glad that Lord Pembroke had forbade Thomas from returning to the estate once Thomas had surfaced. Donald had said that Thomas was a liar and schemer. But Peter had seemed to like Thomas.

She withdrew a sheet of paper from the drawer and began to write. When she was finished, she put the note in an envelope, addressed and sealed it.

She would post it tomorrow, on her way to see Charles.

—⚌—

Lamb pushed the starter on the Wolseley. Again, the thing responded on the first try.

He thought of how, a few hours before, he'd liked his luck. Now Harry Rivers was sitting next to him, quietly staring out the window at the dark environs of Quimby. Seeing Rivers emerge from the rear seat of Harding's car had been like watching a specter rise from the grave.

Neither of them spoke as the Wolseley crossed the stone bridge over Mills Run and left the village. Thanks to the blackout, Lamb had to maneuver the old machine in near darkness along the narrow road, as the dim beam from his hooded headlights illuminated only the portion of the road directly ahead.

Twenty-two years earlier, nearly to the day, he and Rivers had sat next to each other in a forward trench preparing to head out, in the black of night, on a reconnaissance of the German positions that lay less than two hundred yards distant. Both had performed such raids several times before and, indeed, Lamb had developed a reputation for being quite skillful at the job, which required stealth and a sharp mind, and depended on Rivers to back and second him. Even then, Lamb entertained no idea that Rivers liked him, though he felt certain that Rivers at least respected him. Rivers's enmity seemed to be grounded in the fact that Lamb wasn't Martin Wells, the man whom he'd replaced as second lieutenant, commanding the squad of south London men that Wells had commanded. But Wells had had the unfortunate luck of getting himself killed in a raid very much like the one that Rivers and Lamb and a half dozen other hand-picked men were about to launch. Lamb often felt as if Rivers blamed him for Wells's death—as if his place in the command pipeline somehow had hastened Wells to the grave. But the main point of contention between him and Rivers had been Private Eric Parker, a cocksure eye-winker and smoker of fags, and Rivers's best friend. Rivers had talked Parker into joining the London Regiment and therefore (or so Lamb would eventually come to discover) felt duty-bound to protect Parker from the ravages of the war, an impossible task. For his part, Parker had felt no enmity toward Lamb and Lamb had come to see Parker as one of his best and most dependable men. But Parker *had* been killed and Rivers had held him—Lamb—responsible.

Rivers spoke first, his head turned to the window. "You're married with a daughter."

Lamb wondered how Rivers knew. Obviously he'd done some checking.

"Yes. You?"

"Married to the job."

"That has advantages."

"It does."

They drove in silence for ten minutes, Lamb doing his best to concentrate on the road. But he hadn't volunteered to drive Rivers to Winchester in order to fail to divine why Rivers suddenly had parachuted into Hampshire. He didn't want a showdown with Rivers, merely an explanation.

"Why are you here, Harry?" Lamb asked.

Rivers shrugged. "I was transferred, wasn't I?" He looked at Lamb. "War shortages in the south—that's what they told me, anyway. And because I'm a good soldier, when they told me to move, I saluted and did my duty."

Lamb knew those last words were meant to pierce him and, to a degree, they hit the mark. "But you haven't answered my question," he said.

"Haven't I?"

"I assume you knew that I was here."

"I knew. But I had no choice." Rivers smiled his lopsided grin. "No reason to lie, after all. Fact is, I bollixed a case. I got a little impatient with the way things were going and pressed the matter; broke into a bloke's house and got the goods. But it wasn't allowed into evidence, so the bastard is a free man today." He shrugged. "My 'mistake,'" he added, in a tone that suggested that he hadn't really considered it a mistake. "Then they suddenly needed men down south and the man I worked for up there saw his chance to be rid of me."

"Does Harding know about your mistake?"

"He knows. But he decided he'd rather have an experienced man with a blemish than someone green. It also didn't hurt that the man I worked for in Warwickshire is one of Harding's old chums." He smiled again—bitterly, Lamb thought. "Lucky for me, eh?"

"A second chance, then?" Lamb asked.

"You might say that."

That seemed to end their initial skirmish. They drove the rest of the way to Winchester in silence, each wondering what the other was thinking.

—⁊⁊—

Wallace walked alone through the blacked-out streets of Winchester to The Fallen Diva.

He arrived a little after nine and was pleasantly surprised to find the woman he'd seen earlier that day sitting alone at the same table, the same half-expectant look on her face. Her purse was on the table, along with a half pint of beer and an ashtray partially filled with stubbed-out cigarettes. As Wallace passed her, he caught the scent of her perfume and glanced at her; she met his eyes and then glanced away. He was thirsty and hungry—hungry for something he hadn't had enough of in too long a time.

He went to the bar and ordered a pint. He told himself that he would limit himself to three beers. "Who's the bird at the table?" he asked the man behind the bar.

"No idea. Never saw her before until three days ago. Just sits there, all alone."

"Is she waiting for someone?"

"If she is, he hasn't shown up."

"Any blokes try it on with her?"

"One did last night. But he gave up."

Wallace took his beer to the woman's table. She looked up at him. "May I join you?"

She smiled, faintly. "Suit yourself."

Wallace offered his hand. "David Wallace," he said. She shook his hand but said nothing. Wallace thought that she must be playing a game. But he didn't mind a game now and again. He smiled. "So, you have no name, then?"

She didn't answer. Her faint smile reappeared.

"Do I have to guess?" Wallace asked.

"If you like."

He pretended to appraise her. "Let me see," he said. "Green eyes, green dress." He pulled his chair back from the table and looked beneath it. "Ha!" he said. "Green shoes! Your name is Miss Green."

She laughed—a kind of twitter. "Not even close."

"You have auburn hair. Miss Brown, then?"

"No."

"Let's see. I'm running out of colors. Miss Yellow?"

She laughed.

"Turquoise? No? I know—you're French! Blanc. Miss Blanc! Hold on! You're blushing. Miss Rose?"

He believed the game to be a test. She wanted to see not only if he was willing to play, but how well he played. Apparently, he'd done well. The bloke of the night before likely hadn't.

"Very well," she said. "I suppose I'll have to tell you."

"I'm all ears," Wallace said. He tugged at his ears, pulling them out from his head.

She laughed again—snorted. She put her right hand over her mouth, as if the unfeminine sound mortified her.

"Seriously, my dear," Wallace said, affecting an upper-class accent. "What *is* your name? Mother *insists* on knowing."

She twittered again. "Delilah," she said.

Wallace sipped his beer, then wiped his mouth with the back of his hand. "Delilah what?"

"Just Delilah."

Another game. Delilah intrigued him. He quietly appraised her plump body. She was *voluptuous*—that was the word. He reckoned she was maybe twenty-one. A good age. She had neither the look nor attitude of a virgin. Her modesty—the hand over the mouth and the rest of it—was affected, which added to her mystery.

She told him that she worked as a secretary in a firm of solicitors and was considering joining the WAAFs. He said that he was a copper, a sergeant. When she asked—as they always did—if he was stalking a killer, he told her as much about the Blackwell case as seemed prudent. She listened, rapt, as he described how they'd found Will Blackwell's body.

"It all sounds so frightening," she said.

Wallace shrugged. "I suppose. Though dead is dead, after all." He smiled.

"Yes, but the *way* he died." She looked at her beer, which she'd hardly touched. "Poor old man."

"It's possible he didn't feel anything beyond a knock on the back of the head. The killer drove in the pitchfork while the old boy was unconscious. So the doc says." He wondered if he was saying more than he should—if the beer was loosening his tongue. He must watch himself.

They talked for another half hour. Wallace tried to get more out of Delilah—who she was, really, and why she had come to The Fallen Diva to sit alone. But Delilah deflected his questions. At closing, she said "I must get home now." She offered no explanation and Wallace asked for none. He wondered if he'd pressed her too hard for information.

She picked up her purse and stood. Wallace escorted her to the dark street. He'd had his three pints and felt within himself. He was prepared to go home, get a decent night's sleep, and appear in the nick on the following morning ready to go, like a loyal dog. Except that he didn't want to go home. Not yet.

The night had grown cool enough for a sweater, though Delilah had none. Wallace removed his coat and put it around her shoulders. To his surprise, she kissed him quickly on the cheek and said "Thank you, David. You're very charming." She drew Wallace's jacket around herself and added, "I'd ask you to walk me home but I'm afraid it's a bit of a distance. It's fifteen minutes, at least."

She was an odd bird, but he liked her. And he wanted her. Their mutual teasing and the beer had loosed something in him. A walk would do him good, he thought. Clear his head.

"I don't mind the walk," he said. "I can't very well let you walk home all alone in the dark."

"Suit yourself," she said, and smiled at him.

She walked beside him, shivering a little. He slipped his arm around her shoulders. She was young and firm, very well put together, and Wallace began to conjure images of what she looked like with her clothes off and that playful smile on her face.

He was surprised to find that she lived in a small, semi-detached brick house with a front garden in the middle of a street of similar houses called Chatham Close. When she'd said that she lived alone on a secretary's salary, he'd imagined her in a tiny flat with just enough

room for a bed and table and a bath at the end of the hall. He walked
her to her door and waited while she unlocked it. She pushed open the
door and turned to face him. "Would you like to come in?" she asked.
"I could make you a cup of tea—fortify you a bit for your walk home."

"I could use a cup of tea."

They stepped into a small sitting room; Delilah turned on a lamp.
Wallace found the room typical-looking, with a couch and coffee
table against the right wall, a couple of chairs facing them, a narrow
stair on the left that led to the second floor, and a small hall, on the
right, which he guessed led to the kitchen. Perhaps her father had
money, he thought.

Delilah turned to him. "Thank you for the coat, David," she said.
Rather than hand it to him, she let it fall from her shoulders to the
floor.

She moved close to him and Wallace caught the full scent of her.
She put her arms around his neck; he felt her breasts against his chest.
He moved his hands to her hips and they kissed—a lengthy, slow
kiss. He couldn't quite believe his luck. Then Delilah let her arms
drop from his shoulders and took a step backward, leaving him hard
and ready.

"Would you rather a nightcap than a cup of tea?" she asked.

"Yes."

She went to a small cupboard against the far wall and withdrew
a bottle of Irish whiskey and two small glasses. She filled them and
offered one to Wallace. They eyed each other as they drank, almost as
if they were sealing a pact, Wallace thought. She drank her whiskey
quickly, tossing it back; Wallace did the same. He was giving in again.
A year earlier he'd gone through a patch in which he'd drunk too
much; he'd shown up late for work in a disheveled state once too often.
He'd confessed his problem to Lamb, who'd verbally kicked his arse,
then helped him to regain a grip on his life. Wallace told himself that
the transgression he was about to make was only temporary, a one-
off. He moved to take Delilah in his arms but she resisted. "Sit on the
floor," she said. She pointed to a place in front of the sofa. "Just there."

Another game. He did as she ordered.

"Take off your shoes," she said. He obeyed.

She stood before him, a few feet away, unzipped her green dress and let it fall to the floor. She unhooked her bra, freeing her effusive breasts, her eyes fixed on Wallace. She pushed off her knickers and stood before him naked, in her black heels. She took the bottle in her hand and raised her chin toward the ceiling, tossing her hair. She poured a stream of the whiskey down the front of her neck; the brown liquid ran quickly between her breasts and over her soft belly and into her sex. She touched herself there, then brought her fingers to her lips. The whiskey glistened on her body. She looked at Wallace and asked, "Are you ready, David?"

Then she put her wet fingers in her mouth.

SEVEN

—∞—

HARRY RIVERS WAS SITTING AT DICK WALTERS'S OLD DESK WHEN Lamb arrived at the nick on the following morning.

Wallace hadn't arrived yet, though he normally just made it under the wire. Eight or nine uniformed PCs, along with a uniformed sergeant named Bill Cashen, milled about the incident room waiting for Harding to begin his morning briefing.

Lamb nodded at the men, then went to his small office and closed the door. He hung his jacket and hat on the coatrack in the corner and went to his desk. He would have to get used to working with Rivers again, though Harding had said that Rivers's posting wasn't necessarily permanent. Obviously, Rivers was on probation. In any case, he refused to allow Rivers to drag him back into the mud of the Somme, into the old discord and recriminations.

On the way to the nick, he'd stopped at the newsagents and bought the latest issue of *Sporting Life*. He looked at the telephone. Several races were scheduled at Paulsgrove that day, and he had the four quid he'd won on the back of Winter's Tail to work with. He reached for the phone, intending to make a call, then withdrew his hand.

No.

Someone rapped on his door. He opened it to find Wallace standing in the hall. Wallace's suit was uncharacteristically rumpled and his shoes scuffed. A blood vessel had burst in his right eye, giving his gaze a vaguely supernatural appearance.

Wallace had awakened that morning alarmed to find the sun slanting through the window and himself in a strange bed with his head aching. He became aware of Delilah sleeping on his arm, her left leg across his stomach, snoring. Only a few hours before, he and Delilah had devoured each other on the floor of her sitting room. He'd never known anything quite so exhilarating. After the second time, they'd drained the bottle of whiskey, then fallen asleep in her bed.

He'd managed to extricate himself from Delilah's grasp without waking her and walked to his flat, where he'd quickly bathed and shaved and downed a cup of tea. Miraculously, he'd made it to work on time. He hadn't had a drink in seven hours and, despite his headache, believed himself sober. Even so, his heart quickened when he saw Lamb.

"Rough night, then, David?" Lamb asked.

Wallace suddenly worried that his clothes smelled of whiskey; Lamb seemed able to detect things about him that he'd missed. "Nothing out of the ordinary." He felt transparent as glass. He tried a smile, though he knew it wouldn't work. "Showtime, guv," he said. "Harding's ready."

Harding stood at the front of the incident room; behind him, Larkin had taped several large photos of Will Blackwell's dead body to a large chalkboard.

Lamb wondered if Harding had noticed Wallace's appearance and figured that the super must have noticed. Although Harding appeared, in manner, to be obtuse, he was nothing of the kind. He noticed *everything.* Lamb knew that Wallace held a low opinion of Harding and therefore badly underestimated him. Lamb liked Wallace very much and considered him to be an excellent detective. He'd already decided that he would do whatever was in his power to keep Wallace out of the war. But Wallace depended in part on charm to make his way, and Harding despised charm.

Rivers still sat at Walters's old desk; Wallace took his place at his desk. Lamb settled himself against the room's back wall and folded his arms.

"Now then," Harding said, "as I'm sure you're all aware, we've rather a brutal bit of business to attend to in Quimby. The macabre nature of the thing is bound to attract press attention. I'll handle that aspect so that you men can stick to the job of finding the killer. I've arranged a twenty-pound reward for information leading to an arrest of a viable suspect, which should loosen tongues in the village."

He nodded at Lamb. "DCI Lamb will take the lead, seconded by DI Harry Rivers and DS Wallace." Harding raised his hand in Rivers's direction. "Rivers arrived yesterday from Warwickshire; he'll be replacing DI Walters. I'll leave it up to you to make introductions among yourselves."

Harding then yielded the floor to Lamb, who spent five minutes reviewing the particulars of the case.

"At the moment, Abbott is our best suspect, though we have nothing solid to connect him to the killing," he said. "We expect to find his fingerprints on the pitchfork and the scythe both. He claims he tried to pull them out of Blackwell's body after he and the niece found the body and the niece went into hysterics—a claim the niece confirmed last night."

He assigned Rivers to take charge of the canvassing of the village for statements and Wallace to take charge of the search of Blackwell's cottage and a grid search of Manscome Hill. A mild look of surprise crossed Rivers's face. He had expected Lamb to assign him to something unimportant—to keep him out of the way.

They drove to Quimby in several cars—Rivers and his team of three constables in one; Sergeant Cashen and the remaining uniformed men in the second and third cars; and Lamb, Wallace, and Larkin in Lamb's temperamental Wolseley (which took only two tries to kick over, causing Lamb to wonder if he hadn't made a mistake in not placing a bet that day).

They rendezvoused in front of Blackwell's cottage, where they found Harris awaiting them. Unlike on the previous night, no one seemed to be about; the village seemed to have shut itself up, as Lamb had feared it might.

"How is Miss Blackwell?" Lamb asked Harris.

"She's gone off to her sewing job."

"Has she now?" The news surprised him.

"Not the grieving type, then," Rivers said.

"What about Abbott?" Lamb asked.

"He doesn't seem to be home, sir. He likes the ponies, so he might have gone down to Paulsgrove. He normally goes midweek." It was Wednesday.

"Also not the grieving type, then," Rivers said. "Neither of them seem too broken up over the old man's death, despite what they said yesterday."

Lamb was thinking the same thing. He found it interesting that Abbott was a betting man and wondered how Abbott's luck had been running recently. Also, Abbott had ignored his admonition of the previous night not to stray too far from the village.

Harris removed from the pocket of his tunic a small, slender book with a red cover and black spine, which he offered to Lamb. "And I have this for you, sir—*Myths and Legends of the Supernatural in Hampshire* by Lord Jeffrey Pembroke." The title was embossed in gold lettering. "It belongs to the wife. She has an interest in the supernatural, ghost stories and the like. She's marked two stories she has an idea might be helpful."

Lamb glanced in the book and found two places marked with blotting paper. "Please tell your wife thank you," he said.

With that, they got down to work. As Rivers and Wallace deployed their teams, Lamb went to the rear of Blackwell's cottage, intending to inspect the toolshed he'd found the previous evening. He pushed open the door and stepped inside; the shed's dark, musty interior was roughly eight feet long and six wide. It was nearly empty, which Lamb found strange. Dusty shafts of light filtered in through the irregularly spaced wall slats. A rusting shovel leaned against the right wall by the door, along with perhaps a dozen pieces of milled wood of various lengths. A wooden crate that appeared to be full of rags lay in the middle of the floor. The stench of something dead assailed Lamb.

He peered at the back of the shed and saw what he thought might be another crate. He moved toward it, catching a dangling strand of derelict cobweb on his fedora. The crate—or whatever it was—was flush against the back wall of the shed and appeared to be shrouded with a white handkerchief. He fished a box of matches from the pocket of his jacket, lit one, and squatted before the box. The flame illuminated what appeared to be a kind of small altar—an upturned apple crate with the stubs of a pair of red candles stuck to it; the white object that he took to have been a handkerchief was a sheet of paper.

The match went out, and he lit another. He saw now that a dead chicken—the source of the smell—lay at the base of the altar, its throat cut, its blood coagulating in the dirt. He retrieved the paper from the altar and took it outside so that he could examine it in the light.

He found on it a pencil drawing that fascinated and troubled him at once—that of a small bird snared in a spider's web. The bird's wings were spread wide and bent unnaturally due to the way in which the web ensnared it. Its head lolled, lifeless, and its eyes were slits. But what struck Lamb most about the drawing was its excellence. The drawing was no mere scribble or approximation of its subject; it was highly detailed and, in its way, beautiful, even touching. The way in which the artist had depicted the bird's face pierced him; he could feel the creature's life spark having gone out. He thought of Peter, the mute boy, whom Abbott and Lydia Blackwell both had described as spending much of his time sketching insects. He put the drawing in the rear seat of his car and headed up Manscome Hill along the well-worn trail that paralleled the wood.

He crossed Mills Run on the wooden footbridge. To his left, he saw Wallace, Cashen, and the constables beginning to walk their patches near the hedge where Blackwell's body had been found, beating the meadow grass with sticks.

He walked to the top of the hill, where he stood for a moment gazing down at Quimby; he thought of how it resembled the kind of bucolic hamlet that inevitably featured in paintings of a pastoral England that was quickly disappearing, along with the pastoral ways.

He took from his jacket pocket the copy of *Myths and Legends of the Supernatural in Hampshire*, sat in the lush grass, and opened the book to the chapters that Harris's wife had marked with blotting paper.

The first, entitled "A Milkmaid's Murder," related the tale of Agnes Clemmons, an elderly spinster who had lived in the nearby village of Moresham. On a cold March afternoon in 1882, she'd been walking near her home when a local farmhand, John Pilson, had attacked and killed her. After knocking Clemmons unconscious with a hefty branch he'd taken from the ground, Pilson had run the tines of his pitchfork through her neck. He'd then carved a crucifix into her forehead with the blade of his scythe before burying the scythe in her chest. Pilson had believed Clemmons to be a witch. When the previous fall's wheat harvest had gone inexplicably bad, he'd fingered her as the source of the failure. He freely admitted to police that he'd killed Clemmons because she had ruined the wheat harvest by running toads over the fields in the dead of night. He believed he'd done the village a favor in dispatching her and genuinely expected to be rewarded for it. Instead, he was hanged.

The chapter entitled "A Black Dog on Manscome Hill" told the story of Will Blackwell's alleged encounter with a demon dog. The incident was said to have occurred in 1880, when Will was ten. At the time, Will lived with his mother and four older sisters on the other side of Manscome Hill. Will was said to have possessed a talent with animals; he seemed able to communicate with most creatures without the aid of prods, whips, leashes, harnesses, saddles, or spurs. Some in the village found his uncanny abilities queer and wondered if their origin was pure. On an evening in mid-July, Will was ascending Manscome Hill from Quimby, along the ancient path, on his way home, when a black dog—an omen of impending death—suddenly appeared to him in the twilight. The dog was said to have had fiery, unnatural red eyes. That same night Will's oldest sister, Meredith, died suddenly—though of what no one ever was certain. Meredith had not even been ill. She'd screamed in the night, and by the time her mother reached her she'd been dead. A rumor spread in Quimby that Will had made a bargain with the black beast to take his sister instead of him. In return, he'd promised to serve Satan through the practice of witchcraft.

"It strikes one as unfair to label Will Blackwell a witch," Lord Jeffrey Pembroke wrote. "He seems merely to have been a quiet soul who had an unusual affinity for animals. But ignorance and fear are powerful masters, particularly in those areas of rural England in which science, the Enlightenment, and the tenets of Progressive thinking have failed to gain an adequate foothold."

Lamb closed the book and headed down the hill to the village. He'd found the stories interesting—especially the fact that the milk-maid had been killed in a way that was nearly identical to Blackwell's murder—though, in the end, unenlightening. Anyone who might have wanted to tart up Will Blackwell's murder in a macabre cloak might have read or heard the story.

As he crossed the wooden bridge, the urchin boy to whom he'd spoken on the previous night emerged from the wood onto the path. The boy froze when he saw Lamb.

"Good morning," Lamb said. He smiled.

The boy's eyes widened in surprise and fear. He turned and ran back into the wood.

"Wait," Lamb said.

But the boy ignored him and an instant later disappeared from Lamb's sight.

—◊—

Vera sat at the small desk in the room that served as the civil defense office of the Quimby Parish Council. The room, which was on the second floor of a building on the High Street that also contained a sundries shop (which occupied the front room of the first floor) and her tiny billet (which was in the back), barely was large enough to hold its furnishings, which, in addition to the desk, included a squat brown metal filing cabinet, a small round wooden table with two chairs, and a telephone. Her accoutrements also included a Great War–era infantry helmet, a ponderous thing with chipped green paint. Outside the door, at the bottom of the steps leading to the small room, was a hand-cranked siren that Vera was required to sound in the case of a German attack.

Her daily duties required her to call her superiors in Southampton and Portsmouth once an hour to ensure that the telephone lines hadn't been sabotaged. Now and again, too, someone from Southampton delivered a box of informational fliers for her to deliver in the village. The latest, which she'd delivered last week to every occupied building in Quimby, had contained instructions on what to do if the Germans invaded, including "Stay put and hide your bicycle."

She tapped the telephone with a pencil and thought with some trepidation of Arthur Lear. She and Arthur had made love again on the previous evening, in the narrow iron cot in her billet. She thought of how quickly and easily Arthur had seduced her; he had not swept her off her feet so much as he had eased her onto her back and relieved her of her virginity, which had left her surprised at her own lenience.

They'd met a month earlier, a few days after she'd begun her job in Quimby. She'd been leaving the sundries shop in the early evening, her arms laden with a loaf of bread, three tins of sardines, a bit of bacon, two eggs, and a packet of tea. As she'd backed out of the shop, hurrying more than she had needed and not looking where she was going, she'd run into a man entering the shop—a young man with dark hair. That had been her first, quick impression of Arthur Lear: that he had nice hair. They'd collided and she'd dropped her bread, tea, and eggs, the latter of which had shattered on the concrete walk in front of the store.

Arthur immediately had taken responsibility for the catastrophe. "I'm sorry," he'd said. "I've caused you to drop your eggs."

He was tall, slender, long-legged, fit-looking. He had dark hazel eyes and—yes, her fleeting impression had been right—luxuriant black hair. His skin also was just a shade darker than that of the boys to which she was used, as if, perhaps, he had some Latin in his blood. And she saw that his right arm was missing below the elbow.

He smiled and bent to retrieve the bread and the tea with his lone hand. She wondered if he'd lost the arm in France. He seemed of the right age.

"Thanks—but it's okay, really," she'd said, even though she'd used up a week's worth of ration cards for the eggs.

"But I've broken your eggs."

"No—I wasn't looking where I was going."

"Yes, but your hands were full."

"I should have brought a sack with me."

"Are you *sure* you won't let me replace your eggs?"

She tried not to look at his arm. "No, I'm fine, really."

A look of something like recognition suddenly lit Arthur's eyes. "You're the new girl."

Vera smiled. "Yes."

"My name is Arthur Lear," he said, unselfconsciously offering his hand.

Vera cradled what was left of her groceries in her right arm and shook Arthur's hand with her left. "I'm Vera Lamb."

"That's a wonderful name—Vera. Like Vera Lynn."

Vera flushed. "Nothing like that."

"Only, you're prettier than Vera Lynn."

"Well, I don't know. But thank you."

"It's true," Arthur said. "Are you staying in the billet, then? Behind the shop?"

"Yes."

"Are you sure I can't replace your eggs?"

"No, I'm fine, really."

She'd taken the groceries back to her billet and prepared herself a bacon sandwich and a pot of tea. She missed the eggs. She had just a bit of cheese, milk, and roast pork left. She found herself thinking of Arthur as she ate. She liked his smile. She would have thought that she would have minded his missing arm. But she didn't. The rest of him obviously was quite fit. And he seemed intelligent and polite.

On the following morning he'd come to her door bearing a dozen fresh eggs from the farm near the village that he ran with his father. His sudden appearance had surprised her and she hadn't quite known what to say, other than thank you.

After that, they'd met a few times for tea and once in the pub at his invitation. She'd decided she liked him well enough. He seemed charming and solicitous. Then he'd surprised her again by showing up at her billet unannounced, this time at twilight, and inviting her out for a walk. She had agreed to go with him with less hesitation than she would have thought she would have shown even a few days earlier. She wasn't sure why she hadn't hesitated, unless it had something to do with the war, the way in which its omnipresence seemed to hurry everything along, forced one to decide things more quickly than did peace, with its false sense of security and everlasting time. Everyone seemed worried about time now; there never seemed to be enough of it. If the British could manage to hold off the German invasion through the beginning of October, then the Germans likely wouldn't invade because the Channel was too rough in the autumn—so the government and the newspapers said. But if the Germans could destroy the RAF quickly, before the summer was done, they almost certainly would come. Either way, no one felt as if they had enough time—to do or say what they must, to devise a plan of action, to face the inevitable.

They'd strolled up Manscome Hill along the well-worn trail by the wood. The night had been warm and dry, the sky clear, the meadows alive with the twilight activities of birds and insects. As they'd walked, Arthur had told Vera about the life he shared with his father, Noel.

Noel had spent twenty years as an English tutor at a public school in Sussex. When Arthur was five, they'd moved to Quimby, where

Noel intended to start life anew as a gentleman farmer. "That was after my mom died," Arthur had said, neglecting to say *how* his mother had died. But he'd made it clear—he'd lost his mother as a very young boy and this tragedy had set him and his father in motion.

Vera had met Noel Lear once, when she'd run into him and Arthur in the sundries shop one evening not long after Arthur had shown up at her door bearing the eggs. Noel was a slight man who wore glasses, spoke softly, and moved hesitantly. He'd smiled at Vera vacantly and she'd noticed that he'd stayed close to Arthur's elbow, as if his surroundings confused him. The scuttlebutt about the village, which she had picked up here and there, was that he'd never had much success with the little farm.

She'd found their walk around Manscome Hill lovely and peaceful. She was certain that Arthur liked her—and that he perfectly well understood what lay beneath the shapeless, bland masculinity of her Home Guard coveralls. A pair of goldfinches had flashed across the path in front of them, two bright yellow birds, new to the world, against a dusky blue-green meadow crowded with obscure, watching, primeval spirits.

Two evenings later, they'd walked up the hill again. As they'd neared the crest, Arthur had sat in the opulent grass and Vera had sat beside him. As they'd gazed down onto the village and its quiet, shrouded corners, Arthur had told her the two defining stories of his life—of his mother's death and the loss of his arm.

He'd cried when his mother had died of breast cancer, though he admitted that he didn't remember much of it. He recalled seeing her body lying on his father's bed, the pain of her disease still etched on her face, and knew then that he'd never see her again. Now, his grief for her assailed him in "patches," he told Vera. He added, "She was beautiful."

He'd lost his arm when he was ten. His father had been trying to repair their old Ford tractor, which had broken down yet again, and had not noticed that Arthur was round the other side, tinkering with the gears and belts, believing he was helping. When his father had suddenly started the engine, Arthur's left arm had been sucked into the whirring machine. His father had carried him into the village, where a doctor had bandaged him and driven him to the hospital in Winchester. His father had held him in his lap the entire drive. In Winchester, the doctors had removed his ravaged lower arm. He smiled at Vera—a smile that pierced her. "Funny, but I still sometimes forget that I haven't got it any longer. I'll reach for something and realize. . . ." He looked at the grass and said no more.

"I'm sorry," Vera said, though those words hardly described what she felt as she glimpsed the ache in Arthur's eyes.

He had smiled again and said, "It's all right. I still have my dad." Arthur's gaze was raw and tender at once.

"What is wrong with your father?" she asked.

He shook his head despairingly. "I don't know. He seems to be losing his memory; he forgets things. He used to have such a sharp mind. He speaks Italian and French and used to read everything. Now, he can't keep his mind on a book long enough to read even a few pages. I worry that he'd be lost without me."

Vera touched his cheek; she couldn't help herself. He put his hand against hers and held it against his face for a few seconds; then he moved his mouth to the palm of her hand and held his lips against it. Vera felt an emotion begin to rise within her—an emotion she'd felt often and believed she understood, though only in an abstract way, as if she'd only observed the feeling from afar and noted it. She'd daydreamed of what it would be like to make love to a man, though her fantasies had not counted on someone like Arthur Lear.

Arthur kissed the palm of her hand; she felt the tip of his tongue move across her skin, sending a jolt of pleasure through her. Then he'd looked directly at her with his dark, sad, searching eyes and said, "I like you, Vera; I like you very much. You mean so much to me." He moved around to face her and she found herself moving to meet him, fending off a feeling of caution. They drew closer and Arthur put his lips against hers and kissed her gently. She closed her eyes and accepted his kiss, parting her lips slightly, the bloom of doubt within her withering. When the kiss was finished, Arthur stayed very close to her, his cheek against hers; she could smell him quite distinctly, a red-brown odor of youthful male virility. She felt as if she was no longer merely observing that feeling that so often had stirred within her. Arthur had teased it to the surface of her consciousness and caused it to take shape. The feeling was one of frank sexual desire tinged with pity, a product of her deepest fantasies and confidential desires.

Arthur kissed her again, and this time Vera opened herself to Arthur and to her ardor. She leaned toward him, probing him with her tongue, hoping to fire him. She felt as if she hardly knew what she was doing—yet her actions came to her naturally. She felt as if all the knowledge she needed was already contained within her heart and limbs and in the secret places from which she'd imprisoned the rising emotion. And she could feel Arthur swelling, his blood rising.

He put his lone arm around her and pulled her closer yet, surprising her with his strength. They kissed for what seemed to Vera like a very long time; and when Arthur finally had withdrawn his mouth from hers, she'd felt herself dangling on a kind of precipice, her lips warm. Arthur began to ease her onto her back and they lay in the grass facing each other, Vera on her right side, and he kissed her again, annihilating the last barriers lying between them.

Since, they'd made love a half dozen times and on each occasion Vera had found herself longing for and dreading the experience. Everything that had come before Arthur Lear now seemed to have occurred in a separate lifetime. She understood that she'd allowed Arthur to seduce her, though he'd done so more quickly than her virginal self had imagined would have been possible. She enjoyed their lovemaking—she couldn't deny that. And yet the way in which she'd allowed Arthur to gain a kind of control of her life soon had begun to worry her. Now that worry had become like a thorn in her shoe that she could not dislodge; it pricked her consistently, wherever she went, whatever she did.

Three nights earlier she'd awakened to find Arthur sitting at the small round table near the gas ring in her billet, fully dressed. When she'd gone to him, he'd raised his head to look at her and said, gloomily, "I know you don't love me. You can't, not with my arm like this." She'd assured him that she didn't care that his arm was gone. But she understood in the moment, too, with a clarity she hadn't known before that, indeed, she *didn't* love Arthur and wouldn't.

Then, two nights later—last night—Vera had noticed a kind of clinging desperation in Arthur's lovemaking that had not been present before. When they'd finished, he'd rolled off and, inexplicably, begun to cry. When she'd asked him what was wrong, he'd abruptly risen from the bed and dressed quickly. "You know very well," was all he'd said. The look in his eyes was one of animosity, she thought, and wondered what she might have done or said to make Arthur angry. When she'd asked him why he was crying, he'd said again that she knew very well why he was crying. Before she could protest that she didn't know, Arthur told her that he must go home to his father and hurriedly left.

Now she considered bringing her affair with Arthur to an end. Something in his character gradually had begun to reveal itself to her, a kind of unpredictable peevishness and a penchant for self-pity. She didn't want to hurt him, but there was something else besides. She also didn't want to make him angry. She realized that at least a part of her feared Arthur—that her newfound pleasure in their lovemaking had blinded her to something within him that he'd managed, at least at first, to keep hidden. In allowing him to seduce her, she'd made a mistake. She hoped that they could remain friends. But they had moved too quickly and she had allowed herself to succumb too easily. It all seemed so clear to her now that she wondered why she hadn't seen it sooner.

She looked at the clock on the wall above her desk. The time was noon. She called Southampton and Portsmouth. All was well.

She was allowed a thirty-minute break daily, during which she normally ate her lunch in the little room. Today, though, she felt the need to escape her post and clear her head. She left the cramped room and stepped into the sunshine. She moved onto the High Street and turned left, away from the center of the village, in the opposite direction from the Lear farm.

She soon found herself among the few stone cottages that stood at the east end of the village. She cut through an open meadow through which a narrow sheep path ascended Manscome Hill a half mile or so east of the main path that crossed Mills Run, which lay to her right. To her left was a wood that marked the boundary between the hill and the estate of Lord Jeffrey Pembroke.

She climbed the path for ten minutes, walking in the sun, reinvigorating her spirits, before turning around. She decided that, come what may, she was finished with Arthur—finished in *that* way, at least. As she turned to head back down the hill, she saw a tall, gangly, sandy-haired boy standing in the meadow, fifty yards below. The sight of him startled her. She had never before seen the boy. He stood in the meadow looking up at her, a leather satchel over his shoulder. He was dressed in a light cotton shirt and pants and leather sandals and had golden hair almost to his shoulders. Despite the distance separating them, she sensed his skittishness. He seemed poised to run, like a rabbit. When she took a tentative step in his direction, he flinched. Despite his size, he seemed very much like a child. She raised her hand and said "Hello."

He raised his hand to her but did not wave it; the motion reminded her of the one the Indians made in the American cowboy movies when they greeted the white men.

She began to move toward him, intending to ask his name. She got close enough to see the focused intensity in his eyes. She was just about to speak to him when he leapt into motion. With a sinewy grace, he moved quickly through the tall grass and thistle of the meadow and disappeared into Lord Pembroke's wood.

EIGHT

—⟁—

AT HALF PAST NOON, LAMB RENDEZVOUSED WITH HIS MEN AT THE
stone bridge over Mills Run, near Will Blackwell's cottage.

No one had good news to report. Rivers and his men had not
fared well. Even with Harris in tow, they'd encountered more shuttered doors and drawn curtains than not. The villagers to whom
they'd spoken claimed to have seen or heard nothing suspicious on
the previous day. Nor had the search of Blackwell's cottage or the
ongoing grid search of the hill turned up anything useful, Wallace
reported.

Lamb described the altar he'd found in the shed and showed
everyone the drawing. He said he reckoned that the mute boy, Peter,
had drawn it, given that he was known for drawing insects.

"It's quite good," Larkin said of the drawing, adjusting his glasses.
"Brilliant, really."

"Yes, but what the bloody hell is it supposed to mean?" Rivers asked.

"Maybe Blackwell is supposed to be the bird?" Wallace offered. He shrugged. "He talked to birds—or so his niece claimed."

"Then Abbott's the spider," Rivers said.

Lamb gave the drawing to Larkin with instructions to check it for fingerprints and to check the shed more thoroughly for further evidence. He instructed Rivers and Wallace and their men to return to their respective tasks after lunch, then headed back to Winchester, hoping that Winston-Sheed had finished Blackwell's autopsy and he could read it.

He was driving through open country, fifteen minutes from Winchester, when he heard the sound of aircraft overhead. He glanced skyward and was surprised to see a formation of German dive-bombers, Stukas, heading north. He'd heard no warning sirens. The German planes appeared to be flying unusually low; their nearness spooked him and he felt exposed. Meadow and crop fields surrounded the stretch of road on which he was driving. Roughly two hundred yards ahead, though, it entered a small wood. He stepped on the gas as the Stukas neared.

In the wood, he pulled the Wolseley to the shoulder and left it running. He got out of the car and moved into the trees. He could hear the droning of the planes not far above. He walked into the wood in part to distance himself from his car; he knew his thinking was partly irrational. The chances of a bomb hitting the Wolseley and it exploding were practically nil. And yet he had seen other men die in far more freakish ways.

His heart throbbing, he moved to the edge of the wood, to a place where he could see over the meadow he'd just passed, and peered at the sky. A formation of perhaps twenty Stukas was passing overhead. On the Somme, he'd never felt menaced by airplanes. Then, most planes didn't carry bombs that could be dropped with impunity on all and sundry. But warfare had changed drastically since, and the German Blitzkrieg attacks on the continent had confirmed the new lethality of the airplane. He was about to retreat into the relative safety of the wood when he saw a pair of British fighters, Spitfires, suddenly appear from the north, one flying slightly above the other. They headed straight at the Germans with such fierce intent that Lamb wondered if they meant to ram the Stukas. The higher of the two Spitfires suddenly swooped upward, while the lower plane kept straight on. The British pilot flew into the midst of the Stukas like a bee attacking a swarm of wasps. Lamb heard a brief cackle of gunfire—and almost immediately one of the Germans began to trail white smoke. A second later the Stuka exploded and plummeted in two flaming pieces. It all seemed to happen in an instant. Then a second Stuka began to trail smoke. It kept its northward course for a few more seconds before its white vapor trail turned black and it veered sharply to the east and disappeared.

Now Lamb saw a Spitfire moving westward with a German fighter, a Messerschmitt 109, on its tail. The Messerschmitt had been hovering nearby, acting as a protective escort to the slow-moving Stukas, and had jumped on the Spitfire. Lamb could not tell if the Spitfire was one of the two British fighters he had seen seconds earlier, but thought that it must be. The RAF man rocked his wings, then circled upward. The German in the Messerschmitt followed.

The British pilot continued to race skyward so that his plane was nearly perpendicular to the earth. Reaching the apex of his climb, he suddenly maneuvered the plane into a backward loop and headed toward the ground in a steep dive. Lamb wondered if the German had managed to hit the Spitfire, though he saw no smoke coming from the plane. He thought: *He's going right into the ground.*

But when the pilot was less than a hundred meters from the ground, from death, he suddenly leveled his plane and raced in Lamb's direction. Incredibly, the German had performed the identical maneuver and continued to follow.

The Spitfire was perhaps a hundred meters above and moving toward the meadow. A second later, it swept past Lamb at what seemed to him an astounding rate of speed—and yet he'd clearly seen the form of the pilot in the cockpit. The Messerschmitt followed. As the German plane passed Lamb, its guns fired a quick burst; it then swept away to the east. Lamb's bowels tightened.

The Spitfire headed sharply upward, trailing gray smoke from its right wing. Once again, when the pilot reached the apex of his climb, he turned his plane into a dive. The plane leveled out and headed back toward Lamb—though as it came on, Lamb saw that that Spitfire was losing altitude and that oily black smoke rippled from the place where the gray smoke had been.

The fighter roared past Lamb; this time he saw that its cockpit was aflame and caught the merest glimpse of the pilot's silhouette among the licking fire. He felt dumb, rooted, irrelevant. The plane sped on for a few seconds more before it suddenly nosed down and headed for the ground. It smacked into the earth about three quarters of a mile distant and exploded in a ball of fire that shook the ground on which Lamb was standing.

He felt his knees give way and, an instant later, he fainted.

—⁓—

He came to a few seconds later, lying on his back. The first thing he glimpsed was a remnant of the smoke from the burning Spitfire dissipating in the blue sky. He managed to pull himself to his feet. The German swarm had passed and the meadow had become so quiet that Lamb could hear the buzz of insects. He looked in the direction of the place where the Spitfire had disappeared. A dense column of acrid black smoke billowed toward the sky.

Dead, he thought. *The boy is dead.*

A memory of Eric Parker's blackened, lifeless face assailed him. He thought that he should go to the plane, but realized there was nothing he could do. He had no desire to see the wreckage. Cleaning up the mess was someone else's duty.

Mildly confounded, he moved back through the wood to his car and drove the rest of the way to Winchester in a daze. Rather than going to the nick, he went directly home, to Marjorie. He found her sitting at the kitchen table, sipping tea. She'd just returned from shopping, during which time she'd spent a half hour standing in line to snag a decent-sized cod, which she intended to bake that afternoon for their tea. Lamb's unexpected entrance startled her. She immediately saw the disquiet in his eyes.

"What's wrong?" she asked. She stood and guided him toward a chair.

He sat and put his hat on the table. "I had to stop," he said. "I was on the road, in the open." He looked at her quizzically. "The Germans didn't come here, then?"

"No." She sat next to him. "Can you tell me about it?"

Since the bombing had begun, Marjorie knew that Lamb inevitably must face a moment when the war returned to him. During the early years of their marriage, nightmares had disturbed his sleep. In the past decade or so, he'd managed to bury his memories of the Somme in the routines and concerns of his daily life, and the nightmares mostly had ceased. Seeing the stunned look in her husband's eyes, Marjorie knew that something Lamb had witnessed had dredged those submerged memories to the surface.

"Stukas; I think they were going for the airfield at Cloverton," Lamb said. "They were so bloody low." He thought of the Spitfire pilot in the burning cockpit. "I saw a pilot die. I was coming from Quimby when I heard them in the sky and realized that I was in the open." He paused, then added, "I suppose I panicked a bit. I found some cover in a wood and went to the edge and watched them pass. They were like wasps. A boy in a Spitfire came in among them—went straight into them. He sacrificed himself. I watched him go down; his plane was burning. He went down in a field and there was an explosion."

He looked at Marjorie. "I fainted. I couldn't help it—couldn't control it."

She touched his cheek. "You mustn't feel ashamed of merely surviving," she said. She had told him this many times, though she hadn't needed to in many years.

He'd hoped not to worry Marjorie with the problem of Harry Rivers. But he saw now that he was wrong to think that Marjorie shouldn't know. And he'd been wrong to believe that he could keep the old war at bay in the midst of the new one. He would need Marjorie's help to keep his balance—to stay on the beam—just as he'd needed her twenty years earlier, when he'd returned from the trenches, and as he'd needed her ever since.

"Dick Walters's replacement came yesterday," he said. "It's Harry Rivers."

"Rivers?" For a second, Marjorie wondered if her husband was delusional. Harry Rivers was among the phantoms of the first war that Lamb had buried.

"He was transferred. He bollixed a case in Warwickshire and was transferred."

"But *here,* of all places. . . ."

"I didn't want to bother you with it."

Many years earlier, Marjorie had heard Lamb's explanation of why he'd tolerated Rivers's enmity and found it unconvincing. She was sure that Lamb felt responsible for Parker's death, when he shouldn't. The bloody Germans were responsible for Parker's death. She believed that Harry Rivers had done too good a job of playing on her husband's sense of guilt in Parker's death as a way of relieving himself of his own feelings of culpability, and she had told Lamb this, too, on many occasions, though not in many years.

But she repeated none of that now. She said only, "I'm glad you told me all the same." She squeezed his hand in hers. "You owe him nothing. Just remember that."

"I know," Lamb whispered.

Marjorie kissed his head. "You know," she said. "But you don't believe. And you must believe."

NINE

—⚉—

LAMB SAT AT THE TABLE SIPPING TEA FOR AN HOUR BEFORE HE FELT ready again to face the world.

During that time, he temporarily put aside his guilt about fouling the kitchen and smoked a half dozen cigarettes to the nub. When he was done, he told himself he must get back to his job and willed himself to leave the kitchen and go out to the Wolseley. Marjorie followed him to the car. She kissed him again and promised that she would have a baked cod ready for their tea when he returned home.

"Thank you," he said. "I'm not sure what I'd do without—"

She put her finger to his lips. "It's all right," she said. She smiled. "Just try not to be late."

He drove to the hospital, where he picked up a copy of Blackwell's autopsy from Winston-Sheed, and from there to the nick. He found himself glancing out the window of the Wolseley at the sky, looking for planes, and told himself that he must stop. He could not afford to give in to his fears and anxieties. He had too bloody much work to do.

When he arrived at the constabulary, Harding confirmed Lamb's guess that the Stukas had been on their way to attack the RAF's Cloverton airfield. The German dive-bombers had set the field's fuel depot aflame, destroyed a half dozen British fighter planes on the ground, and left the grass landing strip scarred with bomb craters. Harding added that he'd put the Hampshire police force on alert in case they were needed to assist the RAF.

Lamb said nothing to Harding of his own encounter with the Stukas. He did not want the super to know that seeing the planes had left him shaken. It was better that he give Harding no reason to doubt his ability. Instead, he delivered to the super a brief rundown of what he and his men had found—or hadn't found—in Quimby that morning.

"Very well," Harding said, displeased by the lack of progress. "When the rest of them return, we'll meet, get everything bloody straight."

Lamb read Blackwell's autopsy in his cramped office, sucking on a butterscotch. The report described the most savage killing Lamb had encountered in his twenty-one years as a police officer. Someone had bashed in the back of the old man's head with an oak branch; the presence of mud in his nostrils indicated that he had hit the ground face-first while still alive. The killer had then spun the old man onto his back and driven the left tine of the pitchfork into the middle of Blackwell's neck, severing Blackwell's larynx and killing him. The killer had then gouged the cross into Blackwell's head with the scythe before thrusting the tool into the old man's chest. The blade had pierced and ruptured Blackwell's heart. Blackwell had lain near the hedge long enough to nearly bleed out. In the end, birds had pecked out his eyes.

Lamb put the report on his desk, closed his eyes, and sorted the evidence he'd so far collected. It wasn't much. They'd find Abbott's fingerprints on the pitchfork and scythe; but Abbott had a convenient story to explain that. And Lydia Blackwell had confirmed Abbott's story of how they'd found the body. He would need to speak with both of them again, press them more forcefully. And he must speak as soon as possible with Lord Pembroke and the boy, Peter.

He felt the need to escape the nick; he could still feel the anxiety the Stukas had called up in him—at seeing the pilot die—sitting at the nadir of his gut. He picked up the issue of *Sporting Life*, walked onto the sunny street and lit a cigarette, then headed for The Fallen Diva. He sat alone at a table near the back of the pub (coincidentally, the same table Wallace had occupied on the previous afternoon, at lunch), smoking and sipping a half pint of ale. Hoping to clear his mind of rubbish, he gazed at the listing of the following day's races at Paulsgrove, circling the names of horses he might bet on. He found a horse in the second race called Summer Wind.

Summer Wind—Winter's Tail? Maybe there was something there, some symbiosis, he thought? He threw his pencil onto the table in a mild fit of self-disgust. *Summer Bloody Wind?* Why did he even entertain such ridiculous notions?

Marjorie was right; he musn't feel guilty about surviving. He'd thought he'd made his peace with that idea, and with the memory of Eric Parker, twenty years ago. Apparently that peace was more fragile than he'd known. He told himself to straighten up and get on with it. He folded the paper, tucked it beneath his arm, and returned to the nick. He found Wallace, Rivers, and Larkin in the incident room talking with Harding. He removed his hat and joined them.

"Any news?" he asked.

Rivers raised his chin. "Man named Michael Bradford claims that someone stole a chicken from his henhouse two nights ago. I took him to the shed and showed him the chicken we found on the altar. He claimed it was his."

"Did he seem surprised that *Blackwell* had stolen the chicken?" Lamb asked.

"No. As a matter of fact, he went on a bit—maybe a bit too much—about how he *wasn't* surprised, given that Blackwell was a witch and the rest of it."

"Do you believe him?"

Rivers shrugged. "He keeps a henhouse behind his cottage. He lives in one of the old mill houses. The place is barely fit for pigs. According to Harris, he's a widower and lives in the house with his three kiddies."

"A boy and two girls?"

"Yes."

"He wants the bloody reward," Wallace interjected. "He'll tell us whatever he thinks we want to hear."

"What else have we got, then?" Harding asked.

Larkin reported that he'd found distinct thumb and forefinger impressions on the drawing of the bird trapped in the spider's web but nothing on the altar. "I checked the prints against Blackwell's but they don't match, nor do they match those of Abbott or the niece. I haven't finished yet with the weapons. Also, I found nothing else of interest in the shed."

He returned the weird drawing to Lamb. Harding sighed impatiently.

"All right," Lamb said. "We'll go at the hill again tomorrow—widen things a bit. And we need to track down Abbott. Harris claims that Abbott plays the ponies, so if it comes to it we'll send a man to Paulsgrove to look for him. We'll rendezvous here tomorrow morning."

Harding followed Lamb into Lamb's office and closed the door.

"I spoke to the man from the *Mail*, so there'll be a story in tomorrow's paper," Harding said. "I'll assign a couple of constables to handle the bloody phones for the next few days, but I haven't men to waste." He laid a hand on Lamb's shoulder—a gesture of trust and camaraderie he never would have displayed in front of the lower ranks. "We need a quick result, Tom. Tamp down the bloody nonsense and keep the press off our backs. This is just the sort of thing they feed on, especially with the bombings and the rest of it going on. People are looking for something to take their minds off the bloody Germans."

Lamb nodded. "Yes, sir," he said, though he was far from a "quick result."

When Harding left, Lamb sat at his desk and made two telephone calls. The first was to Brookings, the ancestral estate of Lord Jeffrey Pembroke.

Lamb never had met Pembroke but knew that Pembroke enjoyed a reputation as a philanthropist and a kind of rebel against his class. Some of the highborn apparently even considered Lord Jeffrey an outright traitor. He had refused to take his seat in the House of Lords for reasons that Lamb was not entirely certain of, except that Pembroke believed that the English class system had endowed people such as himself with too many advantages and that he hoped to break down those class barriers.

Pembroke was well known for his practice each summer of playing host to two dozen boys from an orphanage in Basingstoke. The boys stayed at Brookings from the beginning of June until the end of August, living in barracks that Pembroke had built for the purpose. The boys spent the summer studying the flora and fauna of Brookings, collecting specimens, and keeping journals on what they'd discovered. They also tended the estate's extensive flower and vegetable gardens. Gardening was among Pembroke's passions and he actively supervised the boys' work. The vegetable gardens provided food not only for the estate but a large surplus that Pembroke distributed free to the people of the neighboring villages, including Quimby, which bordered his estate to the west.

Lamb found a listing for Brookings in the Hampshire telephone directory. He called the number and, after a half dozen rings, a ponderous, ancient-sounding voice answered, "Brookings. How may I help you?"

Lamb identified himself and asked to speak to Pembroke.

"I'm sorry, sir, but Lord Pembroke is not available at the moment," the voice said. Lamb imagined an ancient butler arrayed in the Edwardian manner, holding the telephone to his ear with lips pursed, slightly suspicious of the voice on the other end and, indeed, of the very existence of the telephone itself. "You may, however, speak with Lord Pembroke's secretary, Mr. Parkinson, sir," the voice said.

"Yes, please," Lamb said. "That would be fine."

"Very well, sir. Please hold the line and I will fetch Mr. Parkinson."

A minute later a clear voice fairly barked, "*Hallo*—Chief Inspector? Leonard Parkinson here. How may I help you, sir?"

"Yes, Mr. Parkinson," Lamb said. "Thank you for taking my call. I'd like to arrange to speak with Lord Pembroke as soon as you can arrange it."

"Well, that should be no problem at all, Chief Inspector. Might I ask what about?"

"I'd like to speak with him in connection with a murder inquiry. You might have heard that an old man was killed in Quimby yesterday. This man was said to have been known in the village as a witch and was killed in a way that seemed to suggest that some sort of black-magic ritual might have been involved."

"Yes, I did hear something about that. And you'd like to consult with Lord Pembroke on this black-magic angle then?"

"Basically, yes. In fact, Lord Pembroke mentioned the dead man, William Blackwell, in his book. Blackwell was supposed to have seen some sort of demon hound in his boyhood. And the manner in which he was killed is similar to that used to kill a milkmaid in the last century—a story that Lord Pembroke also mentions in his book."

"Well, it sounds a terrible tragedy and I'm sure that Lord Pembroke would be happy to help you in any way he can. Can you meet him here tomorrow morning at ten?"

"That would be fine," Lamb said.

"I should say, though, Chief Inspector, that Lord Jeffrey doesn't have much of an interest in the supernatural these days. That was more a youthful fancy. He's moved on to more weighty concerns."

"All the same, I believe that speaking with him could prove helpful."

"Of course, of course," Parkinson said. "We look forward to seeing you tomorrow morning, then. Just come to the front door and Hatton will fetch me."

"Thank you."

"My pleasure, Chief Inspector."

Lamb hung up the phone and, playing a hunch, called the number of a man he'd known for twenty years. Indeed, Albert Gilley had provided Lamb his first big success as a detective, when he'd shut down Gilley's numbers ring in Portsmouth. Gilley had done three years for that, then sworn off criminal enterprise—or so he'd claimed. He now spent his days at Paulsgrove racetrack in what he liked to call a "consulting" role. He placed bets on horses for Lamb and other "clients" and then sent the clients their winnings in the post, after deducting a ten-percent fee for his trouble. It was penny-ante stuff and perfectly legal, if not necessarily savory. Gilley knew Paulsgrove and its denizens perhaps better than anyone.

"Gilley," he answered.

"It's Lamb, Albert."

"A pleasure to hear your voice, as always, guv. What can I do for you?"

"Have you sent the four quid I won on Winter's Tail yet?"

"I was just about to put it in the post as you called, guv."

"Don't bother. I've got a job for you; if you come through, the money is yours."

"I'm all ears."

"I want you to ask after a man named George Abbott. He's from up this way, a farmer. He's an older man but powerful looking—looks as if he might be able to handle someone half his age if it came to it. He likes a drink and probably shoots off his mouth more than he should."

"I think I might know the gentleman, guv."

"I'd like to know if he's in deep to anybody and if so, by how much."

"That shouldn't be a problem. Anything else?"

"Not for now, Albert."

"All right then, guv. I'll call when I have something. The usual number, then?"

"Yes."

"Appreciate the business, as always, guv. Say hello to the missus for me."

Lamb hung up the phone feeling slightly more hopeful about his chances than he'd felt even an hour before. Still, he could not rid himself of the image of the young pilot burning in the cockpit and the sound and sensation of the Spitfire shattering in the distant meadow. He reached for the butterscotch tin in his right jacket pocket, then withdrew his hand, whispered "Sod it all," found his cigarettes in the left pocket, and lit one.

He lay back a bit in his chair, closed his eyes, and tried to relax. But the first thing he saw in his mind's eye was Eric Parker's frozen-eyed face staring back at him.

—⁓—

Wallace wanted a drink and to see Delilah.

He'd been thinking of Delilah all day; the way she'd poured the whiskey over herself had driven him fairly wild. Even so, he'd nearly bollixed things that morning by coming in to work looking like something the bloody cat dragged in. He was surprised that Lamb hadn't interrogated him more thoroughly. Even so, he decided that he could continue with Delilah if she was willing. But he must be more careful with her, just as he must be careful with his drinking.

After returning to the nick from Quimby, he spent nearly an hour laboriously typing a report for Lamb on the results of the grid search. He hated typing and, in any case, found it difficult to compose a report that said, in effect, "I found nothing."

It was now getting on toward teatime. He glanced toward Lamb's small office; the door was closed. Lamb seemed to have gone home. Rivers also seemed to have disappeared and Larkin had gone to the lab to dust the murder weapons for fingerprints. Wallace was just about to knock off when Harding entered the room.

"The RAF have asked for our assistance manning a roadblock near Cloverton," the super said. "The thing is on the main road into the base, just south of it. Round up three men and get out there. Someone there will give you your marching orders."

Bloody fucking hell. He stood. "Yes, sir," he said.

Harding nodded. "I'll see that you're relieved in due time."

"Thank you, sir."

"Get going, then. It sounds as if the bloody place is burning up."

Wallace rounded up three uniformed constables and headed to the airfield, which was roughly four miles northeast of Winchester. He found the roadblock about a half mile from the base. A youthful RAF lieutenant, a dozen soldiers, and a Bren gun crew surrounded by sandbags manned the post. Columns of black smoke rose from the airfield and an acrid smell filled the air—a mixture of burning wood, gasoline, oil, and cordite.

The young officer was waving a tanker truck full of water and a heavier truck with a bulldozer on its bed through the barrier. Wallace ordered the constable at the wheel of the Wolseley to pull off the road onto a slight hill near the gate, just beyond the Bren gun crew. He saw an anti-aircraft emplacement just to the west, its gun pointing skyward. Its crew, having engaged the Stukas, now lounged about the sandbags, sipping coffee. Wallace approached the boyish lieutenant, who was kicking one of the rear tires of the truck transporting the bulldozer and yelling at the driver to "get the bloody goddamned thing moving!"

Wallace offered the man his hand and introduced himself. The officer replied by telling Wallace his last name: Glendon.

"I've a pair of ambulances coming up the road any minute," Glendon said. "Keep the bloody goddamned civilians out of the way. Bloody nuisance. Tell them to go home."

Without waiting for Wallace's reply, Glendon turned back to the trucks and shouted at them to move.

Wallace returned to his squad of constables and deployed them along the road, two on each side, about fifty yards from the roadblock. "No civilians," he told them.

Over the next thirty minutes, he and his men turned back seven people who arrived in motorcars—four men, one of whom was quite old, and three women. None resisted or argued when told that they must turn around and go away. Wallace wondered who they were;

some likely were relatives of those who were stationed at or working at the airfield; others might have been mere curiosity seekers. His job had taught him that some people possessed a bottomless fascination with death, were drawn to it as flies to a corpse.

Over the next two hours, his crew turned away an additional dozen civilians and waved through the ambulances Glendon had been waiting on, along with another four trucks full of water, a fire engine from Portsmouth, several trucks carrying Home Guard men, and a single RAF staff car flying on its front bumper the standards of a very senior officer. Wallace stole a glance into the back seat and thought he spied the severe visage of Hugh "Stuffy" Dowding, the head of RAF fighter command. Glendon saluted the vehicle as it passed.

The traffic at the roadblock had begun to thin and the smoke from the airfield to abate when Wallace saw a woman on a bicycle pedaling toward the checkpoint from the south. The woman came on, steadily and stoically in the twilight, until one of the constables intercepted her. Wallace watched as the constable spoke to the woman. She was a good-looking girl, with longish auburn hair—a bit windswept now from the bike ride—and particularly nice legs. She raised her voice to the constable, though Wallace couldn't hear exactly what she said—something about "having a right."

He watched the girl get onto her bicycle and attempt to pedal past the constable; the constable grabbed the bike's handlebars and stopped her progress. Wallace guessed that love—or some semblance of it—was urging her on. Women fell for the bloody pilots like bowling pins.

He approached the woman and the constable barring her way. "Hold on there, miss," he said. "It's not safe ahead." He nodded to the constable. "I'll handle this, Boyce."

Emily Fordham looked fiercely at Wallace. "I don't care," she said. "I'm going forward. I've been through this gate before. I know what I'm doing. I've a right to go in."

"I'm afraid that doesn't count today, miss," Wallace said.

Emily Fordham dismounted the bike and pushed it to the side of the road. "Then I'll wait," she said. She folded her arms.

Wallace smiled, hoping to disarm her. "You could be in for a very long wait. Perhaps all night."

"I don't care," Emily said. She sat in the grass by the side of the road.

"You'll get cold when the sun goes down. I assume you brought a blanket with you."

Emily didn't answer.

Wallace liked her spunk. He envied the flyboy who'd aroused such passion in her. He went to the boot of the Wolseley and withdrew from it a dark green wool blanket that was part of an emergency kit with which the constabulary equipped its vehicles. He also withdrew a packet of tea biscuits. He laid them in the grass next to Emily. "Are you certain I can't give you a ride back to wherever you're from?" he asked.

"I can take care of myself." She looked at him. "Thank you for the blanket."

"I'll tell the officer at the checkpoint that you're here," Wallace said.

"Thank you," Emily said. But as she spoke, she was looking at the airfield and not at Wallace.

A half hour later, Sergeant Cashen and a trio of fresh constables arrived to relieve Wallace and his men. Wallace told Cashen about Emily. She remained sitting by the road, the blanket lying, still folded, on the ground next to her.

He hoped her lover boy hadn't been killed in the raid. She was, he thought, too young to cry over someone's grave.

TEN

—⟋⟍—

LAMB WOKE ALONE. HE HEARD MARJORIE PUTTERING ABOUT downstairs in the kitchen and hoped she'd made coffee.

He washed, shaved, and dressed. On his way downstairs, he stopped at Vera's room. He wasn't certain why he stopped, other than that he missed Vera. Her bed, with its pale green cotton blanket, was neatly made, as always, though she hadn't slept in it since taking the job in Quimby. Certificates on the wall honored her school accomplishments: one for being crowned champion of her primary school spelling bee in her fifth year, one for having completed a swimming and life-saving course, and one for having earned the runner-up spot in the junior girls division of the 1939 Hampshire cross-country championships.

He thought of the nursery rhyme from which he'd taken his nickname for her, "Doodle Doo."

Doodle Doodle Doo,

The Princess lost her shoe;
Her Highness hopped—
The fiddler stopped,
Not knowing what to do.

The rhyme had been one of Vera's favorites when she was a toddler. As Lamb read it to her, she'd acted out the parts of the princess searching for her shoe, her highness hopping, and the fiddler stopping. As the fiddler, she always came to an abrupt halt and looked around the room with a baroque look of confusion on her little face, which always made Lamb laugh.

He saw on Vera's vanity the accoutrements of her young womanhood that she'd left behind—several hairbrushes, a jewelry box, some odds and ends related to makeup, the small dark blue bottle of perfume he and Marjorie had given her the previous Christmas. It had a French name he couldn't remember; Marjorie had picked it out. He hadn't thought much of it at the time but now realized that young women wore perfume for one reason.

He left the room, closing the door behind him.

He was surprised to find that Marjorie was not in the kitchen, though she'd indeed made coffee. The morning edition of the *Mail* was on the table, its front page given over to stories detailing yet another German raid on the Blenheim factory on the previous night. Lamb glanced at it. Once again, the Germans had bollixed the raid, dropping more bombs around the factory than on it. But in the process they'd killed fourteen people, innocents whose houses and farms had inconveniently been in the path of the errant bombs.

The paper also contained a story on Will Blackwell's murder that included prominent mention of the rumor that he practiced witchcraft. The story quoted Harding as saying that the police were inquiring into the black-magic angle, but downplaying it.

Lamb looked out the kitchen window to the rear yard, where Marjorie kept a small flower and vegetable garden. The sky was blue, the weather clear, sunny, and unseasonably hot, which meant that the Germans surely would come again that day and probably that night.

The summer was fast shaping up as the driest and hottest on record. They'd had no rain in two weeks and none was forecast for the following three days.

Marjorie was standing by her small rose garden, her arms wrapped about herself, as if she were cold. He poured two cups of coffee—adding a drop of milk to Marjorie's—and carried them outside. He came up behind Marjorie and kissed her on the back of the neck. "Good morning," he said and handed her the coffee. He dispensed with "cheers."

He handed Marjorie the warm cup. "Thank you," she said; she allowed Lamb to draw her in close to him and they stood together for a minute, not speaking. When the war had begun, he and Marjorie had tried to persuade Vera to take a "safe" war job, perhaps as a typist or telephone operator. But she had resisted this advice, declaring her intention to do her part.

"They bombed the Blenheim factory again last night," Marjorie said after a moment.

"Yes. But they bollixed it."

"That's what frightens me."

"I know."

"It's all down to chance; there's no guarantee that any of that will bleed into the countryside." Marjorie looked away. "Damn her muleheadedness," she said.

"She's determined to do what she will do and we must let her." He pulled Marjorie closer. "We can't protect her—not entirely. She must learn to protect herself."

Marjorie emitted a sigh of resignation and shook her head.

"Let's have breakfast," Lamb said. He took her by the arm and led her back inside.

—⁊⁊—

At the nick, Lamb found Harding sequestered in his office, speaking on the phone. Neither Rivers, nor Wallace, nor Larkin had arrived—though on his desk, Lamb found Larkin's report on the murder weapons. Larkin had found two sets of fingerprints on the handles of the pitchfork and scythe—Blackwell's and Abbott's. Neither matched the thumbprint he'd found on the drawing. He'd found no usable print on the makeshift altar.

His phone rang. "Lamb."

"Morning, guv," Albert Gilley said.

"Hello, Albert."

"Your Mr. Abbott's into it for at least two hundred, total, with a couple of different blokes, both of whom are losing their patience."

Lamb whistled, impressed. Two hundred was more than a year's wages for a man like Abbott. "Thank you, Albert," he said.

"Anything else, guv? There's a nice-looking filly in the second, name of Summer Wind. Five to one."

"I'll pass today, thanks."

"Suit yourself. Give my best to the missus."

On the previous night, Wallace had made it to The Fallen Diva just before final call. Delilah was waiting for him. He'd downed a pint and then they'd gone back to her little house and devoured each other, as they had the previous night. This time, though, Wallace had curbed his drinking. When, finally, he'd fallen asleep next to Delilah, he'd done so sober.

He'd also brought with him a razor, soap, and fresh clothing, which he'd stuffed into a kit bag. He'd therefore felt confident and on top of his game when he'd awakened. But Delilah was lying with her back to him, softly crying. He put his arms around her; she grasped his right hand to her breast and held it. Her skin was warm and moist. He asked her what was wrong.

"Nothing," she said without turning to look at him. "I just cry sometimes. I don't know why."

He'd held her for some minutes. The smell of liquor lingered on her breath. He felt a slight pity for her and realized that he did not know her surname. He told himself he would ask her later. He'd then washed and shaved and gone on his way, managing to arrive at the nick only a few minutes after Lamb.

Rivers had arrived next, followed shortly by Cashen and Larkin. Lamb conducted a quick meeting in which he reiterated their duties for the day. He told them he would join them in Quimby after speaking with Lord Jeffrey Pembroke. He briefly told them the stories of the murder of Agnes Clemmons and its similarities to Blackwell's killing, and of the tale of Blackwell having seen the black dog on Manscome Hill.

"It's likely our killer has read the book," Lamb said.

After the meeting, he briefly took Rivers and Wallace aside and told them that he had a source in Paulsgrove who'd said that Abbott was deeply in debt to a pair of Portsmouth bookies.

"You'll be in charge in Quimby in my absence," he told Rivers. "Check Abbott's cottage first. If he's not there, then I'll probably send you to Portsmouth."

"But he could be bloody anywhere," Rivers said, barely masking the impertinence in his tone.

"All the same, I want the lead checked," Lamb said evenly to Rivers. "If you're unwilling to go, then I'll send someone else and you can stay here and answer some of the many telephone calls I expect we'll get today in response to the newspaper story."

Rivers nodded and grumbled his assent.

Wallace wondered what Rivers was on about. He'd sensed the tension between Rivers and Lamb from the beginning; then Rivers had made the crack about "backing the wrong horse." But Rivers seemed to be the one who was making the wrong bet, challenging Lamb.

—⁓—

Brookings sat perched above the Solent between Quimby on its northwest side and the village of Lipscombe on its northeast.

Lamb found the main house to be much like other fine old manor houses he'd seen—large, elegant, and decrepit-looking. To the left of the house he saw the large gardens in which the boys who stayed at Brookings in the summers worked. All these, save one, which sprouted a variety of low green vegetables, lay fallow because the war had kept the boys away.

Hatton, the aging butler who'd answered Lamb's call of the previous day, showed Lamb into an echoing foyer. Hatton was just as Lamb had imagined, with a deeply lined, ancient face than nonetheless retained a kind of ageless haughtiness. He was dressed in black and sported wide gray sideburns. Although Pembroke was reputed to be a man of modern ideas, he apparently retained an old-fashioned taste in household staff, Lamb thought. "I'll tell Mr. Parkinson that you are here, sir," Hatton said.

Two minutes later, a small, wiry man dressed in a well-cut blue suit and red tie appeared. Leonard Parkinson walked toward Lamb with such speed that Lamb at first feared that Parkinson might ram him. When still a good seven strides away, Parkinson thrust out his hand.

"Chief Inspector!" he said. "So very good to meet you! Leonard Parkinson!"

Lamb had the feeling of fending off a friendly though slightly frantic terrier. Although Parkinson could not have been more than five feet, four inches tall, he possessed the grip of a stevedore. *Here* was Pembroke indulging in the modern, Lamb thought. Parkinson possessed the glad-handing openness of an American on the make. The people from whom Pembroke had sought to distance himself likely saw Parkinson as a kind of thumb in the eye.

"Lord Pembroke is eager to meet you," Parkinson said. "He finds this business with Mr. Blackwell absolutely a horror and is willing to help in any way he can." He gestured toward the back of the house. "Lord Pembroke is waiting for you in his wildflower garden."

Parkinson led the way through French doors at the rear of the house that gave onto a slate terrace fronting wide marble stairs that descended to a trim lawn about twenty meters wide and a hundred meters long that sloped toward bluffs above the sea. The central feature of this manicured space was a circular fountain perhaps ten feet in diameter that was topped by a bronze mermaid perched upon a rock. Either side of the lawn was bordered by a trimmed box hedge roughly five feet high; along the hedge, spaced every twenty or so feet, were marble benches at the ends of which sat cherubs strumming lyres.

Lamb followed Parkinson along the hedge until they reached a place in which the hedge opened, through an arch, onto one of the most singular and striking private gardens Lamb had ever seen. The garden was roughly fifty meters long and thirty wide; in nearly every square inch, wildflowers grew among delicate-looking bushes that sprouted a profusion of many-colored blossoms. The space was absolutely alive with bees and butterflies flitting among the blooms. A narrow, S-shaped flagstone path led through the blooms to an oval-shaped patch of lawn at the center of the garden; at the center of this green space, Jeffrey Pembroke sat at a black wrought-iron table that was set upon a circular patio of smooth stone, reading a book, a white canvas hat atop his head. At the center of the stone terrace was a sapphire tile mosaic of a butterfly with wings four feet wide. Pembroke was dressed in the Bloomsbury style: a pair of khaki cotton trousers, a green open-necked cotton shirt, and open-toed leather sandals. Pembroke seemed so lost in his reading that he failed to notice their arrival.

Parkinson cleared his throat. "Inspector Lamb has arrived, Jeffrey," he said.

Lamb was surprised to hear Parkinson refer to Pembroke by his Christian name rather than his title. Pembroke looked up from his book—Lamb could not quite read the title—in a way that suggested that someone had just tapped his shoulder to awaken him. He took a second to focus on Lamb and then grew animated. He stood and offered his hand in greeting. "Welcome, Chief Inspector," he said. "How nice of you to come."

Pembroke possessed a high forehead, thinning sandy hair, a long aristocratic nose, and elegant fingers. He was long-armed and long-legged. "I see that you've already made a friend, Chief Inspector," Pembroke said. "Have a look at your shoulder."

Lamb found a tiny butterfly perched on his left shoulder. Its indigo wings moved once—almost as if it were acknowledging Lamb's sudden awareness of its existence—then became still. He found it beautiful.

"The Large Blue," Pembroke said. "Rather a strange name, given its size, I know. I'm afraid it's becoming quite rare. But we've managed to attract a few around here, mainly by constructing the right kind of habitat. I'm not certain you realize how lucky you are, Chief Inspector." He smiled. "I know lepidopterists who gladly would trade their first-born children for the chance to experience what you are now experiencing."

Despite its beauty and apparent rarity, Lamb hoped the butterfly didn't decide it liked his shoulder. He didn't want to swat it away, given its supposed rarity and Pembroke's clear affection for it. He settled for blowing the tiniest of breaths at the thing, which caused it to rise and return to the surrounding forest of flowers.

Pembroke gestured for Lamb to sit.

"Are you a collector, my lord?" Lamb asked.

"No. Were I a collector, I would have had my net on the thing, rare or no. True collectors, despite their protestations to the contrary, are never conservationists. They'd take the last grain of sand in the world for their collections if the need and opportunity presented itself. I enjoy butterflies simply for their presence in the world and their beauty. I find them calming, don't you?"

"I suppose so," Lamb said.

"It's something to do with that rather self-possessed knack for still-ness they possess, I suspect. And by the way, you needn't worry with the 'my lord' business. I'm not *that* impressed with myself, despite appearances to the contrary."

The remark caught Lamb off guard—it suggested that Pembroke had successfully read him even as he was reading Pembroke.

Pembroke turned to Parkinson. "Could you fetch us some tea, please, Leonard?"

Parkinson nodded and smiled. "Right away," he said and disap-peared through the arched portal in the hedge.

Pembroke sat back in his chair and tented his fingers. "Now then, Chief Inspector," he said. "How can I assist your inquiries?"

"I read the chapter in your book on Will Blackwell's boyhood encounter with the black dog and the subsequent whisperings about his practicing witchcraft. Also, the manner of his murder very much mirrors that of Agnes Clemmons, the milkmaid, even down to the use of the pitchfork and scythe. I was hoping that you might provide a bit of perspective on that. How likely is it that these superstitions have persisted in the rural places?"

"You're right, of course. Blackwell's murder is similar to that of Agnes Clemmons, though in the earlier case the victim's connection to witchcraft existed only in the killer's head. I've uncovered no evidence—nor did the police at the time—that Clemmons practiced witchcraft."

"Does it appear likely to you that someone might have killed Blackwell because they believed him to be a witch?"

"It's a possibility, I suppose, though a much more remote one today than it would have been when Miss Clemmons met her end. Still, Blackwell's killing had several obvious hallmarks of the vanquishing of a witch."

"Do you mean the cross gouged into his forehead?"

"No—that's rather too obvious, actually. Even someone who knew nothing of witchcraft but was motivated by religious fervor might have gouged the sign of the Lord into what he considered an evil body. No—the cross is rather too much like the vampire stories. I'm speaking of the pitchfork in the neck. If our man did kill Blackwell because he believed him a witch, he might have run the pitchfork into Blackwell's neck for a couple of reasons."

"Such as?"

"Some occult legends say that the blood of a vanquished witch must be drained away and the body firmly secured to the killing spot, lest the spirit of the witch rise again. The pitchfork in the neck would accomplish both of those."

"What do you think of the notion that someone who is not in the least mad or motivated by religious fervor—but wanted it to appear that way—might have convincingly pulled this off?" Lamb asked.

"Well, they obviously would need to know at least a little something about the lore of witchcraft, which they could achieve, of course, with a little reading. I would have to ask, in turn, whether someone who was out to kill Mr. Blackwell for more prosaic motives would have thought to bother with so many macabre touches. I'll leave it to you to decide whether someone motivated to kill for commonplace reasons would have gone to the trouble this killer obviously has. If you are asking for my opinion, I'd say the crime points to someone with a very diseased mind—although his disease might not be readily apparent." Pembroke leaned back in his chair again. "Might I be allowed to play the role of amateur psychologist?" he asked.

"Please do."

"Well, if the killer is mad, his lunacy could nonetheless be hidden from the general run of humanity. But for that to be so, the man would have to enjoy little intercourse with the rest of the world, given that such a deep disturbance of the mind couldn't be entirely cloaked. Given that, if your killer is a madman, I would guess that he is a loner or hermit, someone who exists without spending too much time in the general hustle and bustle of life. I don't believe, for example, that he'd likely be a publican—just to take an example—or an estate agent." Pembroke smiled. "Or a police detective."

Lamb nodded and returned a smile of lower wattage. "Yes," he said. "I believe you're right."

"Just a thought," Pembroke said. "I doubt if it's of much help in the end."

"On the contrary," Lamb said. "It's quite helpful. Such a man could very well be a farmer—someone who might live and prosper, if he so chose, having little contact with the larger world, as Blackwell himself apparently did."

A maid arrived with the tea. Pembroke thanked her; she bowed slightly and departed silently. Pembroke prepared a cup to Lamb's specifications—no milk and one cube of sugar. The sugar bowl and creamer were full and the tea was something flavored and scented that Lamb had never before tasted.

"Did you know Will Blackwell?" Lamb asked.

"I didn't really, I'm afraid. I tried to talk to him when I was writing my book but he refused to speak with me. I had to rely on the testimony of others—the local folklore, if you will—in order to write the chapter on him. I'm afraid my including his story in the book upset him. I've always been sorry about that; I hadn't meant for that to happen."

"Do you believe the story that he encountered some sort of ghost dog on Manscome Hill?"

Pembroke smiled again. "You might find this strange, Chief Inspector, but I don't believe in ghosts. When I wrote the book, I was merely interested in the occult as a natural outgrowth of the human experience with the world, of our need to explain the irrational. Not to bog us down in metaphysics, but what role, after all, does religion play in our lives save to explain the irrational?"

"Do you remain interested in the occult?"

Pembroke placed his cup on his saucer and then dabbed his lips with a napkin.

"No," he said. "The subject was a passion of my youth. But a time eventually arrived in my life when I realized that my interest in witchcraft and the occult was just that—a fancy. I realized that I had 'other fish to fry,' as the Americans say. The persistence of poverty and the barriers of class concern me very much. Ending those has become my central concern."

Around them, a dozen butterflies of various hues and sizes fluttered, instinctively searching for the nectar that compelled them to take wing. Lamb needed a fag. He rummaged in his pocket and found the butterscotch. He withdrew it and, feeling sheepish, offered one to Pembroke, who declined it with a smile and said, as if he'd read Lamb's mind, "You're perfectly welcome to smoke, Chief Inspector."

Lamb smiled. "I'm trying not to."

Pembroke nodded. "I understand. Isn't it funny how the worst habits always are the most difficult to shed?"

"Very true."

"Anyhow, as I was saying, what we do here is not much, in the end, but it's something," Pembroke continued. "That, I think, is the lesson I've taken from it all—that you do what you can. There is nothing else, really. I realize, of course, that given the circumstances of my birth, I'm able to do more than most. But I'd hate for you to come away from our chat thinking that I understand the genesis of those privileges to be, at bottom, the result of anything beyond the sheer, blind luck of my birth. That said, one can be given the opportunity and resources to perform good works and waste them. I like to believe that I haven't wasted mine."

"I understand you have a boy living on the estate who once had been one of the orphans who visited Brookings. He apparently knew Will Blackwell and occasionally spent some time with him, sketching insects. Several people in Quimby mentioned him."

"Peter Wilkins—yes," Pembroke said. "He first came to us five years ago, when he was in the care of the orphanage, then stayed on. He's a special case, Chief Inspector—a kind of genius, really. The medical term for people like Peter is idiot savant. They have a tremendous amount of trouble understanding and navigating the world. Peter is extremely shy and rarely speaks, for example, even to me. But these people often possess, as a kind of balance, a rare talent at something. Many of them, for example, possess musical or mathematical genius. Peter's genius is as an artist. His favorite subject—his only subject, really—is insects, which he paints and sketches in the most exquisite ways. In my opinion and in the opinion of some others, Peter's renderings of insects rival those Audubon created of birds. A publisher friend of mine in London arranged a couple of years ago to publish some of his renderings in a book, which sells quite well among lovers of insects. The problem with Peter, of course, is that he is incapable of producing any worthwhile or meaningful research or findings to accompany his work. He neither reads nor writes. It's nothing save the art, but the art is beautiful and valuable in its own right. Frankly, I didn't know that he knew Blackwell, though it doesn't surprise me that he did. He has the run of the estate and wanders off it when it suits him."

"When does it suit him?"

"When he is searching for the subjects of his art, particularly butter-flies, which are the center of his life. He makes an annual count of them in and around the estate every summer. It's all very detailed and rather obsessive. He keeps in sketchbooks excruciatingly detailed records, consisting of drawings and renderings of what he finds each year. This need to tote things up is part of his disorder. Peter is comfortable only when he is allowed to follow an ironclad routine and brooks no effort to disturb it. He can become angry if he perceives that you intend to prohibit him from following his routine."

"He sounds difficult," Lamb said. "Was it his genius, then, that prompted you to adopt him?"

"I haven't adopted him. He is merely a resident on the estate. When I first met Peter I could see that he was special but that his disorder would not allow him to make his way in the world. At the time, I discussed his situation with the director of the orphanage and we agreed that he might do best here, on the estate, rather than cooped up with the other children. He doesn't relate to other children—or most people, really. He is sixteen now and comes and goes pretty much as he pleases. He lives in what was once a small summerhouse on the estate, by the sea, which I had converted for his use. He lives there and has his studio there, though he comes and goes from the house, as he needs. I'm afraid he will never be able to go out into the world as a normal person would."

"Do you intend to keep him here, then?"

"If he wants to stay, yes. If he doesn't, I'm confident he will make that known to me. At that time, we'll have to make other arrange-ments for him. But he seems happy here. Allowing him to stay is no burden; Peter is no burden, despite his handicaps. In fact, he is prob-ably less of a burden than a normal sixteen-year-old boy would be. Mostly, he dwells in his own private world."

"Do you find it unusual that he struck up a friendship with Blackwell? Apparently, he sometimes sat with Blackwell as Blackwell worked in the fields around the village."

"It does surprise me, yes, though I suppose it's possible that Peter found Blackwell less threatening than he finds most people. From what I knew of him, Blackwell was a loner and a bit of an outcast. His quiet nature might have made Peter feel at ease. When most people meet Peter, they normally try either to assist or bully him, depending on the quality of their character. Either way, they demand something of him, which Peter resists. But I suppose Blackwell might have merely accepted Peter's presence."

"Is Peter now in the midst of one of his butterfly counts?"

"Yes."

Lamb produced the drawing of the spider and the bird he'd found at Blackwell's cottage. "Is this Peter's work?" he asked.

Pembroke studied the drawing. "Yes," he said. "The quality of it is unmistakable." He looked at Lamb. "Where did you get this, if I may ask?"

"I found it in a toolshed behind Blackwell's cottage, lying on what I believe was a kind of black-magic altar—an apple crate upended upon which someone had burned some candles. I also found a chicken with its throat cut lying nearby. A local man claims the chicken was stolen from him."

Pembroke nodded, a grave look in his eyes. "I see," he said.

"Have you any idea what the chicken was supposed to represent?"

"Well, it sounds like voodoo, some kind of blood sacrifice."

"To who—or what—exactly?"

"I'm afraid I couldn't say."

"Can you venture a guess as to the meaning of the drawing?"

Pembroke looked again at the sketch. "I don't know, Chief Inspector," he said. "I wish I could be more help. I can tell you, though, that Peter doesn't often draw spiders. Though as you can see, he can draw them beautifully."

"Blackwell apparently liked birds and even told his niece that he was able to communicate with them. Is it possible that the bird represents Blackwell?"

"It might," Pembroke said. "But it might be anything, really."

"Is Peter capable of subduing a man such as Blackwell?"

Surprise animated Pembroke's face. "Certainly you don't believe that Peter might have hurt Blackwell?" he said.

"I'm not ruling out anything at the moment."

"I don't know," Pembroke said quietly. "I suppose that Peter is strong enough to subdue a man of Blackwell's age." He looked at Lamb. "But I simply can't see it—especially the manner in which Blackwell was killed. Violence frightens Peter."

"And yet you just said that he resists any effort to change his routine. Perhaps Blackwell upset that routine in some way."

Pembroke was silent.

Lamb leaned forward. "What if Peter saw something related to Blackwell's killing? Is it likely that he would fail to exhibit evidence of that—that he could be upset but have buried his distress?"

"Peter is very difficult to read, though a few people, including myself, have been able to reach him, at least to a degree."

"Might it be possible for me to speak with Peter?"

Pembroke hesitated before answering. "I suppose it would be all right," he said. "But I can't guarantee that he's even around the estate at the moment. When he's off on his census I don't see him for days. And I should warn you that, even if we do manage to track him down, he probably wouldn't speak to you. He is not mentally retarded. He knows what has happened to Blackwell and he knows what policemen do."

"I understand," Lamb said. "I've no wish to upset him."

"Very well, then." Pembroke rose. "I'll take you myself to his cottage. If you went alone he would run for certain the instant he saw you."

Pembroke led the way out of the butterfly garden to the sweeping lawn.

From where they walked, Lamb could see far out into the Channel. He just made out, along the horizon, a convoy of ships slowly heading west. In the first days of the battle for Britain, the Germans had concentrated their efforts on dive-bombing British shipping in the Channel, resulting in stupendous dogfights that were visible from the coast.

"I had quite a show out here for a bit in the beginning," Pembroke said as they walked. "The Germans came nearly every day. As much as I hate to admit it, it struck me as rather like watching a play. I could see everything clearly, and yet they were so far off that it didn't seem real. I never felt afraid."

Before they reached the cliffs above the sea, Pembroke led them to the right, through another arch in the hedge that gave onto a path laid in fieldstone. This path led, in switchback fashion, down the side of a bluff, toward a glen. Lamb noticed that Pembroke's portion of the coast contained no barriers against attack, though nearly all of the southern and eastern coast of England bristled with barbed wire, bunkers, and mines designed to stop a German invasion from the sea.

"I see that you're not fortified here," Lamb said as they descended the trail.

"No need for it," Pembroke said. When they made it to the glen, he turned toward the sea. "Allow me to show you something." He led Lamb to the cliffs. Thirty feet below, the sea crashed against jagged rocks and a slender spit of sand.

"You see, Chief Inspector," Pembroke said. "No one in their right mind would attempt to land there."

Lamb wasn't so sure. He stepped back from the precipice before vertigo overcame him. He'd never been comfortable looking down from heights.

"Well, I suppose we should see if Peter is in," Pembroke said. He turned and led Lamb back toward the glen, which gave onto a clearing in which stood a small, white, wood-shingled cottage. "This is it," Pembroke said. Lamb followed him to the cottage's front door.

Pembroke knocked. "Peter?" he said. "Are you home?"

No sound came from the house. "Peter?"

He turned to Lamb. "He doesn't appear to be in, though we can try the back."

He led the way to the back of the cottage, which faced a wooded hill. A dirt path led up the hill, at the top of which stood a dead tree, its branches crooked and barren. The tree resembled a lone sentry guarding whatever lay beyond the crest of the hill. As they rounded the side of the cottage, Pembroke gently took Lamb's arm. "There," he said. Lamb at first thought Pembroke was turning his attention to some animal, perhaps a fox or badger.

About twenty yards distant, he saw a sleeping boy, his back against the trunk of a tree and his chin fallen toward his chest. A leather-bound notebook lay in his lap and a butterfly net at his feet.

"Can we wake him?" Lamb asked.

"We can try. But the experience of coming awake in the presence of a stranger might be more than he's willing to countenance." He turned to Lamb. "I'll wake him. Once he's on his feet and sentient and I've explained that he has a visitor, I'll signal for you. In the meantime, it might be best if you kept out of sight."

Lamb moved behind the edge of the cottage as Pembroke approached Peter. He peered around the corner to watch Pembroke gently shake Peter awake. Peter stood immediately, as if the sudden interruption of his sleep had frightened him. He had straw-colored hair that came to his shoulders and wore a simple khaki-colored cotton shirt and shorts and a pair of brown boots. His face was fine-featured and he looked to Lamb younger than sixteen, though he was nearly six feet tall. His arms and legs were sinewy and tautly muscled, like those of a long-distance runner. Even from his slightly compromised vantage point, Lamb could see an animal-like wariness in Peter's eyes and believed him easily capable of thrusting a pitchfork into someone's neck.

Pembroke stood very close to Peter and spoke to him, though Lamb could not hear what Pembroke said. Pembroke then stepped back and looked in Lamb's direction. Lamb took this as his cue and moved around the corner of the cottage into Peter's view.

"Hello, Peter," he said.

Peter's eyes widened. Before Lamb could take another step, Peter turned and ran up the hill along the dirt path, passing beneath the dead tree and disappearing, as if he were a rabbit fleeing a fox.

Lamb joined Pembroke by the place where Peter had slept. Peter had fled so suddenly that he'd left behind his notebook and net.

"I'm sorry, Chief Inspector," Pembroke said. "I warned you."

"I understand," Lamb said. He turned toward the cottage. "Do you mind if I look inside?"

"If it's all the same, I'd rather you didn't," Pembroke said. "This is his house, after all. Merely because he's different doesn't mean he would see your entering without his permission as any less of a violation of his privacy than would I—or would you, if the situation were reversed. In any case, I'm sure he's watching us, and if he sees you enter the house I'll have a devil of a time convincing him that it's safe for him to return there. Never mind the fact that if you so much as touched even a single thing of his in there, he would know. The placement of everything within that house is designed to serve a kind of order and predictability that is known to Peter alone."

"I see," Lamb said. He felt chastised, delivered a lesson in the proper sensitivities. He stared at the path up which Peter had fled. "Very well, then. I suppose the only thing left is to thank you for your time."

Pembroke smiled. "Please don't take it personally, Chief Inspector. It's merely that most people never have met anyone quite like Peter. They expect him to act with something approaching normality, despite what they've been told about him. But when they finally actually encounter him, they are surprised to discover how truly unique he is. There's no preparing for it, really. I'm afraid it can leave one feeling quite confused."

ELEVEN

—⟋⟍—

IN QUIMBY, RIVERS TOOK CHARGE OF THE WIDENED SEARCH OF Manscome Hill. Harris met them by Blackwell's cottage and reported that Lydia Blackwell had not come home from work on the previous night and that Abbott also had not returned home.

"So she's gone away with the old man, then," Wallace said.

"Looks like it," Rivers said. "I said that those two were hiding something." Rivers believed for certain now that Lamb had bollixed his initial chance to solve Blackwell's killing by being too solicitous toward Lydia and wasting time looking into the nonsense about the ghost dog on the hill.

Rivers had last been in charge of an investigation more than six months earlier, in Warwickshire. The case was one of murder—the wife of a prominent local man had been gunned down in the couple's bedroom. The man had told what Rivers believed to have been a

107

concocted story about a burglar having come into the bedroom in
the dead of night and shot the wife when she'd confronted the man.
The husband claimed that he and his wife had argued earlier in the
day and he'd therefore slept on a sofa in his study and hadn't seen
the burglar. The shot—which police later determined came from a
.38-caliber revolver of American manufacture—had awakened him
and he'd gone to their bedroom to find his wife dead. By then, the
intruder had fled. An initial search of the house had turned up nothing
incriminating the husband. Still, Rivers mistrusted the husband and,
in probing his background, turned up a mistress—a stripper. He'd
then broken into the house while the husband was away and found
an American-made .38 lying in a suitcase and wrapped in a tea towel.
The bloody arrogant bastard had kept the gun, certain that he was in
the clear. And indeed he was—the case against him was thrown out,
thanks to Rivers's transgression. At the time, Rivers had been up for
an opening as detective chief inspector in Warwickshire. But the case
killed his chances, and shortly thereafter his superintendent bluntly
had told him that he was looking to transfer him.

Just as Lamb had been shocked to find Rivers standing with
Harding in front of Blackwell's cottage two nights earlier, so Rivers
had been stunned to learn that he was being transferred to Hampshire. Rivers had kept tabs on Lamb and knew that Lamb was a DCI
in Hampshire. He had thought at first to appeal the transfer. Then
he'd decided that avoiding Lamb amounted to a kind of cowardice.
He intended to make a fresh start in Hampshire, Lamb or no. And if
Lamb was unwilling to do what was necessary to solve the Blackwell
case, then he was happy to step in.

He sent Sergeant Cashen, the constables, and Harris to search
the hill from the place where they'd left off on the previous day, and
Wallace and Larkin to search the wood.

Playing a hunch, he went to the pub, from where he called
the coat factory where Lydia Blackwell was a seamstress. The
man on the line said that Lydia had not shown for work that day,
confirming his hunch. He then went to Abbott's cottage and banged

on the farmer's door, but received no answer. The old bastard clearly had done a runner. Still, there was no guarantee that he'd gone to Paulsgrove as Lamb believed. He went round to the back door and found it locked. Though he lacked sufficient cause, he could kick in Abbott's door. Were it not for the bloody rules, he could accomplish something, he thought. He bottled his anger and went down the trail to join Wallace and Larkin in the search of the wood.

Lamb arrived an hour later. He first went up the hill to check on the grid search. He was pleased to see that Rivers had deployed Cashen and his men correctly. He found Harris, who informed him of Abbott's and Lydia Blackwell's absence. Lamb asked Harris about Michael Bradford, the man who claimed that Will Blackwell had stolen from him the chicken they'd found on the altar in the shed. Lamb intended to speak to Bradford and the boy he believed was Bradford's son—the waif he'd encountered in front of Blackwell's cottage on the first night—and wanted to know what sort of man Bradford was. Rivers had described Bradford's cottage as unfit for pigs, and the filthy, ragged manner in which Bradford's children were dressed had distressed Lamb.

"He's a drunkard, sir," Harris said. "His wife died of consumption two years ago and left him with the three kiddies. He squats in one of the old mill houses, across the bridge."

"What's the boy's name?"

"Michael Junior, sir. 'Little Mike,' they call him. He's a villain in the making. Minor vandalism, pinching trinkets and things from the shops—that sort of thing. Bradford leaves the three of them pretty much to their own devices."

Lamb then hunted down Rivers, who by then was helping Wallace and Larkin search the wood. "What's the story with Abbott?" he asked Rivers.

"Done a runner, obviously. The niece, too, I'd say. I called the place where she works and they told me that she didn't show this morning." Rivers derived genuine pleasure from informing Lamb that he'd obviously been mistaken about Abbott and the niece. But that was Lamb, Rivers thought—always wanting things his own way, even when it bollixed all else.

Lamb asked Rivers to show him where Michael Bradford lived, which surprised Rivers. Rivers considered Bradford unimportant but held his tongue. The two men descended the hill, crossed the stone bridge in the middle of the village, then headed back up the hill on the opposite side of the wood, toward the ruins of the mill and its attendant houses. At first, they walked together in an uncomfortable silence. Then Lamb spoke.

"What are you thinking, inspector?"

Rivers found the question odd. "About what, exactly?"

"All of this—Abbott, Bradford, all of it."

Rivers wondered if Lamb was trying to bait him into somehow blundering. "Abbott and the niece did it," he said. "I don't buy the rest of it. I say we search Abbott's house. There's evidence in there. I'll bet my last shilling on it."

"We've no grounds to search it."

"No. But there are ways around that. Accidents."

Lamb thought of reminding Rivers that such an "accident" had led to him cocking up the case in Warwickshire and his transfer to Hampshire. But Rivers didn't need to be reminded of that. Still, he agreed that Abbott and Lydia might have run off together. If so, Lydia might eventually end up in some danger, if Abbott decided she had become an encumbrance or liability. If Abbott didn't return soon, they would have to enter his cottage. But Lamb wanted to do that legally, if possible.

"There won't be any accidents," Lamb said. "But if we need to, we'll move."

They reached the abandoned grain mill. Its windows were hollow, void even of wood framing, and its slate roof was on the verge of collapse. The low stone wall that surrounded the mill yard was crumbling and covered in moss and ivy; the iron gate that had opened onto the yard was gone from its rusted hinges, and the yard itself was overwhelmed by weeds, high grass, and a variety of industrial and domestic junk: machine parts; broken bottles; sodden, filthy rags.

Lamb stopped and turned to face the mill. "I want you to search it," he said to Rivers.

Rivers didn't mask his surprise. "It's a bloody ruin. There's nothing there." He wondered again if Lamb somehow was setting him up for a fall.

"All the same," Lamb said evenly. He turned to face the cottages. "Bradford is squatting in the one farthest up the hill, then?"

"Yes," Rivers said. Lamb hadn't really needed to be led to Bradford's house, he thought. Lamb had brought him up the hill merely to set him to the useless task of searching the mill.

Lamb turned back to Rivers. He believed he knew what Rivers was thinking.

"I'll see you on the way down, Harry," he said.

The squat fieldstone houses faced Mills Run.

The yard of the one in which Michael Bradford had installed himself and his children was awash in rubbish. As Lamb approached the house, he saw that its door was open; he detected the lingering smell of fried kidneys coming from within. He saw no sign of Little Mike or his sisters.

He pushed open the gate and made his way through the yard to the door, called "Good morning," and peeked inside. He saw a wooden table on which sat unwashed plates; just beyond the table was a shelf containing food. A worn wooden chair stood by the hearth, next to which sat a pair of boots. Bits of wood, paper, and sundry household items—including a rusting pot Lamb guessed was there to catch water leaking from the roof—littered the floor.

A small man appeared from the gloom to the right of the door. He was shirtless, barefoot, unshaven, though well muscled. He squinted at Lamb as if his eyes had not yet grown used to the light of day. "Yeah?" he said.

"Michael Bradford?"

The man put his hand to his brow and barred the door with his short, squared-off body. "Who are you?"

"Chief Inspector Thomas Lamb of the Hampshire Constabulary."

"Police, then?"

"Yes."

"You here about my chicken? The one old Blackwell nicked?"

"I'd like to speak with you about a couple of matters, Mr. Bradford."

Bradford removed his hand from his brow. "My boy done something, then?"

"No," Lamb said. "But I do think he might be of some help to me." Before Bradford could answer, Lamb added, "There's still the matter of the twenty-quid reward to be settled."

"That's the same as the other one told me. Said I'd get twenty quid if I cooperated and I did—told him as what Blackwell had done. Nicked my chicken and cut it up for one of his bloody sacrifices, like. But I haven't seen a penny of no reward."

Lamb stepped across the threshold. Bradford took a slight backward step but didn't protest. "Come in, then," he said. He did not offer Lamb a seat. They faced each other near the table. Lamb's eyes began to adjust to the light and he saw that Bradford's eyes were a clear, bright blue that hinted at intelligence.

"We're still sorting out the matter of the reward, Mr. Bradford," Lamb said. "Had Blackwell stolen other of your chickens in the past?"

Bradford hesitated and looked away from Lamb for an instant. "Yeah."

"How many times?"

"A couple. I didn't keep count."

"Did you confront him about that? For most men, that would be a problem—someone stealing their food."

Bradford glanced away again. "No, I didn't say nothing to him."

"Why not?"

"I didn't want him to put one of his hexes on me, did I? I've got enough trouble."

"Were you on the hill on the morning Mr. Blackwell was killed?"

"Nah. I was right here all morning."

"Doing what?"

"This and that."

"So you did not see Mr. Blackwell that morning, then?"

"Like I told you, I was here."

"Did it surprise you that Mr. Blackwell was killed?"

"Surprise me? Well, I guess it surprised me, yeah. I knew as how some around the village didn't trust him—thought him a witch and up to mischief, like. But I left well enough alone. I figure Blackwell and his kind are like bees. You don't bother them, they don't bother you."

"And yet you claim that Blackwell stole your chicken. Why would he do that? Did you bother him in some way—swat at him, like a bee, then, Mr. Bradford?"

"No!" Bradford protested. "I don't know why he stole my chicken. I never did him any harm."

"Do you know anybody in the village who ever harmed Mr. Blackwell or wanted to?"

Bradford looked at the floor, as if he were contemplating the question. He shook his head. "No. Like I said, stories is one thing, black dogs and that. But murder is another."

No one in Quimby seemed to be on Will Blackwell's side, Lamb thought. No one, perhaps except his niece, seemed sufficiently shocked or outraged by the old man's murder. And though nearly everyone spoke of how Blackwell was an unwelcome presence in Quimby, they also took pains to point out that they *personally* meant him no harm and claimed to know no one else who might have harmed him. Lamb normally was not a believer in conspiracy theories; still, he sensed that the residents of Quimby possessed almost a kind of unspoken agreement about Will Blackwell's status as a pariah and had decided that his death was a subject unfit for conversation or inquiry.

"I'd like to talk to your son, Mike," Lamb said. "He seems to get about the village and the hill and I'm hopeful that he might have seen something that might help us in our inquiries."

"He saw nothing, either. He would have told me if he had."

"All the same," Lamb said—the same words he'd used with Rivers. "It would save me from having to take the two of you to Winchester to answer my questions there."

Without taking his eyes from Lamb, Bradford yelled for his son. "Mike!" A moment later, the boy appeared in the threshold of the door. Lamb guessed that the children had been watching him since at least the time he'd arrived at the mill with Rivers, and had followed him to the house, keeping out of sight, little goblins of Manscome Hill.

"Come here," the elder Bradford said to Mike. He didn't look at the boy when he spoke. "Policeman here has some questions about old Blackwell. I want you to tell him what you know." He added: "And no lies. If you lie, I'll know."

Mike wore short black trousers with no shirt or shoes; his knees were scabbed. Lamb sensed that the boy's fear of his father kept him rooted to the spot on which he stood. He noticed that Mike had a bruise on his upper right arm.

"Hello, Mike," Lamb said. "You and I met a few nights ago in front of Will Blackwell's cottage and then, the next day, on the path up Manscome Hill. Do you remember?"

Mike did not speak or move.

"Mike!" his father said. He glared at the boy.

"Yes," Mike said.

"It's all right, Mike," Lamb said. "You're in no trouble."

Mike looked at the ground.

"I want you to think back to the day on which Will Blackwell died. Did you see anything strange or unusual on the hill that day? It's very important that you tell me the truth, Mike. I give you my word that you are in no trouble."

Mike glanced at his father. Lamb wasn't sure if Michael Bradford nodded.

"I only seen the man," Mike said.

Lamb tried not to appear as stunned as he felt; he had not expected that Mike had seen anything so important as a man on the hill that morning—a man who very well could be the killer. "Who was this man?" he asked.

"The man on the hill," Mike said.

"Did you recognize him?"

Mike hesitated a hitch, then said "No."

"What did the man look like?"

"He were tall."

"How was he dressed?"

"In regular clothes."

"Tell me what he was wearing."

Mike seemed to consider the question for a couple of seconds. "He were wearing a white shirt and tan trousers and a brown hat."

"Can you tell me anything more specific about him? Did you see his face?"

"No."

Lamb wondered now if Mike might be telling a lie cooked up by his father and rehearsed with him under the threat of violence. Michael Bradford badly wanted the reward money, after all, and might have anticipated that the police would want to speak with Mike. If Mike was lying, then Lamb would have to expose that lie—and yet in so doing, he might also expose Mike to a beating from his father.

"When did you see this man?" Lamb asked, treading carefully.

"In the morning."

"The morning of the day on which Will died?"

"Yes."

"Was it in the early morning, or late morning?"

"Late morning."

Lamb turned to the father. "Does this sound like anyone you know?"

"No," Michael Bradford said.

Lamb turned again to Mike. "Did this man see you, Mike?"

"No."

"How do you know that he didn't see you?"

A look of surprise—leavened with fear—crossed Mike's face. Lamb guessed that this was because, if Mike was lying, the boy and his father hadn't anticipated the question and so had rehearsed no answer to it. "He were far off," Mike said after a pause. "Far off down the hill."

"You mean by the village?" Lamb asked. He could sense Mike struggling.

Mike stole another glance at his father. Michael Bradford made no move or expression. He was leaving the child on his own, Lamb thought, like an animal in a trap. "Just down the hill," Mike said.

"I see," Lamb said. He smiled. "You're doing fine, Mike. We're almost finished."

Mike continued standing at attention, his eyes darting from Lamb to his father, who stood just to the right of Lamb with his sinewy arms crossed against his naked chest.

"Did you ever speak to Will Blackwell, Mike—or did he ever speak to you?"

"No. Old Will were a witch. He seen the Shuck. He'd put the evil eye on you."

"How about a boy named Peter, who draws insects? Do you know him?"

Mike glanced quickly at his father, then back to Lamb. This time, Bradford definitely nodded.

"He don't talk," Mike said. "The devil has his tongue. Old Will were teaching him about the devil."

"Is it possible that the tall man you saw on the hill the day Will was killed was Peter?"

Mike glanced at his father. "It were Peter," he said, turning back toward Lamb.

"Are you sure?" Lamb asked.

"It were Peter." He sounded like a parrot.

Lamb wasn't convinced. "Why do you say now that it was Peter when before you said you weren't sure, Mike?"

Mike froze. For a second, he seemed unable to speak.

"Mike!" his father barked.

"Because you said so," Mike said to Lamb.

"Because I said so."

"Yes. You said it were Peter."

"So that's why you're telling me now that it's Peter?"

"Yes."

Lamb realized he'd blundered in suggesting to Mike that the man might have been Peter Wilkins. "Forget for a moment what I said, Mike. I'm interested in what *you* saw. Did you see Peter on the hill that day?"

"Yes. It were Peter."

Lamb saw no reason to continue. He touched Mike on the head and said, "You've done well and I believe you."

"Do we get the twenty quid, then?" Bradford asked.

"We'll have to see," Lamb said. To protect Mike from Bradford, he added, "The information Mike has given me has been very useful."

"All right, then," Bradford said. He seemed pleased. He absently mussed Mike's hair. Mike flinched at his father's touch.

"Can I go?" Mike asked.

"Yes," Lamb said.

Mike ran through the door and disappeared.

Michael Bradford stood with his arms crossed. Lamb moved a step closer to him. "If I find out the boy is lying, then you, not he, will pay the consequences, Mr. Bradford," he said.

Bradford uncrossed his arms and thrust out his chest, as if preparing to defend himself. "Wot?" he said. "I've done nothing wrong."

"I hope for your sake that's true," Lamb said. He straightened himself to meet Bradford's physical response. "More importantly, if I find out you've laid a hand on the boy, or any of your children, I will come back here and personally do the same to you, twice over."

Bradford threw his shoulders back. "Wot?"

"Don't test me, Bradford." He smiled. "You know as well as I that we policemen can do whatever we damned well please and get away with it. Don't test me. And don't disappoint me."

With that, Lamb turned and walked through the trash-strewn yard to the path.

TWELVE

—⁓—

RIVERS HOISTED HIMSELF OVER THE LOW WALL AND MOVED through the mill yard.

He stopped at the opening that once had held the mill's main door and peered in. The interior was damp and dark, penetrated here and there by dust-choked shafts of sunlight. It stunk of mildew and other rot.

He stepped inside and moved carefully through the wood-and-metal detritus that littered the floor; the floorboards creaked beneath his weight. He knew enough about how such mills worked that he was certain that the room below him contained the water-driven mill machinery. The floor he was now in had been a kind of warehouse in which the milled grain had been packaged for transport. The far right side of the room contained the wide frame of what had once been a door that gave onto a loading dock.

He moved to the wall that was opposite the door; it contained three high windows from which the frames had long ago been broken out and used for firewood. He peered out of one and saw, ten feet below, Mills Run and the five-foot-deep stone race that had diverted the rushing stream to the wooden mill wheel. The wheel was gone and the place where the race met the stream had long ago become clogged with deadfall, though a trickle of water continued to move through the race and over and around the bits of wooden shingles, broken pieces of the slate roof, and chunks of ruined masonry that had fallen into it. He thought again of how Lamb was wasting his time, undermining him.

To his right, a steep, narrow wooden staircase led to the floor below. He moved down the stairs carefully, testing each before he put his weight on it to ensure that it wouldn't give way. The stairs ended in a room that was much like the one he'd just left, though darker and damper. At its center lay the rusted and broken remnants of the machinery that had crushed and milled the grain. The iron shaft that had connected the machinery to the mill wheel protruded from a damp moss-covered fieldstone wall.

On the wall opposite the steps was an opening—its door also was gone—that gave onto a lower yard of packed dirt that, like the front yard, was choked with weeds and detritus. As Rivers made his way into the yard, picking his way through the rubbish, something caught his eye among a pile of charred boards. He knelt to look closely at the object and saw that it was a red tin box with silver edges. The box appeared to be nearly new; unlike the rest of the metal rubbish that littered the yard, its paint was bright and clean.

He flipped the box's latch and opened it. He found in it three photographs of Will Blackwell and his wife, Claire, on their wedding day. He recognized the couple from the photographs he'd found in Blackwell's bedroom. In the photos, Blackwell posed, rigid, in a black suit with waistcoat, a high-collared, starched white shirt, and dark tie. Claire wore a white dress with a veil. She clutched a bouquet of light-colored flowers to her chest and smiled faintly.

"Bloody hell," he said to himself.

The box must have belonged to Will Blackwell, he thought. If Blackwell had squirreled away any cash, then he likely would have kept it in such a box, with his other keepsakes. His suspicions of Abbott and Lydia Blackwell hardened into a credible narrative: the pair of them had killed the old man, taken his cash, tossed away the box, and done a runner.

He extricated himself from the lower mill yard and headed up the path toward Bradford's cottage. He met Lamb coming down the path.

"I found something," Rivers said. He stood next to Lamb beneath a clearing sky and opened the box. "It hasn't been there long, obviously. The photos look like the old man's keepsakes, the ones that were most important to him. My guess is that he kept his valuables in there. Whoever took it had to have been close enough to him to know he had the box and where he kept it—which means the niece and Abbott."

He considered saying that Lamb had been right about searching the mill. But he couldn't quite bring himself to do so. He wasn't sure if Lamb was as surprised as he that he'd actually found something worthwhile in the ruins—whether Lamb hadn't in fact sent him on a wild goose chase that unexpectedly had turned up a gold nugget.

"Good work," Lamb said.

"Right," Rivers said. "So do we toss Abbott's house, then?"

Lamb's first thought was the same as Rivers's had been—that Abbott or Lydia likely had thrown the box into the mill yard. Only someone who was close enough to Will to know something of his daily life would be aware that he'd kept such a box of photographs and known where he'd kept it—and known, too, whether Will had kept anything else in the box, including cash. In any case, Rivers was right: it was time they had a closer look at Abbott's house, if only in the hope of finding some clue as to where he and Lydia Blackwell might have gone. But they must do it legally. He thought that the discovery of the box, and the argument that only someone close to Will likely would have had access to the photos, constituted sufficient cause for a warrant.

"Yes," he said to Rivers.

Rivers grinned in triumph. Lamb finally seemed to be seeing sense.

"But we'll do it legally."

He sent Rivers to Winchester to get a warrant to search Abbott's and Lydia Blackwell's cottages. Less than two hours later, Rivers returned with the warrant, and the group of them left the hill and trudged up the path to Abbott's cottage, sending Abbott's sheep trotting away yet again.

Rivers banged on the front door. "Open up—police!" He stepped back and looked at Lamb. "He's not there."

"Try again."

"He's not bloody there," Rivers protested.

"Again," Lamb said evenly.

Rivers sighed peevishly. "Abbott, police!" he yelled. "Open the bloody door!" He turned back to Lamb.

"Excuse me, sir, but I thought I might have heard a woman scream inside just now," Wallace added. He smiled and winked at Larkin.

"Okay," Lamb said. "Break it down."

Rivers heaved his shoulder against the door. The old metal latch that held it fast splintered away from the jamb and the door popped open.

Rivers and Wallace headed up the stairs to Abbott's bedroom, while Lamb searched the sitting room and Larkin the kitchen. It took Rivers a scant five minutes to find something worthwhile. Beneath Abbott's bed he found a leather satchel stuffed with cash. "Here," he said to Wallace. He pulled the satchel from beneath the bed and he and Wallace performed a quick count of its contents. It contained nearly two hundred pounds in cash.

"A bloody fortune," Wallace murmured.

They took the money downstairs. "There's nearly two hundred quid here," Rivers said. "No way a man like Abbott saves that much, especially if he's up to his arse in it at the bloody track."

Lamb agreed—though he wondered where *Blackwell* had gotten so much cash—if indeed the money *was* Blackwell's. And if Abbott had done a runner with Lydia, then why had he left the cash behind? He pulled a pencil and pad from his pocket, wrote Albert Gilley's name and telephone number on it, and handed it to Rivers.

"Get back to the nick and call this man," Lamb said. "He's my contact at Paulsgrove. He knows everything that goes on at the track. I want you to get down there this afternoon and meet him. If Abbott's there with Lydia Blackwell, I want you to find them and bring them back."

Rivers took the paper and held his tongue. He continued to believe that the chances of Abbott having run off to Paulsgrove were slim. Still, Lamb had been right about the mill—or he'd at least made a lucky guess that it might contain useful evidence. Even so, Rivers couldn't resist asking the obvious question. "If he's on the run, why didn't he take all of it?"

Lamb looked at Rivers. "Because he intends to come back."

They descended the hill. Rivers went on his way, while the rest of them went to Lydia Blackwell's cottage. Lamb knocked on the door but received no answer. He tried the knob and found the door unlocked. He stepped into the house, followed by the others. "Miss Blackwell?" he said. Nothing.

He set Larkin to search the ground floor while he and Wallace mounted the narrow stair to the second. He entered Blackwell's sparsely furnished bedroom, stood in the middle of it and looked around. He pulled the drawers from the dresser and put them on the bed, but found no place within the dresser or the drawers in which Blackwell might have hidden the tin box. He moved close to the walls and examined them but saw no sign of concealed panels. He checked the frame of the wooden bed but also found nothing.

He went to the closet, knocked on its walls, and found them to be solid. He glanced at the floor of the closet and noticed a small notch in the right side of a floorboard that was wide enough to accept a man's finger. He bent, put his finger in the hole, and lifted the board; it came away easily from its narrow slot. The space beneath it was empty.

Lamb went to the top of the stair and asked Larkin to bring the box into Blackwell's room. The three of them stood by Blackwell's closet as Larkin slipped the box into the space.

It fit perfectly.

"We've got him," Larkin said.

―〰―

That evening, Wallace arrived at The Fallen Diva an hour before last call. But Delilah wasn't there. He asked the landlord if she'd been in.

"Not tonight, mate. Sorry."

Fifteen minutes later, having made his way through the blacked-out streets to Delilah's little house, he rapped on the door. He waited for what he considered a reasonable time for her to answer before knocking again. "Delilah?" He listened but heard no movement within the house. He tried the knob but found the door locked.

He moved to the window that faced the street but could see nothing through the blackout curtains. He rapped on the window. He wondered if she was sleeping.

"Delilah? It's David."

He moved to the door again and knocked, but received no answer. He looked for a note at the foot of the door but found none. He'd thought she would have left him a note, or perhaps even a key, some signal that she expected him.

He stood on Delilah's doorstep for a few seconds deciding what to do. "Delilah," he called again, louder this time. He heard the sound of the lock being unbolted from within. Finally she'd heard him. But the door did not open. He pushed the door open onto a darkened foyer; he could just make out Delilah's figure standing several feet from the door. She was in her sleeping gown. Every light in the house was out.

"Close the door," she whispered.

She was playing another game, like the one she'd played on the first night when she'd doused herself in whiskey, he thought. Wallace did as she instructed. But she merely stood there, indistinct and silent. He stepped toward her. "Delilah?"

She didn't answer. He found her arms with his hands. He could barely make out her features in the darkness. "I can't see you. Why have you turned out all the lights?"

"I was trying to sleep."

"But I can't see you." Something was wrong; she was not in a playful mood—unless that, too, was part of the game. He moved toward the door and the light switch he knew was next to it. Delilah grabbed his sleeve. "No," she said. "Don't."

"Why?"

She pulled him back toward her. "Just don't."

"What's wrong?" he asked. She began to cry, just as she had done in bed that morning.

He found the switch and flicked on the light in the foyer. Delilah covered her face with her hands.

Wallace moved to her; she buried her face in his shoulder. "Tell me what's wrong," he said. He gently maneuvered her away from his shoulder so that he could see her face.

She looked at him, tears streaking her cheeks. Her eyes were blackened and swollen. The sight of her wounds shocked him.

"By God," he said. "What happened?"

"I fell." She looked away.

He didn't believe her. Someone had beaten her; that was obvious. "You didn't fall. Someone hit you. Who was it?"

"It's nothing," she said. She looked at him. "Please, David, forget it. It's nothing."

"What do you mean, it's nothing? Tell me who did this to you."

"I can't. Please promise me you'll let it go."

"Let it go? I'll bloody fucking kill him. Who is he?"

"Please, David."

"Delilah."

She looked away. "I deserved it."

"What in bloody hell are you talking about?"

She threw her arms around him and pressed her face against his chest. "Please, David," she said. "I love you. Please don't ask me any more questions."

—⁂—

At twilight, Arthur Lear had knocked on the door of Vera's billet. She went to the door with trepidation. She had become firm in her decision that she must tell Arthur that they could no longer be lovers. She hoped he would understand and accept her reasoning, but doubted that he would—doubted that he would merely accept what amounted to her rejection of him.

She opened the door to find Arthur holding a bunch of purple foxglove in his hand. He smiled and held out the flowers to her. "For you," he said. The gesture touched her but did not change her mind.

"Thank you," she said. He stepped inside. She put the flowers in an old jam jar she found in the cupboard above the gas ring and placed the makeshift vase in the middle of the table. She and Arthur stood near each other. Vera understood that Arthur expected something in return for his flowers and this notion only steeled her against giving it to him. She'd allowed herself to be too easily bought. But no more.

"I'm sorry about the other night," Arthur said. "I shouldn't have said those things. I wouldn't blame you if you're angry with me."

He looked at her with a pleading look in his eyes that she found pathetic.

"Why don't we go for a walk," she suggested. She wanted to get him out of her billet. They would walk and, hopefully, Arthur would relax. Then, when they returned to her billet, she would beg off, claim that she was tired. In that way, she might be able to fend him off gradually.

They walked up the hill at an easy pace. When they reached the wooden bridge over Mills Run, by the dead sycamore, Arthur said, "Let's go see the place where old Blackwell was killed."

"Do you really think we should?" Going to the site seemed ghoulish. Still, Vera was curious.

"I just want to see it."

They turned off the trail into the meadow. Farther up the hill, George Abbott's sheep grazed placidly, while the crows that had pecked out Blackwell's eyes silently watched Vera and Arthur from the crooked branches of the sycamore.

"He didn't talk to people much, old Blackwell," Arthur said as they moved through the meadow. "When I was a boy, we kids mocked him—pointed at him and called him a witch and the rest of it. And we told stories about him—that he would boil you in a big black pot and eat you if he caught you. He might have saved himself a lot of trouble if he'd just been a little friendlier. It doesn't pay to be stand-offish in a village. I don't think anybody in Quimby will miss him, save his niece."

"That's very sad," Vera said.

Arthur shrugged. They were nearly to the hedge.

"I saw someone up here yesterday—an older boy with long blond hair," Vera said. "I was on the other side, near the estate. He stood below me, just off the path, and stared at me; I thought he wanted something. But when I tried to speak to him he ran into the wood, as if I'd frightened him."

Arthur turned to her, alarmed. "He's loony," he said. "Stay away from him."

"He seemed harmless."

"He can't speak—or he doesn't," Arthur said. "He's unpredictable. I shouldn't wonder that he killed Blackwell. He's capable of it." Arthur looked at Vera disapprovingly. "You shouldn't let yourself be fooled by him, Vera. Just because he looks harmless doesn't mean he is. I've seen him around; he lives like a wild animal." He thrust his chin in the direction of Brookings. "He's one of Lord Pembroke's experiments in breaking down the social order—a kind of Frankenstein's monster."

They reached the hedge and walked around to the place where Blackwell's body had lain. Speaking of the boy seemed to have made

Arthur angry. Vera wondered if the walk hadn't been a bad idea. Perhaps she should have just turned him away at her door and been done with it. But she had been afraid of turning him away—afraid of how he might have reacted.

The ground along the base of the hedge still was black in the places where Blackwell's blood had saturated it.

"Let's go, Arthur," she said.

Arthur touched her arm. "Hold on." He moved closer to the killing site and crouched. He pushed the index finger of his lone hand into the soil, then quickly withdrew it; he looked quizzically at the tip of his finger, which was stained a vague reddish color that made it appear as if he'd been picking berries.

"It's still wet," he said, staring at the ground. "With the old man's blood, I mean." He looked at his finger, then held it toward Vera. "Witch's blood."

Vera crossed her arms. She wanted to leave. She glanced up the hill and saw something that startled her. "Oh!"

"What is it?" Arthur stood.

She pointed up the hill. "It's him," she said. "The boy." Peter stood along the crest of a rise, watching them. His shoulder-length hair moved in the twilight breeze. Otherwise, he was still.

Arthur stood. "Go away—shoo!" he yelled at Peter, thrusting the back of his hand in Peter's direction. "You're not wanted here."

Peter didn't move.

"I said to go away," Arthur said angrily. "Go back to where you came from."

"What's his name?" Vera asked.

"You don't want me to come up there," Arthur said, glaring at Peter. He made a feint in Peter's direction; Peter flinched.

"What's his name?" Vera repeated.

Arthur whirled to face her. "What bloody difference does it make!"

"Don't yell at me," Vera said angrily. "I'm not a child." She looked past Arthur to where Peter had been standing. But Peter was gone. He seemed to have left something where he stood—a piece of paper. Vera thought it might be a note. She began to walk up the hill, intending to fetch it.

"Where are you going?" Arthur asked. "I told you he's dangerous."

She ignored him.

"Vera." Arthur's voice suddenly had lost its heated edge and again taken on the vague character of pleading. "I'm sorry I yelled at you. His name is Peter."

He followed her up the hill. By the time he reached her, she had picked up the paper that Peter had left. On it was a penciled sketch of a spider devouring a butterfly. The drawing possessed an amazing quality; Vera found it frightening and beautiful all at once.

"Does he draw these?" she asked Arthur.

"I'm sorry I yelled at you, but you don't understand how dangerous he is," Arthur said. He tapped the picture. "Look at this. It's bloody bizarre. I told you, he's unpredictable."

"We should go. I have to get up early for work tomorrow." She began to walk down the hill with Peter's picture.

"But you're not going to take that bloody thing with you?"

"Yes." She kept walking. The twilight was waning.

"But it's morbid," Arthur said. He tried to hide any hint of anger or exasperation in his voice. But the loony boy seemed to have touched something within Vera and this made him jealous. He suddenly wondered if she'd paid *him* attention merely because she pitied him his lost arm.

He caught up with her and took her elbow. "You should leave that here," he said. "Something like that is not fit for a girl like you to have."

She moved her elbow free of his hand. "I'll decide that, Arthur."

"Suit yourself, then," he said, finding it harder to rein in his growing resentment at Vera's interest in Peter. "I can't stop you if you want that sort of bloody stuff."

Vera didn't answer. She reached the path, crossed the bridge, and started down the trail, with Arthur at her heels. When they reached her billet, Vera put herself between the door and Arthur. She tried to be pleasant. She smiled. She still feared Arthur's reaction to her rejection, but standing up to him on the hill had lessened that fear.

"Good night, Arthur," she said firmly. "Thank you for the walk."

"Can I come in?" Arthur asked.

"Not tonight. I'm very tired."

"You're angry at me; angry because of what I said about the . . ." He caught himself, so as not to do any further damage. ". . . about Peter."

"I'm sorry, but I don't like being yelled at, Arthur." She paused, then added "All the same, I'm very tired." She turned to open the door.

"Vera," he said. She turned to face him and he moved to kiss her. He kissed her deeply, almost pinning her to the door. She allowed him to, but did not respond in kind. When he finished, he withdrew, his chest heaving slightly. "I've made a terrible mistake," he said. "I've upset you." He made a move to take her into his arm, but she fended him off with her forearm.

"Please, Arthur," she said firmly. "We'll talk about it tomorrow."

"But I've upset you," he said desperately. "Tell me I haven't upset you."

"You haven't upset me," she lied. "I'm fine."

She opened the door, stepped inside, closed the door and bolted it. She leaned against the door for a second clutching Peter's drawing, her heart pounding.

THIRTEEN

—⁂—

SOUTHAMPTON HARBOR LAY FAR BELOW, IN UTTER DARKNESS.

Hermann Seitz, the twenty-five-year-old pilot of Luftwaffe Heinkel HE-111 207, a medium-range bomber based in Cherbourg, knew from the readings on his instruments that he was over the harbor. But he had no clear idea of where his target lay. His quarry was the Supermarine factory, the place where the British made the fighter planes, the Spitfires, that had shot down so many of his comrades, men like him—men in slow-moving Heinkels who were supposed to be able to find a target in utter blackness, with nothing useful to guide them and without the fighter escort that might fend off the British in their Spitfires, give them a chance to at least drop their bombs in the right vicinity and still have half a prayer of returning to France, to live. At night, the Messerschmitts didn't even go aloft; fat Goering had said it was useless for the fighters to go along, given that no one could see anything. That's why they had instruments. The best available, Goering said. *Ha!* Seitz would like to see that fat bastard find his fucking toes beneath his gut, much less the Spitfire factory in the dark from eighteen thousand feet!

On the journey across the Channel, the British had shot down three of the planes in his squadron—shot them into the sea. Now, they'd been flying through ack-ack for nearly five minutes. An eternity. That's the way it was every night. They were torn to bits and never succeeded in knocking out a damned thing. They'd tried to knock out the Blenheim bomber factory southeast of Winchester three times now and hadn't even come close. During those raids, he'd dropped his payloads regardless; he'd had no idea, really, where his bombs had fallen or whether they'd done any damage. He knew only that he must never return to Cherbourg without an empty bomb bay. Now Goering had set his sights on the Spitfire factory. And now they were over Southampton and, as usual, none of them knew where the hell they were.

Seitz felt something strike the Heinkel that made it shake and rock. They'd been hit. For an instant the plane began to heel to the south. He gripped the wheel and brought the plane under control, though he had to put all of his strength into the effort. Next to him, the navigator, Henning, yelled, "We've been fucking hit. Lucius is dead." Lucius was the man—a boy, really—who manned the machine gun in the turret on the plane's roof.

Seitz looked at Henning.

"Time to go!" Seitz yelled, and Henning nodded. They were running now, fleeing, giving up on the Spitfire factory, though neither of them considered this wrong. After all, they were nothing but sitting ducks on a suicide mission. Seitz turned the plane to true north and began to climb, away from Southampton. As the plane rose steadily, relief filled Seitz. They were not mortally wounded. Not yet.

He turned east. To their right a plane exploded in midair, close enough that the shock waves engendered by its vaporization shook the Heinkel like a rabbit in a fox's mouth. "Holy Christ!" Henning yelled.

Despite the enveloping calamity, Seitz hoped that luck was with them. They sped east for little more than a minute; then he heeled the plane south, toward the Channel. Below them lay pasture and woodland and the occasional village.

They had just crossed the coast and were over the Solent when the Heinkel suddenly shook and rattled again, as if God had thrown down a handful of rocks upon it. Seitz looked at his port wing and saw that it was aflame.

Dear God, he thought.

He must get away, be as fast as possible. Nothing must weigh him down. He remembered that he still was carrying his payload. Why hadn't he released it over Southampton? But too much had happened at once. Too goddamned much!

The bombardier sat just below and in front of him in the glass-and-steel cockpit. "Let them go," Seitz shouted. They were back over the Channel now and the bombs began dropping into the sea.

The Heinkel shook violently and began to roll toward the east. The fire on the port wing continued to burn. Seitz said a Hail Mary. Then the plane nosed down suddenly and Seitz saw the black water rushing at him.

—⁂—

Emily Fordham pedaled along the darkened road toward Lipscombe. The night was clear and she could see well ahead. Behind her, to the southwest, the sky was lit from the fires that had begun to burn in Southampton harbor.

Her mother would be frantic by now; Emily would find her lying on the parlor floor, curled like a fetus from worry. But she was finished playing at her mother's sick game. The bloody woman could lie on the floor all night as far as she was concerned. In the past few days Emily had reached a kind of epiphany: she'd realized that her mother could not control her if she refused to allow it.

That day, she'd gone to Cloverton and met Charles in the little pub in the village near the airfield. Their meeting had been too brief.

Still, it had been better than having not seen Charles at all. She felt thankful to God that Charles had lived through the attack on the air-field. Now it was only a matter of him—of the three of them—getting through the rest of the war. She had exhibited what she considered to have been exceptional patience and bravery in recent days; she had waited by the checkpoint near the airfield well past dark before she'd gotten word from one of the ambulance drivers that Charles was unhurt—though as soon as she saw Charles at the pub she'd dissolved into tears. They'd spent a few minutes sitting on a bench outside the pub holding each other. Still, she had not told him about the baby. She could not forgive herself if he was killed because she'd distracted him by worries about their child.

As she maneuvered her bike around the big bend by the marsh, she saw a figure standing just off the road, about a hundred meters distant. The person appeared to be wearing a hat, though she could not, from that distance, tell whether the person was a man or a woman.

As she moved closer, the figure waved to her.

PART TWO

—⁓—

A Blue Butterfly

FOURTEEN

—◊—

LAMB COULDN'T REMEMBER IF TODAY WAS A MARMALADE DAY.
He'd awakened with much on his mind. The Blackwell case had
suddenly gained a head of steam; Abbott was in his sights now, as was,
perhaps, Lydia Blackwell. Even so, a notion that he was somehow missing
the mark nagged at him. Peter's drawing of the spider snaring the bird
bothered him, even though he was not yet sure if the sketch had any value
or connection to the inquiry. He knew very little about children such as
Peter—children who seemed to have been dealt profoundly bad hands
in life; children whose handicaps cut them off from most normal human
intercourse and therefore the normal amounts of attention, love, praise,
security; children whom many people saw as freaks of nature. He could
not be sure what the spiders and the bird represented, and yet he sensed
that the drawing was important and that Peter was intelligent and even
purposeful despite the ways in which the gods had seen fit to cripple him.

He told himself to forget the case for the moment and enjoy breakfast with Marjorie—or, at the very least, not to force her to sit at table with a distracted companion. As he descended the stairs he smelled the coffee, which whetted his appetite. He decided that even if today was not a marmalade day, they were going to have bloody marmalade regardless.

Marjorie was at the kitchen table intently reading the morning edition of the *Mail*. Lamb saw from the headline on the front page that the Germans finally had hit the Spitfire factory in Southampton. Marjorie put down the paper. Lamb saw the worry in her eyes.

"They bombed Southampton harbor last night," she said.

"Yes, I see."

"I called Quimby this morning; I know I'm not supposed to tie up the phone like that, but I couldn't help it. I let it ring and ring and she finally answered. She's all right. None of them came near the village."

Lamb thought of going to Marjorie, to physically comfort her, but sensed that she did not want to be held, or touched. She did not want to be condescended to—told yet again that everything would be fine.

Lamb sat at the table and read the story. A few of the German bombs had hit the factory but failed to knock it out or even to damage it badly. Scattered memories and images began to fill his mind—of mud, rats, flies, drenching rain, lice, dysentery, cold food; of freezing in the night curled in a blanket underground and listening to the sounds of dying men outside the trenches begging for water. Eventually, the begging stopped and the night grew quiet. He'd seen many men die. Eric Parker had been one; the pilot he'd seen go down in flames was another. The same mess, twenty years on, he thought. He went to the larder and got the marmalade.

He was just biting his toast, tasting the tang of the jam on his tongue, when the phone rang. Annoyed at the interruption, he went into the hall.

"Lamb."

It was Harding. "We've another body, Tom. Young girl—seventeen, eighteen. She was found early this morning lying just off the main road into Lipscombe. Someone has bashed in her head."

He knew Lipscombe; it was on the eastern side of Brookings.

"How far from the village?"

"A half mile or so."

Feeling cheated of a minor pleasure, he went to the kitchen and crammed what remained of his toast and marmalade into his mouth.

—⚊—

The road bent south around a stretch of meadow and bottomland. Beyond this, Lamb spied the church spire of Lipscombe. A few hundred meters on, he reached a pair of police cars that were parked along the right side of the road, one of which was Harding's. A uniformed constable stood along the shoulder.

Harding stood at the edge of the meadow in the company of three constables, Wallace, and Larkin. Wallace had fallen asleep the previous night in Delilah's bed, holding her. They had not made love; she was too beaten up for anything like that. Even so, she had stubbornly refused to tell him who had beaten her.

In the meadow, a young woman lay face-down in a damp depression about ten feet from the road. She wore a dress of green gingham that was hiked up to her bottom and a black shoe on her left foot. Her right shoe lay two feet to the right of her body. Her auburn hair was inundated with blood and spotted with green-black flies. The grass by her feet was splattered with blood; a black bicycle lay to the left of her body, almost parallel to it. Above this tableau, four seagulls circled and shrieked.

"Her name is Emily Fordham," Harding said, nodding to Lamb in greeting. "Age seventeen, from Lipscombe." He pointed to the bike. "That's her bicycle. A local farmer found her. He was cycling into Lipscombe and saw the body. He couldn't see the girl's face but recognized the bike. I sent a man into the village to see what he could find out about her. She lives with her mother; the father's dead and her older brother's in the Royal Navy. She apparently volunteered at the RAF infirmary near Cloverton." He handed Lamb a slip of paper. "This is the mother's address."

"Do we know what she was doing out here?"

"No. She hasn't been dead long by the look of it, though."

Winston-Sheed arrived and joined them. He looked at the sky, at the seagulls.

"It's the bloody war," the doctor said, thinking aloud about what had become an unusual spate of murders. "It's changed the rules. Some people simply are taking earlier advantage of it than others." He smiled in the languid way he normally did.

"Well, that may be, Doctor," Harding said. "But the rules haven't changed as far as I'm concerned. I'd like to get things moving here, if you don't mind. I've been here nearly a half hour and hardly a damned thing has happened, save the lot of us standing around speculating."

The three of them, along with Wallace and Larkin, moved in to examine Emily Fordham's body. Lamb immediately noticed several places on which the seagulls had defecated on the girl's dress. Winston-Sheed shooed away the flies and examined the wound in the back of her head.

"At first glance, I'd say she was struck with a blunt object, perhaps of metal or smooth, finished wood," he said. "I don't see any sign of splinters. I'd say our man hit her once, which probably knocked her down, though I can't say for certain that it knocked her cold. Once she was down, he struck her several more blows to make sure."

He glanced up at Lamb and smiled. "All that's speculation for the moment, of course."

Lamb nodded.

The doctor continued. "This killing looks very much like Black-well's—*sans* the macabre touches, of course. But the basics are the same—a blow to the head and the job finished as the victim lies on the ground, unconscious." Lamb had been thinking the same thing.

Winston-Sheed took the body's temperature and examined the skin and limbs more closely. That done, he and Lamb carefully turned the body over. Although the girl's face was filthy from having lain in the mud, Lamb could see that she had been strikingly beautiful. She had a small nose, high cheeks, a slender jaw, and fierce green eyes that now were frozen open, icy. Lamb couldn't help but think of Vera. She and the dead girl were about the same age.

"Bloody Christ," Wallace said.

"What is it?" Lamb asked.

"I know her."

"You know her?"

"Well, I don't know her, exactly. I just met her, at the roadblock near Cloverton airfield, the evening of the raid. She bicycled right up to the place, pretty as you please. I stopped her but she wouldn't turn round. She insisted on waiting. She went off about a hundred meters or so and sat in the grass with her bike. I gave her a blanket and a packet of biscuits."

"You mean she stayed there the entire night?" Harding asked.

"I believe so, sir."

"And you allowed this?" Harding asked.

"She seemed harmless enough," Wallace said. He knew it sounded weak.

"Harmless?" Harding said. "How do you know she was bloody harmless? Did you search her?"

"No, sir."

"Good-looking, you mean. She was good-looking and so you let her stay and chatted her up a bit. Gave her a blanket and biscuits, did you? Hoping to get lucky, then?"

"No, sir, it wasn't like that."

"Don't tell me it wasn't like that, man!" Harding said. He was yelling at Wallace now. "How dare you! Of course it was like that. Good-looking girl and you let her stay, when your duty was to turn people away!"

"The officer in charge didn't mind." Wallace instantly regretted saying this. He knew he should not seek to defend his mistake.

"The officer in charge had other duties to attend to, didn't he?" Harding shouted. "It was your job to keep these damned, bloody people clear!"

Lamb agreed with Harding—Wallace had buggered the situation.

"I want this looked into, Tom," Harding said, glaring at Wallace.

Wallace looked at Lamb, as if seeking an ally. But Lamb gave him only a hard, uncompromising stare. Harding turned his back on them and stared toward the road, as if he'd had quite enough of it all—the killings, the lack of results, *the bloody damned incompetence.*

The seagulls circling above the body had increased to about a dozen. One suddenly, brazenly, dived toward Emily's body but pulled up before it reached her.

"Keep those damned birds away from the body," Lamb said to no one in particular.

One of the constables hurled a stone at the seagull but missed the bird by two feet. A wet morsel of seagull excrement struck Winston-Sheed squarely on the head. The doctor delicately touched his head with the fingers of his right hand, then withdrew them quickly. He looked at his fingers, which were sticky with excrement, and shook his head slightly. Absently, he wiped his fingers on his trouser leg.

Larkin, who had been searching the area directly adjacent to the body, appeared, holding a green leather purse. "I found this tangled in a small bush about five meters away," he said, handing the purse to Lamb. "It contains a wallet and some cosmetics, but no money."

Harding continued to stand with his back to the group. Lamb thought it best that he get Wallace away from the superintendent. He gestured for Wallace to follow him to his Wolseley, where he carefully dumped the contents of the purse onto the bonnet. The purse contained a wallet of the same green leather as the purse, a small cosmetics kit, a faux-tortoiseshell hairbrush, and a packet of chewing gum.

The wallet contained no money, not even the odd coin, which argued that the motive could have been theft. One of its flaps contained a small cellophane window under which Emily had placed a photograph of herself standing in a small flower garden with an older woman whom Lamb assumed was her mother. He could see the family resemblance—the older woman had the same dark hair and fine facial features. He slid his finger beneath the photograph but felt nothing. The other slots in the wallet contained nothing more than a card for the library in Winchester and several ration cards.

Wallace was poking his fingers into the purse.

"Anything there?" Lamb asked.

"Hold on," Wallace said. He turned the purse over and shook it vigorously. A slender piece of cardboard—a kind of false bottom—fell onto the bonnet. Wallace thrust his fingers into the purse again and withdrew from it several pieces of what appeared to be folded paper.

"Here we go," he said, placing the items on the bonnet. One was indeed a slip of paper; the other two were small wallet-sized photographs. One of the photos was of a young man in the dress uniform of an RAF pilot. The pilot had dark eyes and an open smile. The other photo was of a dark-haired boy of about ten years old.

Lamb flipped the photo of the pilot and found "With love—Charles" written on the back in blue ink. "I think I've found the man she was waiting for at the roadblock," he said. He handed the photo to Wallace.

"Reckon he's still alive?" Wallace asked.

"We'll find out soon enough."

The flip side of the photo of the boy contained only three encrusted brown spots, like the points of a triangle, at which the photo appeared to have been glued to something, perhaps the page of a photo album.

"One of the girl's relatives?" Wallace said. "Maybe a younger brother, or nephew?"

"According to Harding, she had only an older brother."

Lamb turned his attention to the slip of paper—a small, square piece of parchment of decent quality that was folded once, lengthwise. One of its edges was slightly ragged, as if it had been torn from a notebook. The paper contained at its center a small but detailed India ink drawing of a spider devouring a butterfly. Except for the difference in the spider's victim, the drawing was nearly identical to the one Lamb had found in the shed behind Blackwell's cottage, of a spider menacing a bird. The drawing was not signed, just as the one from the shed hadn't been. But Lamb was certain he knew the artist. Emily Fordham had known Peter Wilkins.

"Do you think it's the boy again?" Wallace asked.

"I'm sure of it."

"Is he our killer, then?"

Lamb looked more closely at the drawing. "I don't know. I think he might be trying to communicate something with these drawings."

"To who?"

"At first guess, I'd say he was trying to communicate something to the girl and maybe to Blackwell."

"Why doesn't he just bloody say it, then? Why the bloody spiders and the rest of it?"

"I don't know that he *can* say it, at least not in the way you and I would expect." He nodded at the drawing. "The drawing's obviously his, so she must have known him."

"But why hide the drawing—and the photos?"

"Why hide anything?" Lamb asked. "To keep someone else from finding it."

As Lamb and Wallace examined the purse, Winston-Sheed had gone to his car. Now Lamb caught a glimpse of the doctor walking back toward Emily Fordham's body carrying a heavy Great War–era pistol, a .45-caliber Webley Mark VI. Lamb had worn a similar pistol on his belt at the Somme.

The sight so surprised Lamb that he said nothing at first. He watched the doctor move silently toward the body, then stop when he reached it. Winston-Sheed raised the pistol and, gripping it with both hands, aimed it at the seagulls wheeling in the sky. Lamb looked at the birds and in that instant heard the pistol fire and saw one of the gulls explode in the air. Its body plummeted to the ground at Emily Fordham's feet. The other birds seem to rise as one, higher into the sky.

"Brilliant shot!" Larkin said.

Lamb ran to Winston-Sheed, who stood still, staring at the sky, the pistol at his side. "What in bloody hell are you doing?" Lamb yelled.

Winston-Sheed raised the pistol and squeezed off another shot that missed the flock.

"Stop it, damn you!" Lamb yelled. "You're fouling the scene!"

The doctor ignored Lamb and fired a third shot; a second bird exploded and fell to the ground about three feet from them.

Winston-Sheed's gaze remained fixed on the birds. "I think we've endured enough trouble from the air these last few days, don't you?" he said without looking at Lamb.

Lamb yelled at Larkin. "Get those bloody damned birds out of my crime scene immediately!"

He turned to Winston-Sheed. "What in hell is wrong with you? This is a murder scene, not a damned shooting party."

Winston-Sheed turned to Lamb and shrugged. His casualness infuriated Lamb.

Lamb spoke sharply to Larkin. "Get in there and mark the places where the birds fell and clean up the mess. I don't want to find out that my evidence comes from a bloody goddamned bird!"

"Yes, sir," Larkin said. He seemed shaken, as if only then realizing what had happened.

"Well, I think we're finished here, then," Harding said. He stood rigid, his hands behind his back. He seemed unperturbed by what Winston-Sheen had just done. Harding's lack of emotion struck Lamb as unusual, given the way in which he'd only just reproved Wallace.

"You've got a hell of a bloody mess here, Tom, no doubt about it," Harding said. "But I'm counting on you to get results quickly. Otherwise we could end up with a kind of general panic. It's bad enough that the damned Germans are due any day now and our men are being shot out of the sky and slaughtered before they can even get airborne. It's too much strain on the average person. The sooner we wrap this up, the better. I understand your frustration and your desire for protocol, but I frankly don't see how a couple of bloody seagulls matter in the larger picture. We'll get this cleaned up and move on."

Harding addressed the other men present.

"I don't need to tell you, of course, that we simply can't speak of this. I'll have the arse of any man I discover has wagged his tongue. Let's do our duties and solve this case before the whole bloody mess ends up becoming another casualty of the war."

Harding turned and walked to his car. As Lamb watched him leave, he wondered if they'd all gone mad.

FIFTEEN

—⁓—

LAMB STRODE TO HIS WOLSELEY, GATHERED UP EMILY FORDHAM'S
purse and its contents from the bonnet, got into the passenger seat, and
slammed the door. He was too angry to drive. Wallace, understanding,
eased in behind the wheel.

Lamb fumbled in the pocket of his coat for his fags and lit one.
"Bloody goddamned fools," he muttered.

Wallace said nothing. He approved of Winston-Sheed having
shot the birds. It was past time that someone had acted. They all had
spent far too much time merely *waiting*. He started the car. "What's
next?" he asked.

"We'll talk to the girl's mother," Lamb said. His task would be
to break the news to the woman of her daughter's death, and then
endeavor to calm her enough to extract some usable information from
her. He hated such interviews because he knew them to be, in their

way, cruel. But there was no avoiding them. He had to speak to the mother as soon as possible in the likely case she possessed some crucial evidence or clue. For that reason, the mother's moment of private grieving would have to wait and he would have to maneuver around that grief, keep it at bay long enough to get what he sought.

Wallace pushed the starter button. Lamb's Wolseley sputtered but refused to start.

Lamb turned to Wallace. "I'm going to ask this bluntly, because I haven't got the time to muck about: Have you been drinking?"

The question stunned Wallace; he'd thought he'd managed to hide his drinking from Lamb. That morning had been particularly good in that he'd even managed to arrive to work early, despite the mess with Delilah. He recovered quickly enough to say, "What do you mean, sir?"

"Damn you, David." Lamb's eyes were fierce. "I'm in no bloody mood for your games. I intend to pull your arse out of this latest mess you've made, but I won't lift a bloody goddamned finger on your behalf if you lie to me. Is that clear?"

Wallace blinked. "Yes."

"So answer my bloody goddamned question."

"No, sir," Wallace said without looking at Lamb. "Only the occasional pint in the pub. Same as anyone else."

"Nothing at all, then?" Lamb said, the sarcasm evident in his voice. "Don't think I haven't noticed—the lateness and the occasional foul-ups and now *this*."

"It's a woman," Wallace said. He thought it a good excuse. It explained everything and was partly true.

"Well, you better bloody well get John Thomas under control, then."

"Yes, sir."

"Don't you see what you're doing? If you lose your warrant card, you're going straight into the thick of it. And don't think you'll get by on your bloody charm. I spent a bit of time in the Army in the last war. They'll chew you up and spit you out. No one there gives a damn about your well-cut suits and your dazzling smile. Being at the front is like swallowing a bucket of shit every day, over and over again. Do you understand me?"

"Yes."

Lamb wondered if he did.

"Then pull yourself together and stop being a bloody damned fool. I can't help you otherwise. And if I find out you've lied to me, I'll have your arse."

Wallace looked straight ahead. "Yes, sir," he said.

He pushed the button again and, to his relief, the car started.

—⁓—

The road narrowed as they entered Lipscombe.

A moment later, they were through the square and on the eastern side of the village, where they came to a row of small stone houses with tiny front lawns and gardens. The third of these was the one in which Emily Fordham had lived with her mother. Wallace stopped the car.

"Be prepared if she collapses," Lamb told Wallace as they exited the car. "Get her off her feet and into a chair as quickly as possible."

They walked along a flagstone path flanked by pink roses to a green door with a small brass knocker. The morning sun shone on them. Wallace lifted the knocker and rapped on the door. Lamb removed his hat.

A few seconds later, a small woman, her shoulders wrapped in a red cotton shawl, opened the door. Lamb recognized the woman from the photo he'd found in Emily's wallet. He guessed that she could not be more than forty-five, though the shawl and the way her shoulders slumped beneath it made her seem older. She appeared ready to speak; her mouth began to form a question. But she stopped and blinked, as if trying to bring the two strangers standing at her door into better focus.

"Good morning, Mrs. Fordham," Lamb said. "I am Chief Inspector Thomas Lamb of the Hampshire Constabulary, and this is Detective Sergeant David Wallace. May we come in?"

Elizabeth Fordham blinked again but did not answer. She did not seem to understand.

Lamb moved slightly closer to the door. There was nothing for it but to plunge ahead. "It's about your daughter, Emily," he said.

Mrs. Fordham did not move. "Emily?" she asked.

"Yes," Lamb said. "I'm afraid we've some bad news." He put his hand gently on her right elbow and began guiding her into the house.

"What do you mean?" Elizabeth asked. "What has happened to Emily?"

"Why don't we sit down," Lamb said and led her toward the sitting room.

"Why is the news bad?" she asked. Lamb could feel her body beginning to stir, almost as if she had been asleep and only now was waking. "What do you mean?"

Lamb maneuvered her onto a yellow sofa that backed against a window that faced the street. Once Elizabeth was seated, her countenance rapidly changed. She glared at Lamb and said "I demand to know what happened to my daughter." Lamb understood this sudden metamorphosis as the initial stirrings of grief. His and Wallace's sudden arrival at her door, her daughter's name on their lips, their solicitousness, had communicated to Elizabeth's deepest instincts all she needed to know. She now must struggle with the nearly impossible job of accepting a hideous, unalterable truth.

"I'm sorry to tell you that your daughter is dead," Lamb said. "She was found murdered this morning about two miles from the village. I'm very sorry. Very, very sorry."

"Murdered?" Elizabeth asked. Her eyes widened, as if she were on the verge of panic. She seemed to be coming to consciousness in stages, Lamb thought. "That can't be!"

"I'm afraid it is," Lamb said gently. He girded for an eruption.

Elizabeth began to move in the chair as if she'd suddenly grown very uncomfortable. Lamb thought she was going to stand. He prepared himself to grab and restrain her. But she looked at the floor. The fierceness she had shown only seconds earlier suddenly seemed to drain from her. "How?" she asked quietly.

"We believe that she was assaulted as she was riding home last night on her bicycle. She was struck on the head. Her body was found near the road, about three quarters of a mile from the village."

Elizabeth wrapped her arms and the shawl about herself tightly. Her behavior surprised Lamb. She seemed to have moved from defiance to despair in the blink of an eye. Although he had seen the transition occur in the opposite manner—first the slumping, then the rage—he had never seen it occur so quickly. He sat next to her.

"Perhaps Sergeant Wallace can make us some tea," he said.

She looked at Lamb. "Tea?"

"Yes. Perhaps some tea would help."

He felt ridiculous. Nothing would help. The life of the woman sitting before him suddenly and irrevocably had entered a kind of final phase and he could do nothing to stop this. Death had joined them in the little sitting room. For the moment, he could only sit next to her on her yellow couch and suggest she take some tea. She had not collapsed, as he had suspected she might, but retreated into a stupor. His job now was to entice her from that refuge long enough to extract some information from her that he might use to track down her daughter's killer. Wallace went into the kitchen to brew a pot of tea. Lamb moved in, hoping to catch Elizabeth before she locked herself away completely.

"Can you think of anyone who might have wanted to harm your daughter?" he asked.

She looked at him, bewildered. "Harm Emily?"

"Did she have any relationships with men, for example—with someone who might have become jealous or angry at her for some reason?"

"Men?" She blinked.

"Yes. A boyfriend, perhaps? A sweetheart?"

Something in that word—*sweetheart*—seemed to resonate with Elizabeth. Lamb expected her to say something about the pilot whose photo he'd found in Emily's wallet. Instead, Elizabeth paused for a few seconds and then, strangely, smiled. "No," she said. "No sweethearts.

At least not since she was five. She was sweet on one of the boys then. Brian Hall. He was a cute little boy, always smiling." She turned to Lamb. "He's dead now, of course. Drowned in the bath, years ago. I can't remember how many. He slipped and hit his head, you see."

She stopped for a moment, as if to think. The shock she'd registered seconds before seemed already to have worn off. The act of remembering Emily as a girl seemed to have occasioned this metamorphosis. She smiled again.

"Yes, five," she said. "Emily was a very pretty girl even then." She sat up suddenly, as if ready for her tea.

"Was there anyone more recent than Brian Hall?" Lamb asked gently.

"Not really," she said. She stopped speaking and looked at the floor. Lamb felt her retreating again. He realized he'd made a mistake in shifting the subject of their conversation away from Emily's childhood.

"But they were cute, the two of them, when they were children— Emily and Brian?" he asked.

"Oh, yes. They were very cute. And then Brian died."

Elizabeth suddenly put her face into her hands, bent forward, and began to weep.

Lamb let her cry for several minutes. She sobbed loudly, her shoulders heaving. Several times she cried aloud, "Oh, God," or "Please God, no!" Eventually, Lamb ventured to touch her shoulder. In response, Elizabeth put her right hand over her mouth for a second and then pressed her index finger and thumb against her eyes.

"She's dead," she said, as if she were informing Lamb of this fact. "Emily is dead."

"Yes," Lamb said. "I'm sorry."

Elizabeth drew in several quick breaths and sniffed. Her eyes, though red-rimmed, filled again with a kind of fierceness. Lamb thought that he had never met anyone like Elizabeth Fordham. Emotions seemed to course through her like unpredictable winds through a canyon. And yet he sensed that, despite this, she possessed some control over her moods. She pushed her hands along her thighs, wiping the moisture from her hands.

"Ask me your questions," she said to Lamb. She had become erect and forthright. "I know that you must ask me questions if you are to find who did this to Emily."

Wallace arrived with a tray containing a pot of tea, three cups, a small cup of milk, and a bowl of sugar. He put the tray on the table in front of the sofa. Elizabeth poured each of them a cup of tea, then abruptly stopped. Wallace quietly withdrew his notebook and a pencil from his jacket pocket.

"I understand she volunteered at the infirmary near the RAF base in Cloverton," Lamb said. "What did she do there?"

"Whatever was needed. She was a helper. She helped with bandages and made tea. She was always a helpful girl."

"Did she have a job?"

"No. I wouldn't allow it. Not with the war on. I didn't want her mixed up in things. She wanted to join the WAAFs, but I wouldn't allow it."

She poured a bit of milk into her tea and sipped it.

Lamb sensed that she was again growing calm. "Do you know of anyone else who might have wanted to hurt Emily?" he asked.

"No." She shook her head and looked away from Lamb. "Who would want to hurt Emily?" She said this almost as if she were speaking to herself.

"Oh, Emily!" she exclaimed. She was looking at the far wall. "Why must you be so difficult?" The tempest in her was rising again.

"Who else did she know?" Lamb asked. "Where did she spend her time?"

Elizabeth daubed at her eyes with her fingers. She thrust out her chin, again seeming to bring herself under control. "She wanted to join the WAAFs, but I wouldn't allow it," she said again.

"Yes," Lamb said. He realized that he had made another mistake. Elizabeth had wanted to explain her reasons for prohibiting Emily from joining the WAAFs and he had tried to guide her away from that.

"She got the idea from Lilly, her friend," Elizabeth said. "We argued about it, but I didn't want her mixed up with it. We argued about it." She hesitated for a second, then turned to face Lamb. "Do you have children, Chief Inspector?"

"Yes. I have a daughter who is about Emily's age."

"Well, then, you know how difficult they can be."

"Yes."

"Emily always has been a difficult child. And she defied me."

Lamb nodded.

"When I forbade Emily from joining the WAAFs, she went instead to volunteer at the infirmary. She came in here one afternoon and announced that she'd done it." She looked again toward the far wall. "I didn't fight it. I was tired of fighting."

"What is Lilly's last name?" Wallace asked.

"What?" She was looking at Wallace but also looking past him.

"What is Lilly's last name, madam?"

"Schmidt—it's a German name. I hadn't really noticed until the war started, but Lilly has a German surname."

"Can you tell us where we might find Miss Schmidt?"

"She's a waitress in the tea room in the village."

Lamb produced the photo of the RAF pilot they'd found in Emily's wallet. He braced himself for another shift in Elizabeth's emotions. "Do you recognize this man?" he asked.

Elizabeth took the photo and stared at it. Lamb saw surprise in her eyes.

"No," she said. "I've never seen him before. Why are you showing me this?"

"We found the photograph in Emily's wallet."

Elizabeth threw the photo onto the coffee table.

"This is the man who killed her, then?" she asked. "This is her killer?"

"We don't know," Lamb said. "We hoped you might identify him."

She seemed to recoil from the photo, pressing herself against the couch.

"No. This is a mistake. Emily wouldn't have that man's photograph in her wallet. She would have told me if she knew this man.

Someone has put that photograph in her wallet." Her eyes widened. "I wouldn't doubt that Lilly gave her the photo. She's still trying to persuade Emily to join the WAAFs, despite my having forbidden it."

Lamb decided not to press the matter.

"She'd have told me if she knew this man," Elizabeth repeated.

"Yes, of course," Lamb said.

He produced the drawing of the spider attacking the butterfly and the small photo of the boy. "We also found these in Emily's wallet," he said. "Do they mean anything to you?"

Elizabeth stared at the drawing fleetingly. "No," she said quickly and with obvious disdain. "I don't know what this is. It makes no sense; it's garish and ugly. Emily didn't do this sort of thing."

"Do you recognize the boy?"

"No. I have no idea who he is. I suppose he could be one of the children Lord Pembroke takes in over the summers. Emily and her brother, Donald, worked there a few summers." She thrust out her chin again. "Lord Pembroke chooses several local young men and women of good character to help out with the children each summer. Donald applied first and was accepted, then Emily."

The news surprised Lamb. He hadn't known that Pembroke hired young people from the villages to assist him with the orphans. Obviously, that was how Emily had known Peter.

"Do you know of a boy named Peter Wilkins who also stays with Lord Pembroke?" Lamb asked. "We have reason to believe he might have drawn this picture."

"No. Why would you think that some boy connected with Lord Pembroke would have drawn this horrible thing?"

"He likes to draw insects."

Elizabeth drew in her shoulders beneath her shawl, as if she'd caught a chill. "They're terrible-looking things," she said. "Frightening. I don't know why he would have sent Emily such a thing unless it was to frighten her."

"Where is your son, Donald, stationed, Mrs. Fordham? We may want to speak to him."

Elizabeth looked away. Lamb sensed that she was shutting down again. "You can't," she said. "He's too far away. He's in the Royal Navy."

"Is he stationed on a ship, then?" Wallace interjected.

Elizabeth looked at Wallace with an expression that seemed to say that she found his question idiotic. "*Nothing* like that," she said. "He's part of an anti-aircraft crew guarding Scapa Flow." Her eyes flared. "Donald also defied me. I told him I didn't want him to become mixed up in the war, but he defied me."

"Do you have the name of the unit to which he is attached?" Lamb asked.

"No. I don't concern myself with such things. Donald defied me."

Lamb decided he'd gotten all he could for the moment from Elizabeth Fordham. The woman seemed to have entirely lost touch with the true substance of her daughter's life.

"If you think of anything else, please call me," Lamb said, handing Elizabeth a card with his telephone number on it. "I can only say once again that Sergeant Wallace and I are very sorry to bring you the news we have brought you and will do everything in our power to discover who did this to your daughter."

"Yes," Elizabeth said, absently. "Thank you." She sat again on the sofa with her hands in her lap, staring at the opposite wall.

"Is there anyone whom you might want us to contact for you, Mrs. Fordham? Perhaps someone who might come and stay with you for a time?"

Elizabeth shook her head. "No."

She looked at her feet. "Emily," she said quietly. "What am I going to do with you?"

SIXTEEN

—⁀—

THE EXCELSIOR TEA ROOM WAS IN THE LIPSCOMBE VILLAGE SQUARE.
Lilly Schmidt was wiping cake crumbs from one of the shop's four
yellow tables as Lamb and Wallace entered. The shop was empty of
customers. Lilly looked up when the bell over the door jingled.

"Good morning, gentlemen," she said. Lamb could see from her
countenance that she did not yet know that her friend had been
murdered. Normally, such news traveled very quickly in the little
villages. Apparently, though, no one yet had gotten around to Lilly
Schmidt.

"Miss Schmidt?" Lamb said. The place smelled of cinnamon and
coffee, which made him hungry. "Lilly Schmidt?"

"Yes."

Lamb showed his warrant card and introduced himself and Wallace. "Do you have a minute or two to spare?"

"Yes," she said. She appeared suddenly confused. "Is something wrong?"

They sat at the table that she had been cleaning. Lamb was glad that the shop was empty. It would allow them to speak frankly about Emily. If a customer came in, he might have to move Lilly outside. "Is anyone else here?" he asked.

"Not at the moment. The owner, Mrs. Beltram, has gone out."

"I'm sorry, Miss Schmidt," Lamb said. "I just wanted to ensure that we could speak frankly without being overheard. I'm afraid that I have some bad news. Emily Fordham was found dead this morning off the main road north of the village."

"Emily?" Lilly put her hand to her mouth.

"Yes, I'm afraid so."

"But why?"

"That's what we're endeavoring to find out. I'm sorry to tell you that she was murdered—she was struck a blow to the head."

Lilly's eyes began to well with tears. "I don't understand," she said. "I just saw her yesterday morning."

Lamb leaned toward her. "I know it's difficult, Miss Schmidt. But if you believe you're up to it, we'd like to ask you a few questions about Emily that might help us to understand what happened to her."

Lilly put her hand over her eyes in an attempt to stanch her welling tears. "All right," she said.

"Do you know of anyone who might have wanted to hurt Emily— someone she might have argued or fought with?"

"No. Emily had no enemies. Everyone loved her."

"How about a boyfriend? Was she sweet on anyone?"

Lilly looked away and put her hand to her mouth again.

Lamb touched her other hand, which was resting on the small blue table. "There can be no secrets, Miss Schmidt," he said gently. "We must know what you know if we are to find who did this to Emily."

Lilly turned to Lamb. Her lips quivered slightly. "Charles," she said.

Lamb put the photo of the pilot on the table. "Is this Charles?"

"Yes."

"How long has Emily known him?"

"They met last fall when she began helping at the infirmary near Cloverton airfield. They met in a pub in the village near there." She looked down for a second, then back at Lamb. "I think Emily was looking for a pilot—that's why she volunteered at Cloverton. She found them romantic, you know. Heroic. And, sure enough, she found one. He's Canadian. She used to see him two or three times a week before the Germans started coming. She hasn't seen him much since, though. She told me yesterday morning that she was going to see him. She'd spent part of the previous night waiting for him after the airfield was attacked. She told me that she was certain he'd survived."

"Do you know Charles's last name?"

"Graham. Charles Graham."

"Would you say that Emily was in love with Charles Graham?" Wallace asked.

"Oh, yes." She glanced away for just a second. "At least she was in love with the idea of him."

"Was he in love with her?"

Lilly looked at the photo of Graham lying on the table. "I don't know," she said quietly. "Emily thought he was."

"But you had your doubts?" Wallace persisted.

Lilly shook her head. "I don't know," she said. She pressed her fingers against her eyes again.

"Is there something about Charles Graham you're not telling us, Miss Schmidt?" Wallace asked. "Something we should know?"

Lilly wiped her eyes, then pushed Graham's photo toward Lamb. "She was carrying Charles's baby," she said. "She found out a couple of weeks ago. She's been waking up sick in the mornings."

The news surprised Lamb—then again, it didn't. Winston-Sheed was right. The war had encouraged a kind of throwing off of the usual cautions and the notion that patience, waiting, usually produced a greater reward.

"Did she tell Charles Graham that she was pregnant?" Wallace asked.

"She didn't want to worry him with it. She said that he'd spoken to her of marriage."

"Did she tell anyone else of this?"

"Her brother."

"Donald?"

"Yes. They were close. They kept a kind of alliance against their mother, who's mad and has been since Emily's father died more than a dozen years ago. Mad with grief, I always said. Donald's letters to Emily come here, to the shop. Emily couldn't allow her mother to know that she was writing to Donald. His letters come here; I gave them to Emily."

"No one else knew of the pregnancy, then?" Lamb asked.

"Not that Emily said." Lilly looked at the floor. "She certainly wouldn't have said anything to her mother."

Lamb put the photo of the boy on the table. "Do you recognize this boy? We found this photo in Emily's wallet, along with the photo of Charles Graham."

Emily studied the photo for several seconds. "I suppose he could be one of those children Emily knew from working on Lord Pembroke's estate. One of them had sent her some letter or something recently that concerned her."

"Did Emily say that this correspondence came from a boy named Peter?" Lamb asked.

"Yes, Peter. Emily felt responsible for him. I told her she wasn't—that she couldn't help the fact that he was daft."

"What do you mean when you say she felt responsible for him?" Wallace asked.

"She was worried that she might have sent him the wrong message somehow—that he might be in love with her when she had never been anything more to him than a friend. She took pity on him, though she admired his talent. She said he is quite a good artist. Brilliant, even. She told me that she wasn't going to go back to the estate this summer, even if the children came, because she was moving on from all that. She was working on getting out of here, away from her mother. She was worried that Peter might have felt as if she'd abandoned him."

Lamb placed the cryptic drawing on the table. "Is this the sort of thing she said she had received from Peter?"

Lilly's face registered surprise at the drawing. "I don't know," she said after a couple of seconds. "I never saw it. She only said that she was worried that Peter was upset about something. That he was trying to tell her that he was upset."

"Do you have any notion of what this sketch might mean—what he might have been trying to tell Emily?" Wallace asked.

"That he was frightened, or angry? It's very ugly and beautiful at the same time. I think Emily was trying to help Peter, but he took everything in the wrong way."

"Did Emily ever mention any of the other children from the estate—perhaps one who could be the boy in the photograph?" Lamb asked.

"No." She paused, as if considering the question more thoroughly, then added, "There was some trouble last summer with one of the boys, though. One of them ran away for a day or so. But he turned up eventually. The boy was one of those who Donald supervised. Donald also worked for Lord Pembroke in the summers. The boy apparently clashed with Donald, though I'm not sure how."

"Do you know if she wrote to Donald of her concerns about Peter?"

"I suppose she must have. They spoke about everything."

"Have you received any recent letters from Donald?" Lamb asked.

"No. I think it's hard for him to find the time to write."

The bell above the door jangled and an elderly couple entered the shop. Lamb smiled at Lilly. "Thank you for your time, Miss Schmidt," he said. "You've been very helpful."

Lilly's eyes welled. "I don't understand it," she said. "Why would anyone want to hurt Emily?"

—⁂—

Lamb and Wallace returned to Winchester, where they each grabbed a cheese-and-pickle sandwich and a cup of tea. Wallace thought of Delilah, had been thinking of her all morning and of what he might do to the man who'd beaten her. He realized that he was willing to risk trouble for Delilah's sake, even with Lamb's warning still ringing in his ears.

Lamb wanted to have another crack at communicating with Peter Wilkins, and had fresh questions for Lord Pembroke about Emily and Donald Fordham and the boy in the photo they'd found in Emily's wallet.

He called Leonard Parkinson and requested another meeting with Pembroke. Parkinson said that Pembroke had gone to London and planned to return on the following morning. He offered to arrange a meeting for eleven the next morning.

Lamb then called Winston-Sheed's office and left a message that Emily Fordham allegedly had been pregnant and would the doctor kindly confirm that as soon as he was able.

Larkin appeared at the door to Lamb's office. He handed Lamb a brief report on his analysis of the tin box Rivers had found in the mill ruins. Abbott's and Lydia Blackwell's fingerprints were all over the box. "I apologize for the incident this morning with the seagulls, sir," Larkin said, standing in Lamb's doorway.

"It wasn't your fault."

"No, but I suppose I approved of it. At least I did at the time."

"Forget about it," Lamb said. "Find me something to use in this latest mess."

He finished his sandwich and drained his tea. It sated his hunger—the empty feeling in his stomach—but nothing else. Even though he must eventually tell Harding that Larkin had found Abbott's prints on the tin box, he had nothing to say to the superintendent at the moment and so stayed away from Harding's office. Harding had been out of line dismissing the doctor's stunt and threatening the men. In any case, Harding seemed to be avoiding him as well. They would have to steer clear of each other for a while, until the emotions attendant to the morning's events subsided.

Wallace had begun to busy himself by typing up a report of their interviews with Elizabeth Fordham and Lilly Schmidt. He started by typing "Elizabeth Fordham is bloody fucking crazy." He stared at what he'd written and began to laugh—he didn't know why. The woman had lost her daughter in the most terrible of ways. It was nothing to laugh at.

Still.

He typed "And spider boy can't fucking talk!" He laughed so hard at this that he spit some of his tepid tea onto the keys of his typewriter. He looked around the incident room and noticed Lamb heading for his desk. He ripped the paper from the machine, balled it, and tossed it into the basket next to his desk.

"Let's go have a talk with Charles Graham," Lamb said.

Wallace choked back a final smile and wiped moisture from his eyes. He put his hat on his head. "Yes, sir," he said.

At Cloverton, they showed their warrant cards to the guard at the roadblock, who waved them through. Wallace wondered where the energetic young Lt. Glendon had got to; likely kicking someone's oversized arse and screaming at them to get a bloody move on.

Lamb drove into the partially ruined airfield, where they got a close look at the damage done by the marauding Stukas. The fuel depot and the area surrounding it for more than a hundred meters in all directions was a charred mess and the flat grass runway still was pocked with a half dozen bomb craters, though work crews, with the aid of a bulldozer, were rapidly filling them with dirt and gravel. The remnants of the six fighter planes the Germans had destroyed on the ground had been bulldozed to the edges of the field and were being carted away, piece by piece, in rumbling lorries. Miraculously, the Stukas had missed entirely the small command post and the barracks in which the pilots lived. Lamb again recalled the pilot he'd seen die. The boy had lived in a place just like it—perhaps he'd even been stationed at Cloverton and lived in that very building. His metal cot and footlocker almost certainly by now had been assigned to his replacement—some other boy whose job would be to risk his life two or even three times a day, every day, for the foreseeable future, until the Germans either smashed Britain or gave up trying.

He parked the Wolseley in front of the small wooden command post and mounted the stair with Wallace at his heels. A uniformed clerk stood as Lamb entered. He was an older man, perhaps thirty.

"May I help you, sir?" he asked politely.

Lamb showed his warrant card. "I'd like to see the commander, if I may," he said.

The clerk took Lamb's warrant card, looked at it closely, then returned it to Lamb with a tight smile. "Very good, Chief Inspector," he said. "I'll see if the wing commander can speak with you."

The clerk went to a door just to the left of his desk and knocked on it. A voice within said "Come." The clerk opened the door and disappeared into the room, closing the door behind him. Thirty seconds later, he emerged.

"Wing Commander Bruegel will see you now," the clerk said.

He motioned Lamb and Wallace into a small office with no windows that contained not much more than a desk, two chairs, and a pair of olive-colored metal filing cabinets along the left-hand wall. Bruegel stood to meet them; he was of medium height and build—not what Lamb would have called impressive. But Lamb immediately sensed Bruegel's confidence of his place in the world, and his rank. And yet Bruegel couldn't have been much older than his clerk; all of these RAF people seemed so young. But it was their youth, and youth's hallmark sense of invincibility, that was responsible for their courage.

Lamb and Wallace introduced themselves and showed Bruegel their identification; he in turn motioned for them to take the two metal chairs that faced his desk.

"How may I help you, gentlemen?"

"The name of a man under your command—Charles Graham—has come up in connection with a murder inquiry," Lamb said. "I'd like to speak with him, if that's possible."

"Am I allowed to know the details of this connection?"

"His photograph was found in the wallet of a young woman named Emily Fordham, who was found murdered this morning near the village of Lipscombe."

Bruegel's face clouded for a second, though he quickly regained his bearing. "How was she killed, if I might ask?"

"She was attacked last night as she rode her bicycle along the road to Lipscombe. It appears that she stopped for some reason and was struck a blow to the head. We have reason to believe that she might have been returning from Cloverton at the time."

Bruegel called the clerk, who entered promptly. "Fetch Lieutenant Graham, please," he said. When the clerk had left, Bruegel looked at Lamb. "You may use my office, Chief Inspector. Of course, if we are called to scramble, then we must cut the interview short."

"Thank you," Lamb said.

Charles Graham was tall and slender, with a boyish face and blue eyes. He appeared harmless, even benevolent, as he did in the photo Emily had hidden in her wallet—though, of course, he might be nothing of the kind, Lamb thought.

Bruegel straightened as Graham entered and saluted. "This is Chief Inspector Thomas Lamb and Detective Sergeant David Wallace of the Hampshire Constabulary," he said to Graham. "They are conducting an inquiry in which your name has come up. I expect you to give them your full cooperation."

Graham's face betrayed no emotion. "Yes, sir," he said.

"Very well, then," Bruegel said. He nodded at Lamb and left the room.

Lamb stood and allowed Graham to have his chair. He sat on the edge of Bruegel's desk, facing Graham, with Wallace to his right. He wanted to see Graham's immediate, unvarnished reaction to the news of Emily's murder. It was likely Graham hadn't yet heard of Emily's death. Unless he'd killed her.

"I'm investigating the murder of Emily Fordham," Lamb said. "Her body was found this morning on the road near Lipscombe. Someone struck her a fatal blow to the back of the head."

Confusion clouded Graham's blue eyes. "Emily? Are you sure?"

"Quite sure. We found your photograph in her wallet." Lamb produced Graham's photo and handed it to him. "Did you give this to her?"

Graham stared at the photo for several seconds. He looked at Lamb, his eyes filled with an emotion that Lamb thought was genuine shock.

"Did you have a romantic relationship with her?" Lamb asked. "You signed the photo, 'Love, Charles.'"

Graham hesitated for a second before answering. "Yes." He glanced at the floor.

"How long had you been lovers?"

Graham did not answer immediately. "Lieutenant Graham?" Lamb prompted him.

Graham looked at Lamb as if he'd temporarily forgotten that Lamb was sitting next to him. "I'm sorry, Chief Inspector," he said. "It's just that I can't believe it."

"How long were you lovers?" Lamb repeated.

"It started last Christmas. We used to meet at the pub in the village—in Cloverton."

"Do you know Lilly Schmidt?"

"Emily's friend from the village? Emily spoke of her, though I've never met her."

"She claims that Emily was pregnant. I've asked the medical examiner to check for certain, though I find Miss Schmidt's claims credible."

Graham opened his mouth, as if intending to speak, but said nothing. He looked away. Then he said, at a near whisper, "She said nothing to me of being pregnant."

"Have you any reason to believe that you were not the baby's father?"

Graham still was looking away. He shook his head absently. "No," he said quietly.

"When did you last see Emily?"

"Yesterday." He put his face in his hands.

"When, exactly?"

Graham looked at Lamb. "I'm sorry," he said. He seemed not to have heard the question.

"When did you last see Emily, exactly?" Lamb repeated.

"In the early evening."

"What did you do?"

"I'm sorry, Chief Inspector. It's just that I didn't. . . ." He looked at the ground again and shook his head.

"I understand that this news must come as a shock to you, Lieutenant," he said. "But I must ask these questions."

Graham looked up. "Yes, of course. I'm sorry." He sat up. "We sat by the pub and talked."

"Did Emily speak to you yesterday of anything that might have been troubling her?"

"No. We had only a half hour or so."

"Had she spoken to you recently of anything that was troubling her?"

"Only her mother. She made Emily's life difficult."

"Did you ever meet her brother, Donald?"

"No. He was gone into the Navy by the time we met. She told me a bit about him; they were close, she said."

Lamb produced the photo of the boy. "Do you know this boy?"

Graham looked at the photo. "No. Should I?"

"We found this photograph in Emily's wallet."

Graham shook his head again. "I suppose he might have been one of the children she worked with on the estate."

"Lord Pembroke's estate?"

"Yes. She worked there in the summers, helping the orphans—disadvantaged children. She was quite proud of that; I thought it quite noble of her. But she was like that—generous." He shook his head and looked away again.

"Did she ever mention a boy she knew from the estate named Peter?"

"Once or twice. She thought he might be in love with her. She laughed about it some, but I think it troubled her."

"Had she spoken to you recently of any trouble she might have been having with Peter?"

"No."

Lamb showed Graham the drawing of the spider. "Did she ever show you this?"

Graham studied the drawing for a few seconds. "No. What is it?"

"I don't know. But I'm sure that this boy, Peter, drew it and believe that he gave it to her in the hope of communicating something to her, perhaps even to frighten her."

Graham shook his head. "I don't know, Chief Inspector. I'm sorry."

"Had she ever shown you anything else that she'd received from Peter?"

"No."

"What time did Emily leave you last night?"

"I suppose it was close to eight."

"What did you do once she left?"

"I came back here and slept."

That would be easy enough to check. He found Graham's reaction to Emily's death convincing. He now took a shot in the dark. "Did Emily ever mention to you a man by the name of Will Blackwell?"

Graham shook his head. "No."

"Very good, Lieutenant," Lamb said. "Thank you for your time."

He stood; Graham and Wallace did the same. Graham nodded. "You're welcome, Chief Inspector," he said. "I wonder if you'll please let me know if you find out anything."

Lamb smiled but promised nothing.

Before he left, Lamb checked Graham's alibi with Bruegel. Except for the time that he claimed to have met Emily at the pub, Charles Graham had been present and accounted for all the previous evening. That said, men were known to go absent without leave or to creep away for a bit and ask their comrades to cover for them.

"It might have been easy for him to have slipped away for a couple of hours in the middle of the night among all the confusion and upset from the German attack," Wallace said as they drove off the base.

"Yes, but what was his motive?"

"He didn't want to be tied down to a wife and child."

"But he claims he didn't know about the child."

Wallace shrugged. "He's lying."

Lamb shook his head. "He doesn't strike me as the type."

"Why, because he's an RAF bloke? They haven't charmed you, too, have they, sir?" Wallace smiled. He thought of how, a few hours ago, Lamb had been chewing him out and threatening to tie his arse in a sling. Now they were chatting away. Lamb was very hard to figure. But he was no bastard. He would rather work for Lamb than anyone else he'd ever known who outranked him. He half considered asking Lamb what Rivers was on about. Perhaps he could be Lamb's ally in that, though he didn't want to seem as if he was kissing arse.

"Do you mind if I ask you a personal question, sir?" Wallace asked.

"That depends on the question."

"What has Rivers got against you?"

Lamb took a couple of seconds to consider the question. He didn't want to jaw on about Rivers.

"It goes back to the war," Lamb said. "He holds me responsible for the death of the man who was his best mate."

Wallace knew he was risking Lamb's ire in seeking more, though he sensed Lamb was willing to talk. "Were you—responsible, I mean?"

Lamb glanced at Wallace. "Yes, I was, in the sense that I was the man's commanding officer and ordered him to perform the duty that led to his death."

"But that doesn't count, does it? Someone must give the orders in war."

"It's a long story," Lamb said, though it wasn't, really.

Wallace took the hint and ended his interrogation.

When they returned to the constabulary, Evers, the duty sergeant at the desk, told Lamb to report to Harding immediately. "Guv's orders." Evers shrugged, as if in sympathy.

Harding stood as Lamb entered his office. He seemed in a great rush.

"Rivers found them—both of them—in bloody Portsmouth, just as you said," Harding said. "Abbott *and* the bloody niece. They've been holed up in a doss house down there flushing the uncle's money down the loo at the bloody track." Harding clapped his right hand on Lamb's shoulder. "Nice work, Tom. Larkin told me about the prints on the tin box." The super's irritation of the morning seemed to have disappeared utterly. He smiled. "We've broken the bloody thing open."

Lamb wasn't as certain of that. If Abbott and Lydia Blackwell had been holed up in Portsmouth, then they couldn't have killed Emily Fordham. He believed that the connections between the two killings were too numerous to be dismissed as coincidence. Still, he was eager to talk to Abbott and Lydia Blackwell.

Lamb found Rivers in the incident room receiving congratulations on the arrest from Wallace. Lamb approached and offered Rivers his hand. To Lamb's surprise, Rivers took it with what seemed genuine civility.

"Good work," Lamb said.

"They'd blown fifty quid already; the niece admitted that much," Rivers said. "All they had left was two bloody pound. I think she's ready to talk; she feels as if Abbott has double-crossed her."

"All right," Lamb said. "We'll talk to her first. Then we'll put the screws to him."

Rivers thought of how he had been in Hampshire only a few days and already was on the verge of cracking a murder inquiry. As much as he disliked admitting it, part of his success was down to Lamb. Even so, *he'd* done the actual work. Lamb merely had pointed him down the right path, which, after all, was Lamb's job. His cock-up in Warwickshire was starting to feel like a bad, distant dream.

—⬥—

At noon, Vera called Southampton and Portsmouth.

The telephone lines remained open, the saboteurs and fifth columnists at bay. That done, she set out on another lunchtime stroll up the hill to clear her mind. She hoped that she might encounter Peter again and perhaps speak to him. She'd spent part of the morning examining the drawing that Peter had dropped on the hill the previous evening. She found its detail and artistry exquisite, despite the disturbing nature of its subject. In the meantime, the events of the previous evening had vexed her; she seemed to have glimpsed Arthur as he really was—callous and frightened. She had hated the way in which he'd tried to bully her and to bully Peter.

She ascended Manscome Hill along the sheep trail, by the wood that marked the western edge of Brookings. The day was hot but overcast, the first cloudy day they'd had in more than a week. She walked to the place where she'd first encountered Peter and stopped. She looked around but saw no sign of him. She sat in the grass by the path and waited. The meadow was dotted with thistle and wildflower and alive in the midday heat with grasshoppers, darting birds, and butterflies.

A large blue butterfly alighted on a clover blossom near her. She did not know butterflies, really, and so did not know that the creature was called an Adonis Blue. She found it beautiful; its delicate wings were indigo and edged in concentric rings of black and white. She'd never really taken the time to closely examine a butterfly. She could easily see how their prettiness and grace might catch the fancy of a boy like Peter—or of a boy like the one she imagined Peter to be. She wondered what motivated him, what his thoughts consisted of. She thought that he must be lonely and frightened.

She moved to touch the butterfly with the tip of her finger, but it sensed her movement and flew away.

She sat in the meadow for twenty minutes, but Peter did not show. The clouds parted and moved to the south, toward the Solent, opening the sky again to the Germans. Disappointed that Peter had not shown himself, she began to walk down the path toward Quimby.

As she neared the place where the path ended near the cottage, she saw lying in the path, about twenty meters ahead, a sheet of paper like the one Peter had left on the hill on the previous night. She knew immediately what it was. She looked around but still saw no sign of Peter.

She jogged to the paper and picked it up; it was a stout sheet of watercolor paper on which Peter had quickly sketched, in pencil and pastel, the same type of blue butterfly she'd seen on the flower. She recognized the color of its wings and their black and white bands. Peter had been watching her.

Despite the haste with which he'd obviously drawn it, the sketch breathed life, animation. The butterfly seemed poised to rise from the page and, she thought, to possess a soul. Beneath the drawing, Peter had written something; the letters were rendered in pencil, in a crude hand, like that of a very small child who was just learning to write:

tommss ded

She had no idea what the words meant. She called toward the wood. "Peter. Come out. I won't hurt you. I want to meet you." She held his drawing above her head, as if it were a flag of truce. "Your drawings are beautiful. But I don't know what sort of butterfly this is. Can you tell me, please?"

She stood on the path and waited for several minutes before she gave up and returned to her post. From the wood, Peter watched her leave.

When she returned to the Parish Council room, Vera found Arthur waiting for her by the hand-cranked siren. Her heart dropped. She had hoped he'd stay away, though she'd known he wouldn't.

"I've come to apologize," he said. He stood between her and the stair that led to the door of the Council room. She didn't want to speak with him. She clutched Peter's drawing in her right hand.

"You've no need to apologize," she said.

"But I've upset you." His voice had the pleading tone that, she now believed, Arthur used to manipulate her emotionally.

"You haven't upset me. I'm fine."

"But I can tell that you're upset. That you hate me."

"I don't hate you, Arthur."

"You do. I can tell." He was being childish now. That, too, was manipulative—and pitiful.

"I can't talk about this now, Arthur. I'm on duty."

"You see," he said. "You could talk to me if you wanted, but you don't. Because I've upset you."

"Please, Arthur."

"It's Peter; you like him. I sometimes think you like him more than you like me. Is that one of his drawings?" He made a move to take the drawing from her, but she yanked it away.

Arthur laughed slightly—a laugh that contained a sarcastic, derisive edge. "And here I thought you might even have loved me," he said.

"Please, Arthur. I must go back to work. I'm on duty."

She tried to move around him, to ascend the stairs, but he blocked her way.

"I see," Arthur said. "Because he draws the beautiful pictures, is that it?" He held aloft the stub of his right arm; his eyes narrowed in a menacing way. "Not all of us can draw, can we, Vera?"

She hated his implication that she disliked him because of his arm. That was the most manipulative of all. *He* used his arm, deployed it. It had made no difference to her.

"Your arm has nothing to do with it and never has," she said.

He hit the railing of the stair with his fist. "Bollocks!" he said. "I know what you want. You want to be rid of me. You'd rather spend your time with a bleeding idiot who draws spiders."

"That's not true. And it's not fair."

He held his stump aloft again, his eyes aflame. "No, *this* isn't bloody fair. You're a liar, Vera, a liar. And you're a whore. Well, I'll tell you something. *He* hasn't got one, has he? Or if he does, he doesn't know what to do with it."

A whore. She would rather that he had struck her in the face. She had given herself to him because she trusted and pitied him. She saw the true extent of her mistake and no longer even wanted to be in his presence.

"Get out!" she yelled, pointing toward the street. "Get the bloody hell out!"

Arthur took a step toward her, as if he meant to strike her. Vera drew back from him, frightened.

He smiled a crooked, contemptuous smile. "You're bloody pathetic," he said. "You and your idiot eunuch." He pointed at her, jabbing. "I better not catch the two of you together, or I'll make both of you regret it."

"Get out!" She moved as if to turn the siren crank, to awaken the village.

Arthur backed away from the stair. He began to cry. "I hate you!" he yelled. Then he ran into the street and toward his father's farm.

Vera ran up the stairs to the Council room, slammed the door, and locked it, her heart beating furiously. She burst into tears and kicked the door in a gesture of shock, sorrow, and anger.

SEVENTEEN

ALBERT GILLEY HAD FOUND IT RATHER EASY TO TRACK DOWN George Abbott and therefore to point Rivers in the right direction. Abbott and Lydia had been hanging around the track since the day after Blackwell's killing, flashing cash and losing badly, Gilley told Rivers. They were staying in a doss house near the track.

A bleary-eyed Lydia had answered Rivers's knock on the door of their room, simple as that. She'd seemed genuinely surprised to see Rivers. Abbott was snoring in bed.

A few hours later, in an interview room in Winchester, Lamb began his interrogation of Lydia by reminding her that people who were convicted of murder were hanged and that, if she had not killed her uncle, the only way for her to avoid the gallows was to tell the truth. In response, she retched up her story in a flood of repressed emotion and bitter tears.

She hadn't expected her uncle to be killed—she truly hadn't. The plan had been for Abbott to set Will to work on his hedges that morning, and for her and Abbott to take a bit of Will's money and go to Paulsgrove. It was supposed to have been a lark, a one-off thing, though she hadn't been convinced that they could do it all in a single day and still return to Quimby before Will came home for his tea. She'd never been to the racetrack or any sort of gambling establishment. But Abbott—she called him George—told her they could do it easily and that Will never would know they'd been gone. And they *had* done it. They'd bet on a few races and lost most of the thirty pounds they'd stolen from Will's box, then gotten back to Quimby on time. But then Will had failed to show for his tea.

She had known Abbott most of her life, but they hadn't begun "relations," as she called it, until about fourteen months earlier. She was lonely, had always been lonely, and had never had much. Abbott had things—a farm and house of his own, sheep, a phonograph, and other possessions. And he *had* helped Will—given him work—when no one else would. Then, about two months after she and Abbott had begun their "relations," the boy ran away from Lord Pembroke's estate and Will brought the boy home. . . .

The words stunned Lamb.

"Hold on," he said. "Which boy?"

"His name were Thomas," Lydia said. "I don't know his surname."

Lamb signaled to the constable who stood by the door. The man came to the table and Lamb whispered something to him. The constable nodded and left the room. Lamb turned back to Lydia.

"You say that Will brought the boy, Thomas, home?"

"Yes, sir." She felt vaguely irritated with Lamb; she was trying to tell him the truth about what had happened on the day her uncle died, and yet he was interrupting her with irrelevant questions about Thomas.

"What do you mean when you say that Will brought Thomas home?"

"Just that. The boy had run away from Brookings—he was one of the orphan boys who stay there summers. And he ran away and ended up on the hill, where Will found him, hiding. He were hungry and scared. The boy took to Will; he told Will he didn't want to go back to Brookings. He'd had some trouble there with someone."

"Donald Fordham?" Lamb asked.

"I don't know, sir," Lydia said. "I didn't talk to the boy, really. Shortly after he found the boy, Will hiked over to Brookings and, an hour later, returned with Lord Pembroke in Lord Pembroke's motorcar and Lord Pembroke took the boy back to Brookings."

The constable returned with the snapshot of the boy they'd found in Emily Fordham's wallet. Lamb placed it on the table. "Is this Thomas?"

Lydia looked at the photo. "Yes, sir, that is the boy."

"Do you know a woman named Emily Fordham, Miss Blackwell?"

Lydia looked genuinely confused. "No. I've never heard of no one named Emily Fordham, sir." Lamb was getting far off the track, she thought. She was trying to tell him about Will's money. She didn't want George to go to the gallows; she loved George. Lamb had said to tell the truth, and she was doing that. Better that she should tell the truth than that Lamb should believe that George had killed her uncle.

"You said when we spoke the first time that Peter Wilkins sometimes came over from Lord Pembroke's estate to sit with Will while Will worked," Lamb said. "Do you know if Peter Wilkins showed Will where Thomas was hiding on the hill?"

Lamb considered the question another shot in the dark. He was beginning to arrange in his mind a scenario in which the killings had occurred and why, though he hadn't a bloody scrap of evidence yet to support such a scenario.

"Peter Wilkins, sir?" Lydia thought the question strange. Peter Wilkins was deaf and dumb as a mule. He didn't even speak, only grunted.

"Yes, Peter Wilkins," Lamb said. "Is it possible that he led your uncle to where Thomas was hiding?"

Lydia shook her head. "I don't know, sir." Her patience finally ran out. "But I'm trying to tell you about the money. I don't want George to hang. He didn't do it."

Seeing that Lydia seemed to know little about Thomas, Lamb returned to the question of Will Blackwell's money. "Yes, please tell me about the money."

"Lord Pembroke gave it to him. A hundred and seventy-five pound. For finding Thomas."

For a second time, Lamb found himself stunned by what Lydia Blackwell had told him. "And what did your uncle do with this money?" he asked.

Lydia nodded at the tin box, which was on the table between them. "He put it in there."

"And how much did he have in the box, all told?"

"About two hundred fifty pound, sir."

"And where did the rest of it come from—the other seventy-five pounds?"

"That was from what he'd saved over many, many years, sir. He didn't like banks."

"And you told George Abbott about the money—about the fact that your uncle had two hundred and fifty quid in cash in a box hidden beneath the floorboards of his bedroom closet."

Lydia drew back from Lamb as if he'd threatened to slap her. "No, sir!" she said with a tone of resolve that surprised Lamb. "I didn't even know about the box until two weeks ago, when Will told me about it. And it was Will told George about the money, for my sake."

Lydia looked away for a second. Tears began to well in her eyes. "Will were worried that he was getting old and that his time was nearly up," she said. She shook her head. "It all sounds crazy to you, sir, I know, but he said that the crows had been speaking to him, telling him that his time was coming very soon. He thought that they were waiting for him to die—the crows—so they could feed on his remains. I tried to tell him that his thinking weren't right, sir—that the crows had nothing to do with anything. That they were only just crows. But he wouldn't believe me."

She put her hand to her mouth, staving off the urge to cry. Lamb reached across the table and gently touched her arm. "Take your time," he said. "Will told you about the money two weeks ago?"

Lydia sniffled. "Yes," she said. "He said that he wanted me to have it, the money, should he . . ." She hesitated. ". . . should he *die*, sir. He told me where the money was and said that if he should die, that I should take it."

"And you say *he* told Abbott about the money?"

"Yes, sir." She pressed her fingers against the wells of her eyes. "I was certain that Will didn't know about George and me. But he did, sir. He did. It was very hard to hide things from Will. He could see right through you, like. He said that he expected George to look after me once he was gone and that he was going to ask George to do the right thing by me." She pursed her lips and shook her head slightly. "I suppose he thought George was more likely to give him that promise if he knew I weren't to be a burden to George—if George knew there was to be money involved."

"And so on the day Will died, you and George went to the track, then?"

Lydia nodded.

"And George told you that you and he would take a small bit of the money from the box—say twenty quid—while Will was working on the hill, on the hedges, and that the two of you would go to the track and come back with twice that amount, maybe more, is that it?"

She nodded again. A tear ran down her right cheek, which she wiped away as if it had burned her.

"And how much did you take from Will's box that morning, then?"

"Thirty." She barely said it.

"And George lost it all, didn't he?"

She didn't answer.

"And after Will died, he took the cash and persuaded you to come again to the track," Lamb continued. "He said that the two of you needed to get away and that he was sure that his luck would change. He wanted to take it all, but I think you put your foot down and told him that you would go only if you took another thirty or so. You were beginning to believe that he was going to squander the money if you didn't stop him. Am I right about that, too?"

"Yes." She put her right hand against her face.

Lamb was nearly finished. He had one more bullet to fire into the void. He produced the drawing of the spider snagging the bird that he'd found in the shed behind Blackwell's cottage.

"Does this sketch mean anything to you?" he asked Lydia.

Lydia found the drawing ugly, frightening. "No."

"It was found in the toolshed behind your cottage lying on a kind of altar—a satanic altar—along with a butchered chicken Michael Bradford claims your uncle stole from him. Did your uncle perform satanic rituals in the shed behind the house?"

"No! As I said before, sir, those are lies! Will weren't a witch! He were a kind man, a good man."

"Did George Abbott kill your uncle, Miss Blackwell? Maybe he surprised you. You hadn't expected him to kill Will; you only expected a day at the track. But once he showed you Will's body, you had to do as he said. You're afraid of him, after all, aren't you? Afraid that he might do to you what he did to Will?"

Lydia threw herself against the table and began to sob. "No!" she sobbed. "No!" She heaved up the words: "George was with *me*. He couldn't have done it. He was with *me*."

"All right, then, Miss Blackwell," Lamb said. He'd gotten from Lydia all he could for the moment. He signaled for the constable to take her back to her cell.

—m—

Will Blackwell's tin keepsake box remained on the table as a pair of uniformed constables brought George Abbott into the interview room and sat him in front of Lamb.

Abbott eyed the box as he sat. Lamb noticed immediately that Abbott had lost the cockiness he'd displayed during their first interview.

Lamb nodded at the box.

"We found that dumped in the mill ruins with your fingerprints all over it, Mr. Abbott," he said. "You took the cash Will kept in the box, which he told you about two weeks ago, then tossed the box into the mill. You persuaded him to tell you where he kept the cash because you promised to take care of Lydia after he died. He told you that he was worried about dying and you used that to your advantage. After Will's murder, you stashed most of the cash, which we found hidden beneath your mattress. Then you took fifty pounds or so and Lydia Blackwell to the track in Portsmouth, where you promptly lost it all. You've been very careless and stupid, I'm afraid, Mr. Abbott. And there's no use in your denying anything; Lydia has told me the whole story. She says she wants to save you from the gallows. As for me, I'm going to give you one chance—and one only—to explain why I shouldn't charge you right now with Will Blackwell's murder."

Abbott had not yet looked directly at Lamb. Now that he did so, Lamb saw genuine fear in his eyes. "I didn't kill nobody," he said with emotion. "I swear it!"

"Then tell me what happened."

Abbott slumped in the chair. "I took the money," he said. He closed his eyes and took a deep breath, as if preparing himself for confession. "Will told me about the money; it were two weeks ago, as you said. He told me where he kept it." He looked at the box. "He wanted Lydia to have it and I said to him, 'How am I to see that she gets it if I don't know where it is?' I hadn't meant to steal it—not at first." He shook his head solemnly.

"I was bloody surprised when Lydia came to my door saying he hadn't come home to tea. I swear it. We went up the hill to look for him. I thought we might find him up there, dead of a heart attack, as I said before. I never expected to find what we did."

"What happened?"

"I didn't quite believe it at first; didn't know what to think. Then I saw the crucifix carved into his head and I thought, 'Someone has finally done him; one of these crazy bastards who believes him a witch. They'd done him for the bad wheat crop.' It was horrible, him lying there, butchered. Lydia went right to pieces. I tried to pull the scythe from his chest but it wouldn't budge. Then I tried the pitchfork. I didn't like seeing him like that. And then I thought, 'What in bleeding hell are you doing, Abbott?'"

He paused, then said, "I was going to tell someone. I even went down the hill to the pub; I was going to call the constable."

"What did you do when you got to the bottom of the hill?" Lamb asked.

Abbott wrung his hands. "Something came over me," he said.

"So rather than going to the pub to call the police, you went into Blackwell's cottage—into his bedroom—and took the money," Lamb said. "*Then* you called Constable Harris."

Abbott's eyes flared with some of his former indignation. "I thought, 'Why should I suffer from this?' I was the only one who paid him any attention. For years, I was the only one who spoke to him, gave him work, treated him with anything like kindness. I meant that Lydia would get some of the money. I told her that it was better that we keep the money quiet for now, or else you lot would say that we'd done Will for it. We told you everything just how it happened, except for the money."

"So you took the cash and threw the box in the mill yard," Lamb said.

Abbott looked dumbly at his hands. "Aye." He looked directly at Lamb. "But I didn't kill Will."

Lamb himself typed Abbott's statement, which Abbott signed.

He then went to Harding's office, where he informed the superintendent that he was not prepared to charge Abbott and Lydia Blackwell with murder. Instead, he would charge them only with obstructing an inquiry, mostly to keep them apart while he sorted out the case. He believed that George Abbott had not killed Blackwell, he told Harding, adding that he'd begun to consider a fresh set of assumptions.

Harding stood from behind his desk, making his incredulity clear. "What the bloody hell do you mean, you're not going to charge him with murder? His fingerprints are all over the box and the weapons. We've bloody nailed the bastard."

"He says he tried to pull the weapons from the old man after finding him dead and that he took the money afterward. I'm inclined to believe him."

"You can't be serious, Tom?"

"I need more."

"More of *what*? What else could you possibly need?"

Lamb stood his ground. He knew that the super was no fool and that Harding had learned, over more than a decade working with him, to trust his judgment. In other cases, he'd taken what Harding had called "flights of fancy," and, yet, in nearly every case, his instincts had proven correct.

"The running off to the track doesn't fit, for one," Lamb said. "If he'd killed Blackwell and then decided to run, then he would have run for real, gone north probably, where we would have had a devil of a time tracking him. As it was, we had little trouble finding him."

"The man's a bloody idiot," Harding said. "Look at where he hid the money—in his bloody mattress. Maybe his mind is twisted in the bargain, as well; maybe he enjoys killing. He had opportunity and motive."

"But he has no connection that I can see to Emily Fordham's killing."

Harding straightened. "What does Emily Fordham have to do with it?"

"The two cases have several connections, including Peter, the mute boy who lives on Lord Pembroke's estate. He knew both victims. Abbott insisted to me that *he* was Blackwell's only friend. But Blackwell had one other friend—Peter, who left the drawing I found in Blackwell's shed. Pembroke definitively identified the drawing as Peter's work. And we know that Peter also gave Emily Fordham a drawing very much like the one I found in Blackwell's shed, and that she believed that something was distressing Peter. Now, a second boy has come up as a connection. His name is Thomas, though I don't yet know his surname. He is one of the orphans who stay at Brookings in the summers. Last summer, he ran away from the estate; he had some trouble with Emily Fordham's brother, Donald, who helped Pembroke attend to the boys. Blackwell found the boy hiding on the hill above Quimby and returned him to the estate. Emily Fordham had a photo of Thomas in her purse, along with Peter's drawing. I believe Peter knows something. I've tried to speak with him, but he ran from me. But I intend to try again. And I want to speak with the other boy, Thomas."

"The mute boy sounds unsound in mind," Harding said. "I shouldn't wonder that *he's* the bloody killer, if it's not Abbott."

"I haven't ruled that out," Lamb said. "But I need more time to sort things."

Harding sighed—theatrically, Lamb thought, which he knew to be a good sign.

"I'll give you two days, but no more," the super said. "If you haven't come up with something by then, we'll charge Abbott with Blackwell's murder. The evidence is there."

Harding glared at Lamb—another theatrical touch. "Don't fail me, Tom."

Lamb smiled—a smile of defiance. "I don't intend to."

—⁂—

Peter sat on the hill above his cottage, among the trees, out of sight.

Old Will was dead and now so was Emily. Emily's death saddened him, and he did not want the girl in Quimby to be dead too. He liked the girl in Quimby, which is why he'd left her drawings. The girl in Quimby was kind, as Emily had been kind, though Emily had been unkind, too. She went away on her bicycle. He watched her go away, day after day.

Once, he had stopped her on the road as she was going away and she had told him in an unfriendly way that she could not stop. She had been cross with him and this had hurt him very much.

He'd left the drawing for the girl in Quimby. The girl had called to him to come out. She'd been sitting on the hill and seen a male Adonis Blue and that had given him an idea. He'd sketched the Adonis for her. *Polyommatus bellargus*; Lycaenidae. The Adonis was a blue butterfly. He'd written the words beneath it the best he knew how.

He hoped that the girl in Quimby would not be unfriendly toward him, too, as Emily had been unfriendly.

EIGHTEEN

—⁓—

AT THEIR MEETING ON THE FOLLOWING MORNING, LAMB EXPLAINED to Rivers, Wallace, and Larkin his reasons for charging Abbott only with obstructing an inquiry.

Rivers considered protesting, but held his fire. He was beginning to believe that some of what Lamb said about the mute boy being involved in the thing made sense. Even so, he still believed Lamb was giving the boy too much emphasis. Abbott had possessed more than enough opportunity and motive in Blackwell's killing, not to mention that his prints were all over the bloody tools.

Lamb instructed Rivers to take Sergeant Cashen and a trio of constables to Lipscombe and begin a door-to-door canvassing of the village to see if anyone could shed any further light on Emily Fordham; he put Wallace to work typing reports of the events of the past two days for Harding. They'd gotten very far behind in their paperwork, and very soon the superintendent would begin to bemoan the insufficiently full "in" box on his desk.

Wallace had spent the previous night with Delilah. Once again, he'd held her in the darkness, then put her to bed. He'd asked her no more questions about who had beaten her. As she'd slept, he'd sat in her small sitting room alone, in the dark, drinking her Irish whiskey, until he'd had enough and fallen into bed next to her.

He continued to walk a razor's edge—though he asked himself why it mattered.

Lamb drove alone to Brookings to keep the appointment with Pembroke he'd arranged on the previous day.

"I'm sorry that such a wicked business has brought you to us again," the brisk Parkinson said as he led Lamb toward Pembroke's wildflower garden. "We all liked Emily very much here; she was a beautiful girl with a kind heart. I can't imagine why anyone would want to hurt her." He added that Pembroke had arrived home from London only an hour before.

Pembroke sat at the iron table among the flowers, bees, and butterflies, reading the *Times*, a carafe of coffee and a china cup and saucer in front of him. He was dressed in a white cotton shirt and trousers and brown leather sandals.

"Excuse me, Jeffrey," Parkinson said. "Chief Inspector Lamb has arrived."

Pembroke lowered the paper. "Good morning, Chief Inspector," he said. He gestured for Lamb to sit and then folded the *Times* and laid it on the table.

"Would you like coffee?"

Lamb looked at the rich, dark coffee in the carafe. He smiled. "No, thank you."

"I've only heard this morning about Emily," Pembroke said. "I've been in London. It's horrible. I can't tell you how terrible it is for us here. We all liked Emily very much. It seems you have your hands very full. I shouldn't wonder that it's partly due to the coming of this dreadful war—all of this sudden killing. People have lost their bearings."

"Yes," Lamb said. He sat. "I wonder if you can tell me what Emily did here, exactly, in the summers."

"She acted as a kind of helper for the children—that's the best way I can put it." He paused to light a cigarette that he pulled from a light blue packet. "The orphanage with which we work is for boys, and so therefore we host only boys in the summer. Until Emily, we had no girls here. But I decided we needed at least a little female presence around the place. Some of these boys never knew their mothers and have grown up around only male caretakers and other boys. Having Emily on the place was, frankly, a bit of an experiment. And although she was wonderful with the boys, I'm not certain the experiment worked."

"Why?"

"Well, I'm afraid that too many of the boys fell in love with her. I should have seen it coming. The only one who didn't, of course, was her brother, Donald, who worked here as a counselor to the boys—though I've often wondered if Emily's presence didn't sour the experience for Donald as well."

"How so?"

"Well, I can't say as I know, exactly. All I know is that during the summer that Emily worked here, Donald became—how should I put this?—rather less easy to get along with. Before, he'd been a model and a wonderful mentor to the younger boys particularly. But he became irritable and, to be frank, a bit of a complainer, a negative influence."

"This would have been last summer, then?"

"Yes. Last summer."

"Has Emily contacted you recently—or tried to contact you?"

"No. I haven't seen her since last summer, when our season ended here and the boys returned to the orphanage."

"What about Peter? Do you know if she contacted him or if he attempted to contact her?"

"If so, I'm not aware of it." He took a drag from his cigarette, then placed it into a glass ashtray next to the coffee carafe. A dozen or so butterflies moved among the flowers behind him. "As I explained earlier, Chief Inspector, I don't control Peter's movements. I only provide for his needs—those he cannot provide himself. Otherwise, he is free to live his life as he sees fit."

Lamb produced the small drawing of the spider he'd found in Emily's purse. "I'm certain that Peter drew this, just as he drew the sketch I found in Blackwell's shed," he said. "Do you agree?"

Pembroke looked at the drawing. "Yes, this is Peter's work."

"I found the drawing in Emily Fordham's purse," Lamb said. "Do you know why Peter might have sent her such a drawing?"

Pembroke's brow furrowed. "I'm afraid I don't. Peter liked Emily. He, too, might even have fallen in love with her—in his own way, of course."

"Emily had told several people in recent days that she was worried about Peter in some way, though she didn't say specifically what that worry was. Do you know what might have upset Peter?"

"As I said, Chief Inspector, Peter is very private—a conundrum, really. I'm not sure that anyone, myself included, can say with any certainty what he might actually be feeling."

Lamb nodded at the drawing. "Is it possible that Peter might have become jealous of the fact that Emily had a man in her life, someone whose presence made it obvious to Peter that she didn't love him in the way that he might have imagined she did?"

"I suppose it's possible. He's no longer a child, after all." Pembroke looked again at the drawing. "I suppose the spider might have been his way of telling Emily that he was angry with her. As I think I said last time, he doesn't like spiders."

Lamb produced the photograph of the boy that Lydia Blackwell had identified as Thomas and laid it next to Peter's drawing. "Do you recognize this boy?"

Lamb saw surprise briefly flash in Pembroke's eyes. "Where did you get this?"

"I'm not at liberty to say at the moment."

Pembroke nodded at the photo. "That is Thomas Bennett. He is one of the boys who spent summers here before the war."

"Had you had any trouble with Thomas Bennett?"

"Yes, we had a bit of trouble with him last summer, though the matter worked itself out in the end."

"What sort of trouble?"

"He ran away. The boys had been here only a month or so at the time."

"And you didn't think to call the police?"

"I didn't consider it necessary. We've had boys run off before, but they always return. I hope you won't take this in the wrong way, Chief Inspector, but many of the boys who come to us have had negative experiences with the police, who tend to see them as vagrants and troublemakers. When we've had trouble with the boys who come here, we've tended to handle it ourselves. Most of our boys are frightened of the police, frankly, and I saw no reason to frighten them further."

"What prompted Thomas to run away?"

"Well, he had a bit of trouble with Donald Fordham, to be honest. Donald caught Thomas stealing melons from the garden—or so Donald claimed. Donald said that he'd caught Thomas throwing the melons into a stream that runs through the estate and that, when he'd confronted Thomas about it, that Thomas at first denied stealing the melons; Thomas said that he'd merely found them near the stream. When Donald said he doubted that, Thomas basically told him to sod off."

Pembroke retrieved his smoldering cigarette and took another drag from it. "Admittedly, Thomas was a difficult boy," he continued. "Donald was the leader of Thomas's group, and Thomas challenged his authority from the beginning. That said, I thought that Donald's punishment of Thomas for the melon business was harsh: he confined Thomas to barracks alone for an entire day. I didn't intervene, however, though I wish now that I had. I wanted Donald to handle it. I considered the thing a learning experience for both of them. But in the end, Donald handled it badly. He overreacted."

"And so Thomas ran away?"

"Yes. We searched the estate but didn't find him. It turned out that he'd gone to Manscome Hill and that Will Blackwell had found him. Somehow Blackwell persuaded Thomas to come with him to his cottage and then contacted me. I went to Quimby and retrieved Thomas from Blackwell. The director of the orphanage then came down and took Thomas back to Basingstoke with him."

"And so Thomas did not return to Brookings that summer?"

Pembroke exhaled. "No. We thought it best he not return."

"So he stayed in Basingstoke, at the orphanage?"

"Yes. Frankly, I left the decision on the matter up to the discretion of the director. We would have welcomed Thomas back, but the director thought it best to forego a return."

"And what is the name of the director of the orphanage, sir?"

"Gerald Pirie. A good man. He and I have worked together for years. He's a Baptist, you see, and the orphanage is run by the Baptists. The Resurrection Home for Boys."

"Do you know where Emily might have gotten this photograph of Thomas?"

"I'm afraid I don't. I suppose it's possible that she got it from Donald. It's also very possible that Thomas himself might have given it to her. As I said, the boys here all were in love with Emily."

"Is it possible that Peter gave her the photo—that he might have sent it to her with the drawing?"

"I don't see how, unless Thomas gave it to him," he said. "But the two of them never were close, from what I saw."

"Why did you fail to mention the incident with Thomas when I spoke to you before? I asked you then if you knew Blackwell and you said that you didn't, really."

"I suppose I felt that the incident with Thomas was irrelevant, if I thought of it at all. Surely Thomas had nothing to do with Blackwell's killing. He's just a boy."

"You paid Will Blackwell one hundred seventy-five pounds for returning Thomas. It seems an unusually large amount."

"I was very grateful to Blackwell for having done us the favor," he said. "As I think I told you before, what I'd written in my book had hurt him and I hadn't meant for that to happen. I believed I owed him something—perhaps you'd call it restitution of a kind. His finding

Thomas and contacting us turned out to be an invaluable help to Mr. Pirie and me and everyone connected with the program we run here. He did us an inestimable favor, when he might just have washed his hands of the matter. And frankly, Chief Inspector—you'll excuse me if this sounds wrong somehow—but one hundred seventy-five pounds is not a large sum of money to me. I've plenty of money. Much more than I need. I give away large sums of it every year."

"I'd like to try to speak with Peter again," Lamb said.

"I'd rather you didn't, if that's possible," Pembroke said. "The last time frightened him more than I imagined it would. He didn't come home at all that night and when he did return on the following morning, he wouldn't let me near him. I understand why you feel you must speak to him. However, I'm sorry to say that, in any case, he's not around. He's gone off on one of his butterfly explorations."

"Does Peter know what has happened to Emily?"

"I don't know for certain. He's been gone for the last two days. I plan to tell him when the time seems right. I expect the news will be a blow to him."

"I wonder if I might have another look around the summerhouse," Lamb asked.

"Well, I suppose it will be all right, if you think it will be worth your while," Pembroke said. "But you mustn't enter the cottage, as I'm sure I made clear the last time."

"Of course."

"Very well, then. I'll let Parkinson know to expect you back in a little while. He'll show you out, if you don't mind."

"Not at all." Lamb stood. "Thank you again for your time."

"It's my pleasure to be of assistance," Pembroke said. "Hopefully, your luck will improve."

"I'm counting on it."

—⁂—

Lamb made his way down the cliff path to Peter's cottage.

He went to the front window but found it shrouded by blackout curtains. The front door was locked. He walked to the back and stood in the middle of the small space between the cottage and the base of the hill. He looked up the path along which Peter had fled from him and at the lonely tree at the hill's crest. He turned toward the house and peered into the back window but again found his view blocked by curtains.

Peter seemed to have left no sign of himself—of his habitation or habits—outside the cottage. With the exception of his drawings, he seemed to prefer invisibility.

Lamb tried to imagine a scenario in which Emily Fordham might have upset the delicate psychological and emotional balance of Peter's ordered existence. Had she done so, she likely hadn't meant to frighten or anger him. Then again, perhaps she possessed a cruel streak. Perhaps she'd told Peter that she intended never to return to Brookings. Maybe she'd even told him of her RAF pilot. Perhaps Peter saw Emily as the spider and himself as the butterfly. Maybe, too, Will Blackwell had rejected or upset Peter.

He went to the back door of the cottage and tried the knob. To his surprise, he found the door unlocked. He decided that he must see inside the cottage, despite Pembroke's objections. He was not yet convinced either of Peter's guilt or innocence in the deaths of Will Blackwell and Emily Fordham. But he was certain of Peter's *involvement* in the events of the past few days. And yet his chances of speaking to Peter seemed dim. Believing that he had no choice but to act, he pushed open the door to the summerhouse. A fly seeking sunlight buzzed past his head into the summer air and a musty smell assailed him. Moving by the light that filtered in through the open door, Lamb went to the window and parted the heavy, black curtains. Sunlight spilled into the cottage's single, small room.

An unmade wooden cot, piled with a crumpled white sheet and feather pillow, lay along the far wall. To the right of this was a sink with a water pump; a metal bucket sat empty in the sink. The rest of the interior consisted of an array of shelves and small tables and a pair of wooden chairs. Some of the shelves were built into the walls, while others were freestanding. All were stuffed with illustrated guidebooks to the flora and fauna of England, along with notebooks and sheaves of paper. The wall opposite the one that held Peter's cot was dominated by a table of about six feet wide on which was spread an array of paints and brushes and pens and pencils and boxes of pastel crayons. Sketchpads of various grades of paper were stacked near the right edge of the table; several small blank canvases leaned against its legs.

The wall above the desk was filled with a dozen framed exhibits of bugs stuck to black felt backgrounds with straight pins—butterflies, beetles, bees, wasps, hornets, spiders. None were labeled. Lamb estimated that the exhibits contained several hundred specimens. Peter had arranged the exhibits in three neat rows of four each. The only anomaly was a framed photograph of the dead tree that stood at the top of the hill. The photo was centered beneath the second and third exhibit—butterflies and spiders—of the bottom row. The photograph had been taken from the bottom of the hill on a cloudy day. The barren branches of the tree stood out against the gray sky like the black, crooked legs of an insect.

Lamb spent several minutes searching the cottage's corners and crannies for something with which Peter might have hit Emily Fordham and Will Blackwell in the head, but found nothing.

He returned to the desk and gently searched the mess of papers, portfolios, books, and paints, making sure that he replaced everything in the way it had been. He opened a leather-bound portfolio and found that it contained a dozen crayon sketches of butterflies. Each was beautifully and richly rendered down to the tiniest markings and variation in color.

He heard a scraping noise by the window. He went to the window and peered into the yard but saw nothing amiss. He stood still and listened. The back door stood open. His first thought was that Pembroke had come down the path and caught him rummaging through Peter's things. He heard what he thought sounded like someone moving from the cottage up the hill. He went to the door but saw no one.

"Peter?" he said.

No one answered.

NINETEEN

WALLACE HAD SPENT THE PAST TWO HOURS LABORIOUSLY HUNTING and pecking away at the reports on the Blackwell and Fordham killings for Harding, hating every minute. He was nearly finished when he realized suddenly that Lamb was standing by his desk. He immediately moved to hand to Lamb what he'd thus far typed, as proof that he hadn't dawdled away the morning.

"I was just about to deliver this bloody mess to you," he said, smiling.

Lamb glanced at the papers for a couple of seconds, then handed them back to Wallace. "I'll read them later," he said, to Wallace's consternation.

Lamb had just finished reading Winston-Sheed's report on Emily Fordham's autopsy, which he'd found on his desk when he'd returned to the nick from Brookings. She had been struck on the head and knocked cold with a blunt object. The killer then had bludgeoned her in the head until she was dead. She showed no sign of other injury or sexual violation. And she indeed had been pregnant—seven weeks.

Even though he still had very little to go on, he could sense cracks opening.

He told Wallace that Pembroke had confirmed Lydia Blackwell's identification of the boy in the photo as Thomas Bennett, that Thomas had quarreled with Donald Fordham, and that Pembroke had sent the boy back to Basingstoke at the suggestion of the orphanage's director.

"I think this boy knows something, just as Peter does," Lamb said. "We need to speak with the director of the orphanage and, hopefully, with Thomas himself. I'm going there now and I want you to come with me." He smiled. "Save you from your bloody typing."

"Does the director know we're coming?" Wallace asked as he grabbed his jacket.

Lamb popped a butterscotch into his mouth. "Of course not."

The Resurrection Home for Boys was housed in an ancient, somewhat decrepit manor house. Lamb and Wallace entered a wide, high-ceilinged foyer. In the middle of the foyer, a small sign atop a metal stand informed visitors that the office was to the right.

The office was housed in what had been the sitting room. A wall had been constructed to divide the room into a small outer office and waiting room and a rather large inner office. As they entered the outer office, a middle-aged woman looked up at them from behind a small desk. She was a good-looking woman, Lamb thought. Her hair was blond streaked with a touch of gray, which showed her age. But she maintained the attributes of classic beauty: high cheeks, large eyes, and an aristocratically slender neck and shoulders.

She smiled at Lamb and Wallace. "Good afternoon, gentlemen," she said. "May I help you?"

Lamb introduced himself and Wallace. The woman smiled again and offered them her hand. "My name is Mrs. Langdon," she said. Her gesture surprised Lamb; he wasn't used to secretaries and clerks introducing themselves.

"A pleasure, madam," Lamb said, shaking her hand. "I wonder if we might have a word with Mr. Pirie?"

"I'll see," Mrs. Langdon said brightly. She got up and disappeared into the inner office. A minute later, she returned. "Go right in," she said.

Gerald Pirie's office comprised the better half of the former sitting room. Behind the wide mahogany desk at which Pirie sat, a trio of high windows looked onto what once had been the estate's east lawn but now was a playing field on which a group of small boys were kicking about a football. Pirie was one of those men whose age Lamb found it difficult to gauge; he guessed that Pirie was in his mid-forties, though he might be older. He was of medium height and slightly overweight, with a round face, plump hands, and dark eyes that radiated melancholy. He wore a dark blue suit that had the look and quality of a railway conductor's uniform; all it needed was brass buttons. He came out from behind his desk to greet them.

"Good afternoon," he said, offering them his hand. His accent was Scottish. "This is a surprise, I must say. I hope one of my boys isn't in trouble." He looked at Lamb with his chin slightly raised, expectant.

"Nothing like that—though I would like to speak to one of your boys," Lamb said. "May we sit?"

Pirie gestured for Lamb and Wallace to take the two chairs that faced his desk. He returned to his place behind his desk. "To which of the boys would you like to speak?"

"Thomas Bennett," Lamb said.

"Thomas?"

"Yes."

"Why Thomas, if I might ask?"

"His name has come up in connection with a murder inquiry."

"A murder inquiry? Thomas?" Pirie hesitated for a couple of seconds, then placed his hands on his desk. "But I'm afraid Thomas is no longer with us, Chief Inspector."

Lamb waited for Pirie to elaborate. When Pirie didn't, he asked, "Where is Thomas?"

"He was adopted."

"When?"

"Six or seven months ago. May I ask how Thomas is involved in your inquiry?"

"His photograph was found in the wallet of a young woman named Emily Fordham, who was bludgeoned to death near the village of Lipscombe. Miss Fordham worked on Lord Jeffrey Pembroke's estate in the summers with the boys from your institution. He told me that Thomas ran away from the estate last summer."

"That is true, yes."

"Did Lord Pembroke say why Thomas had run away from the estate?" He wanted to see if Pirie's version of events matched Pembroke's.

"Thomas had gotten into some sort of trouble with one of the boys down there who work on the estate. I'm afraid I didn't press Lord Pembroke on the matter; I merely took his word that he was satisfied with its resolution."

"And Thomas did not return to the estate?"

"Yes."

"Was that because you forbade him?"

"Yes. I didn't think it wise to send him back."

"Did he ever mention the names of Donald or Emily Fordham to you after his return?"

"I gathered that Donald Fordham was the boy with whom Thomas had the trouble. He never mentioned anyone named Emily."

"Did you inform Lord Pembroke of Thomas's adoption?"

"I must have told him, yes."

"But you don't remember?"

"I must have done." He smiled again. "I'm sorry, Chief Inspector, but as you might imagine I have my hands rather full here. I have learned to avoid trying to manage every detail. Otherwise, I fear I'd go mad. As it is, I've given my life to this place. My main concern is that the boys are getting what they need."

"Do you know Peter Wilkins?" Lamb asked.

"Of course. He was one of our boys before Lord Pembroke became his guardian."

"Has Peter tried to contact you recently?"

"No. Peter has a great amount of difficulty communicating."

"Lord Pembroke is one of the orphanage's primary benefactors, I suppose?" Lamb asked.

"Yes."

"So you must please him, then?"

Pirie straightened in his chair, in mild defiance. "I'm sorry, but I'm afraid I don't follow you."

"I'm only saying that Lord Pembroke must exercise influence in how the orphanage is operated—perhaps even in the decisions you make."

Pirie's face reddened. "I'm sorry, Chief Inspector, but I must say that I resent any insinuation of improprieties on Lord Pembroke's part, or on mine. As I've already told you, I have dedicated my life to this place. I can't even imagine what you might be implying. And if you are indeed implying something, I'd prefer that you just state it outright."

"I apologize," Lamb said. "I was merely trying to better understand your relationship with Lord Pembroke."

Pirie's injured expression softened. "It is a relationship dedicated to helping the boys—to seeing that we give them the best that we can offer them."

"May I know the name of the people who adopted Thomas?" Lamb asked.

"It's irregular. As you can well imagine, we do our utmost to protect the privacy of our boys. We are privately funded and therefore are under no obligation to release such confidential information."

"I was hoping that, under the circumstances, you might make an exception. I could get a warrant, of course."

Pirie thrust out his chin. "Then I'm afraid you must do so, though I can't think on what grounds. I'm sorry, but I can't be party to your bothering Thomas. For the first time in his life, he's in a secure situation. I can personally assure you that he had nothing to do with this mess to which you refer. He's only eleven."

"This *is* related to a murder inquiry," Lamb reminded Pirie.

"I understand. But I can only say once again that I'm certain that Thomas had nothing to do with it."

"How can you be so certain, sir?" Wallace interjected.

"For one, he's merely eleven; for another, he lives in Glasgow." He lowered his brow and peered at Wallace. "Now, I ask you, Sergeant, do you really believe it possible for a boy of eleven to hop on a train in Glasgow, travel to the south of England, commit murder, then hop back on the train for home, especially under the circumstances in which we presently find ourselves?"

"No one said he committed murder, sir," Wallace said. "We merely said we found his photograph in a wallet."

"But that's what you're implying, certainly," Pirie said. "That he's involved in some way with this young woman's death."

Lamb abruptly stood, startling Pirie. "Very good, Mr. Pirie," he said. He made the displeasure evident in his tone. "I suppose there's nothing left for Sergeant Wallace and me to do but to thank you for your time. We will return with a warrant."

Pirie did not rise. "I trust you can see yourselves out," he said.

Mrs. Langdon waved at the two of them as they left. "Good-bye, gentlemen," she said.

They returned to Lamb's Wolseley.

"He was moving along rather nicely until you jabbed him," Wallace said.

"Yes."

Lamb peered at the boys who were kicking the soccer ball around the vast field. He was beginning to believe that his latest flight of fancy might be correct.

—⁂—

That night, Wallace went straight to Delilah's and rapped on her door. Delilah opened the door a crack, just wide enough for Wallace to see her. She was in her sleeping gown. Her eyes were still hideously bruised.

"David, you shouldn't have come," she said. Despite the heat, she hugged herself, as if cold. She didn't open the door wider and invite him in.

"What do you mean?" Wallace asked. "Don't you want me here?"

She didn't answer; she looked past him, then opened the door wider. A single lamp burned in the parlor, on the small cupboard in which Delilah kept her whiskey. He stepped into the foyer. She stood before him, naked beneath her flimsy cotton sleeping gown. He could see the swell of her breasts and the dark color of her nipples beneath it. Still, he felt no specific desire for her—not with her face that way. He couldn't. He feared he might break her. He gently touched her chin; she raised his face toward him. "Let me see," he said.

She complied.

"Who did this to you?"

She looked away. "I told you; I fell."

"Why are you lying to me, Delilah? Who are you afraid of?"

"Please, David. Let's not talk about it."

"Why won't you tell me who did this?"

"Why must you know? Why can't you just let me live with it? Why can't it just be my problem?" She went into the sitting room.

"I can't pretend it's nothing."

She went to the cabinet where she kept the whiskey and withdrew from it a half-empty bottle and two glasses. "Let's just have a drink," she said.

Wallace understood that she was trying to put him off. Perhaps she hoped he'd become drunk and stop asking questions. But he wanted a drink.

He went to the cupboard. She handed him a drink, which he downed quickly. Almost immediately, he felt a change come over him. Delilah's erect nipples poked at the flimsy fabric of her sleeping gown. She took a drink of the whiskey and licked her lips. She poured him another, which he also drank quickly. She looked at him and smiled. He couldn't believe what he was feeling. She was keeping secrets from him, playing her game.

She put her finger over the mouth of the bottle and tipped the bottle so that some of the whiskey poured onto her finger and her hand. She moved close to him, lifted her chin, and drew her moist finger down both sides of her neck and then across her lips. Then she put her finger in her mouth and sucked on it; she pulled her finger slowly from her mouth and then made a kind of purring sound. The whole thing struck Wallace as ridiculous, given her swollen face, and yet he could not help himself. And Delilah knew it.

He yanked up her sleeping gown, exposing her to the neck. She raised her arms and he pulled the gown off her, causing her hair to fall over her face. He took the bottle from the top of the cupboard and doused her breasts and the front of her body with whiskey. He moved his mouth to her breasts and began to suck at them. She arched her back, thrusting herself into him. He pressed his right hand against the small of her back and began to lower her to the floor. *Damn the whole bloody fucking mess*, he thought. He was beyond caring, exhausted from keeping himself in line.

He lowered her to the floor; she lay before him naked, voluptuous, fervent, her face a terrible mask. She grabbed at his shirt as he struggled to unbuckle his belt. She pulled him down onto her and their mouths came together. She tasted of whiskey. He moved his mouth down her throat and across her breasts and onto her stomach.

An air-raid siren sounded.

Wallace thought at first that he must have heard wrong. But there was no mistaking the sound. It was close. Thus far, the Germans had spared Winchester. It contained nothing valuable, no ports or armaments factories.

Wallace lifted himself to his knees, still hard. He and Delilah were silent for a few seconds as they listened to the insistent wailing. Wallace looked at her. The siren had cooled their fire. "We've got to get you dressed," he said.

He rose and buckled his belt and tucked in his shirt. He offered Delilah his hand and helped her to her feet. They moved into Delilah's bedroom, where she slipped on her clothes as quickly as she could manage. "Have you a house key?" he asked.

"Yes." They went into the sitting room, where they found her purse on the sofa. Wallace turned out the small lamp on the cupboard. The floor was slick from the spilled whiskey.

When they reached the door, Delilah asked "Can we go apart, David?"

"What do you mean?"

"Can we go apart to the shelter?"

"It's black as coal out there."

"I'm sorry."

"Why do you keep saying that?"

"Please, David."

"No, Delilah; I don't know what you mean. Of course we can't go apart." He put his hands on her shoulders and tried to turn her back round toward the door. She twisted out of his grip and faced him. "We must go apart. Please, David."

"What in bloody hell are you talking about?" He turned her roughly toward the door and opened it. Several small groups of people were in the street, heading for the nearest shelter, which was three blocks away. He tried to push her out the door but she resisted. "Stop it, damn you!" Wallace said.

Delilah spun around and heaved herself back into the foyer. Wallace turned to face her.

"I'm married!" she said.

Wallace felt as if he'd been shot—as if the bullet had entered him suddenly, though he had no idea from where the shot had come and whether it had wounded him mortally.

"I'm sorry," she said. She ran past him into the street.

Wallace watched her move into the swelling group heading for the safety of the shelters. "Go," he heard himself say. He looked around, unsure of how to respond. He closed the door and followed.

He stayed apart from her but tried to keep her in sight. Around him, strangers hurried in the same direction; men led women by the arms and women led children by the hands. Most of them carried gas masks and he realized that Delilah had forgotten hers. His was on the other side of Winchester, in his flat. A baby cried. He heard a man yell "Come now, make it snappy!" Just ahead he saw the beams of torches directing people to the shelter entrance.

He cursed himself for having been so damned stupid. The signs had been there—her coming to The Fallen Diva alone, the house, her secrecy—but he'd ignored them, chalked them up to a game. He understood now who'd beaten her—some member of her husband's family or one of his mates who'd discovered that she been fooling around while her husband was at war. He should have seen it. Perhaps he had.

The sirens continued to wail. Wallace found himself moving down a narrow side street that was utterly dark, save the bobbing torch beam of an air-raid warden at the other end. There, he lost sight of Delilah. He glanced at the sky to find searchlights crisscrossing it. He moved out of the narrow lane and made for the shelter, which was a block away. He followed the throng into the shelter and took his place on the benches with the rest of them. He looked for Delilah but did not see her. He hoped to God they wouldn't emerge from the shelter to find her little house blown to bits.

They waited with their hands in their laps. A young woman read from *Peter Rabbit* to three small children who huddled against her; an old man sat with the back of his head against the tiled wall, his eyes closed and mouth open. Besides the young mother, hardly anyone spoke, and those who did whispered; everyone was listening for the sound of airplanes.

They sat that way for nearly an hour, the silence broken only by an occasional cough and the soft, low voice of the young woman reading. But the sounds of the airplanes—and of bombs—never came. The all-clear sounded; the Germans had gone elsewhere. The room filled with a palpable sense of relief and a sudden buzz of conversation that reminded Wallace of the sound of bees swarming. The man next to him grabbed his arm, shook it and said "I say!" and then turned and did the same to the woman sitting on the other side of him.

The senior air-raid warden set to the process of emptying the shelter. The young mother closed her book and shepherded her children toward the door. The old man who had been sitting with his head against the wall got up slowly and patiently waited for the crowd to clear. The man next to Wallace also stood and began to pat random people on the back.

202

Wallace emerged from the shelter onto the darkened street. He stood near the entrance to the shelter scanning the faces of the people who emerged from it, but did not see Delilah.

He walked up the street and turned back into the dark, narrow lane. He could scarcely see his way and this time saw no bobbing torch beams at the other end. He slowed so as not to stumble. He was nearly to the place where the lane gave onto Delilah's street when three people entered the lane coming the opposite way. They were no more than dark shapes, though he could tell by the way in which they moved that they were men. His adrenaline spiked; he moved to the left to allow them to pass. The figures moved toward him shoulder-to-shoulder.

"Hello," Wallace said into the darkness in case the men had not seen him. For good measure, he added "Ship ahoy."

None of the three answered. They were just about to pass when, suddenly, they rushed him; Wallace had just begun to instinctively raise his arms in defense when he felt something hard hit his left shoulder. The blow staggered him. He fell against the wall, his shoulder throbbing. He turned back toward the figures, hoping to find someone to strike. But before he could get his bearings, one of the men slugged him in the right eye, sending him reeling against the wall. He put his hands to his face, then caught two more sharp blows, one to his chest and another to his stomach. He doubled over, clutching his gut, breathless and in pain, helpless. He caught a glimpse of the three figures closing in, cutting off his routes of escape. Before he could raise his hands again, he took two more sudden blows to the face, almost simultaneously—one from the right and one from the left—which rattled his skull and forced him to his knees, his nose spouting blood.

"That'll teach you to fuck another man's wife," a voice above him hissed. Something cracked down hard on the back of his neck and he slumped to the ground, unconscious.

A minute later, he came to with his mouth full of the sharp taste of blood.

Darkness surrounded him. His right eye was swollen, his left cheek bleeding. His right arm and head ached. With effort, he pulled himself up so that he sat, slumped, with his back against the stone wall. The men seemed to be gone. He spit some of the blood from his mouth. Then he heard a woman speak his name.

"David."

He felt the presence of someone to his right and turned in that direction, expecting another blow. "David," the voice said again. "Oh God. I'm so sorry, David."

Delilah knelt next to him and brushed his hair back from his blackened eye.

Wallace looked at her. "Delilah."

"Don't talk."

He pressed his right hand against the ground in an effort to push himself up. He winced and drew in a sharp breath. "Bloody hell," he said.

Delilah slipped her right arm around his back. "Let me help you." With her help, he stood. She held his arm.

Wallace took a couple of tentative steps. "I'm all right," he said.

"I'm so sorry, David. I've been such a damned fool."

"Who did this, Delilah?"

"We should try to get you to a doctor."

"No—no doctor. I'm all right. The doctors have better things to do."

"Let's get out of here," she said and led him down the dark lane toward her house.

She settled him on the sofa and helped him to remove his jacket and shoes. "Lie down here," she said. "I'm going to get you some ice."

Wallace rubbed the back of his neck, then lay back on the sofa. He wanted a drink; he wondered what he would tell Lamb and Harding. His face would be a mess for days, as Delilah's was. He decided that he would say that three men had jumped him on his way back from the shelter and stolen his cash.

Delilah returned with a handful of ice cubes wrapped in a tea towel and a glass of water. "Put this on your eye," she said. She disappeared again for several minutes and returned with a warm, soapy cloth. She sat on the sofa. "Your cheek is cut," she said. "I'm going to wash it."

Wallace lay on the sofa like an obedient child as Delilah washed his barked cheek. It stung; he winced. She patted the wound dry and put a gauze bandage on it.

"I need a drink," Wallace said.

"Water first." He sat up and she brought the glass to his lips. He took several tentative sips, which only partially washed his mouth clean of the taint of blood.

"Now can I have a proper drink?" He managed a smile.

She went to the cabinet and poured two fingers of whiskey into a glass. Wallace downed it in a single gulp. "Another, please."

Delilah poured him another shot, which he drank in two sips. "All right," he said, speaking more to himself than to Delilah. "That's it."

Delilah put her hand gently on his damaged face. "You should sleep," she said.

He put his hand over hers. "Not until you tell me what happened."

She looked away.

"Who was it? His mates?"

"I don't want them punished." She looked at him. "They are only sticking up for Bill."

"Is that his name—Bill?"

She glanced away. "Yes."

"Which branch?"

"The Army; he was called up."

"Do you know where he is?"

"The Mediterranean." She looked down and shook her head. "I don't know where, exactly," she added in a whisper, almost as if speaking to herself.

Wallace sat up on his elbow. "Do you love him?"

"I don't know. I suppose I must."

"You don't have to stand for it, Delilah."

"You don't understand, David."

He put down the ice pack and took Delilah's hand. "What don't I understand?"

She looked away. Wallace touched her cheek. "What don't I understand?" he repeated.

When she turned back to face him, she was crying. "I deserve it."

"That's ridiculous. Did *he* beat you, too?"

"No," she said softly. She looked at Wallace. "I was pregnant with his child; that's why we married." She looked at the floor. "I miscarried. I know it sounds terrible, but a part of me was glad. I wasn't ready for a child. And yet losing it devastated me. He blamed me. He stopped coming home—started spending more time with his mates. That was a year ago. I was actually relieved when he was called up, and I hate myself for feeling that way. It's not right."

He touched her cheek again. "Delilah."

"No, David," she said, touching his hand. "Nothing you can say will help."

She looked at him with pleading in her eyes. "You must promise me you won't go after them." She put her hand gently against his shoulder, encouraging him to lie back.

"You should sleep now," she said.

—◆—

In the moonlight, Peter crept down the hill to the summerhouse.

The policeman had gone into the house; he'd seen the policeman. No one could see him now; no one was watching. Everyone was sleeping. He found the kerosene lantern, lit it.

Everything was as he had left it except for his drawings. He could see that the policeman had looked through his drawings.

A barn spider had spun its web across the knot in the tree. He went to the photograph of the tree and moved it so that it was off center. Then he went to his desk and began to draw—first the dark oval, then the spider and its web.

He worked quickly.

He left the photograph as it was, off-center. Then he returned to the darkness.

TWENTY

—⚬—

THE NEXT MORNING, WALLACE AWAKENED ALONE ON DELILAH'S SOFA.

His head and neck ached. He sat up gently and decided that he was in good enough shape to go to work; he couldn't afford to give Harding an excuse to kick him about. He looked at the clock; he had just enough time to make it if he didn't tarry.

He went to the tiny loo at the rear of the house and studied himself in the mirror. His right eye was black and swollen and his collar, shirt, and tie bloodstained. He looked at his trousers; they were muddy and torn at the cuff and right knee. He realized that he must go home to bathe and change, which would make him late for work. But he had his story ready for Lamb—he'd been beaten and robbed.

He mounted the stairs to Delilah's room. He expected to find her curled into herself, sleeping. But her bed was empty. A note lay on the pillow.

David,

    I think it would be best if we didn't see each other for a while. It will be safer that way. I'm sorry for what happened to you; I feel as if I might never forgive myself for it. I've acted a fool and don't want to hurt you anymore, or see you hurt. I've made my bed and must lie in it. I truly hope that you are feeling better and I'm dreadfully sorry I'm not there to comfort you.

    Delilah

Wallace stared at the note for nearly a minute before he dropped it on the bed and left.

—⁂—

On the previous night, Lamb and Marjorie also had spent nearly an hour in a shelter waiting out the air raid that never came. They worried more about Vera than themselves, but when the planes failed to show, their worry lessened. To their surprise, Vera had called them later that night from Quimby wanting to know if they were all right; she'd heard that the sirens had gone off in Winchester.

In the morning, Lamb obtained a warrant to see the adoption records of Thomas Bennett on the grounds that the boy might have information that was material to the inquiry into Emily Fordham's murder.

On the previous day, Rivers and the constables had managed to knock on roughly half the doors in Lipscombe but turned up nothing useful on Emily Fordham. Before setting out for Basingstoke, Lamb sent them back to Lipscombe to finish the job.

Wallace was just arriving, a half hour late. He didn't bother trying on his smile with Lamb. "I'm sorry I'm late, sir," he said. He stood before Lamb, vaguely at attention.

Wallace's battered face shocked Lamb. His first thought was: *He's done it; he's gone over an edge.* "What in bloody hell happened to you, David?"

"A couple of blokes jumped me last night, took my cash. I fought back—stupid, I know."

Lamb thought, *You were drunk and got into some bloody row.* Still, the sight of Wallace's swollen face filled him with a strange pity. "Are you sure you're all right?" he asked.

Wallace straightened. "It's just a black eye. I've had my share."

"I don't suppose you got a good look at the men who jumped you?"

"No. It was black as pitch out."

"Do you want to file a report?"

"I don't see the need. They only took me for a few quid. Drunken kids."

Lamb was silent for a couple of seconds; Wallace felt as if Lamb was looking directly into his soul.

"You're certain you're all right, then?" Lamb repeated.

"I'm fine, sir."

"All right, then." He held up the warrant. "We're going to Basingstoke."

—⁂—

The small football pitch was empty as Lamb brought the Wolseley to a stop by the door of The Resurrection Home for Boys.

Mrs. Langdon looked up from her desk as Lamb and Wallace entered. "Back with us so soon?"

"Yes," Lamb said. "I wonder if I might speak with Mr. Pirie?"

"Well, you could, I suppose, except that he's not here." As Wallace stepped out from behind Lamb, she noticed Wallace's eye. "My goodness, Sergeant. What happened to you?"

Wallace smiled. "A bad fall, I'm afraid."

"Oh my. I do hope you're all right."

"I'm fine, thank you."

"Mr. Pirie is not in?" Lamb asked.

"No. I'm afraid he's running late."

"Do you expect him soon?"

"Well, I don't know, really. He hasn't called, which is unlike him. But it's possible he's been detained on some business or another. He's often called away."

Lamb produced the warrant. "I have here a warrant authorizing Sergeant Wallace and myself to see the adoption file of Thomas Bennett. I'm going to have to request that you produce it for us."

Mrs. Langdon read the warrant. "Oh, dear," she muttered. "I don't think I understand."

"What don't you understand, madam?" Lamb asked.

"Well, we have a file on Thomas Bennett, of course. But we have no adoption file."

"And why is that?"

"Well, Thomas has never been adopted, Chief Inspector. You see, he never returned to us after he went to Lord Pembroke's last summer. Mr. Pirie told me that he'd had some trouble at Brookings and that he and Lord Pembroke had arranged to have Thomas transferred to another orphanage—St. Christopher's, in Norwich. Mr. Pirie came to an arrangement with the director there. Thomas was a troubled boy—we had our troubles with him, too, you see. And we've taken in other boys who found it hard to adjust to other institutions."

"Mr. Pirie told us yesterday that Thomas had been adopted by a family in Glasgow," Wallace said.

Mrs. Langdon's face clouded. "Oh, dear," she repeated. "I'm sorry, Sergeant, but I don't know why he would have said that. He must have confused Thomas with someone else."

"May we see Thomas's file, please?" Lamb asked.

"Of course." She rose from her chair and went to a pair of wooden filing cabinets that stood against the left-hand wall. She spent a few seconds flipping through the files before turning back to Lamb with a look of confusion and worry on her face.

"I'm afraid the file isn't here, Chief Inspector, but for the life of me I can't say why." She looked back at the cabinets. "I keep the files in good order."

"Did you handle the paperwork related to Thomas's transfer, Mrs. Langdon?" Lamb asked.

She looked at him. "No. Mr. Pirie handled it personally because he considered it delicate."

"Do you have a telephone number for St. Christopher's?"

"Yes, we do, of course." She opened a metal filing box on her desk that was full of index cards and found the one pertaining to St. Christopher's, which she gave to Lamb. "The director's name is Hoskins, as you can see there on the card."

"Thank you," Lamb said. "Do you have a telephone that I can use privately?"

Mrs. Langdon glanced at Pirie's office. "I suppose Mr. Pirie wouldn't mind if you used his," she said tentatively.

"Thank you."

Lamb went into Pirie's office with Wallace. On the telephone, Mr. Hoskins emphatically denied that any boy named Thomas Bennett ever had been transferred to St. Christopher's from The Resurrection Home for Boys.

"Why didn't he cock up some sort of phony adoption papers?" Wallace asked after Lamb hung up.

"What good would it do him? Something like that can't be faked; it's too bloody easy to check. His only hope was that he'd never be questioned on it."

"So demanding the warrant was to give him enough time to do a runner?"

"That's the way it looks."

"What's happened to the boy, then?"

"I've a terrible feeling he's dead."

They returned to the outer office and asked for Pirie's address, which the helpful Mrs. Langdon supplied to them. "I do hope there's nothing wrong."

Wallace smiled. "Nothing at all."

Lamb then briefly returned to Pirie's office, from which he called Harding and requested that the superintendent send Larkin and a half dozen constables to Basingstoke, along with a warrant to search Pirie's house.

"What's this bloody man Pirie done?" Harding asked.

"I think he might have killed Thomas Bennett, the boy I mentioned to you yesterday."

"Bloody hell."

"Yes, sir."

"All right, I'll call the railways and request that their people be on the lookout for Pirie," he said. Lamb gave Harding a brief description of Pirie and then rang off.

Lamb instructed Wallace to wait at the orphanage on the off chance that Pirie might risk a return to the orphanage to pick up something of value. He then went to Pirie's small detached house on the east side of Basingstoke. When no one answered his knock, he kicked in the door and stepped into the foyer.

The living room was to Lamb's right; to the left a narrow flight of stairs led to the second floor. A hall led through the center of the house to the kitchen. Lamb peeked into the living room but found it empty, the blackout curtains drawn. He moved down the hall to the kitchen but found that empty also. He went back down the hall and mounted the steps to the second floor, where he found two rooms. The first was a kind of study. A desk was pushed against the window on the wall opposite the door; the other walls were lined with books in shelves, with the exception of a small space by the desk in which sat a file cabinet. Piles of papers and files lay on the floor near the desk. Lamb entered the room and looked through the papers but found nothing related to Thomas Bennett.

The second room was Pirie's bedroom. It contained a dresser, a single bed against the far wall, which was unmade, and a night table next to the left side of the bed.

Lamb carefully picked through the drawers of the dresser but found only socks and underwear, along with several wool sweaters and cotton shirts. The bottom drawer contained a blanket. He checked the closet and also found nothing but clothes—trousers, shirts, jackets, a pair of dark suits—and three identical pairs of well-shined black shoes. He checked the pockets of the trousers and the jackets but found nothing, not even lint. He pulled back the covers on the bed but found nothing beneath them. He got onto his hands and knees and looked beneath the bed, where he also came up empty. He saw no sign of the presence of a woman in the house; Gerald Pirie appeared to be a bachelor.

He stood and looked around the room. He glanced at the night-stand; its top contained nothing save an alarm clock that had wound down. He pulled open the drawer and found that it contained several religious-themed books and a volume of Wilfred Owen's Great War poetry. He leafed through the books but found nothing in them.

A leather portfolio lay at the bottom of the drawer. Lamb tossed the books on Pirie's bed and picked up the portfolio. It contained a sheet of plain white paper lying atop a photograph. Lamb removed the sheet and found beneath it a photograph of a dark-haired boy of about ten, who stood facing the camera utterly naked in what appeared to Lamb to be a kind of white-walled cell. The boy stood with his hands on his hips, his eyes brimming with fear and confusion. The boy was standing on a white sheet and in front of a second white sheet that appeared to have been pinned to the wall behind him.

The boy was Thomas Bennett.

The emotions that Thomas's face betrayed pierced Lamb to his soul; the child was a prisoner, held against his will. He was small and weak and had no recourse but to obey whatever power dominated and threatened him. His neck and chest were bruised in several places.

Lamb's mind raced with scenarios of what might have happened to Thomas and why. He thought that Thomas might have run from Pembroke's to escape going back to Pirie. But then Pembroke had sent Thomas back to Basingstoke. Blackwell had assisted in that, if unwittingly. Thomas's running had spooked Pirie, who was used to Thomas's obedience. So Pirie had killed Thomas and concocted the fake transfer to cover the boy's sudden absence. None of the boys who had gone to Pembroke's the previous summer—nor, perhaps,

Pembroke himself—had even known that Thomas was gone from the orphanage until the summer had ended and they'd returned to Basingstoke, when Pirie had told them that Thomas had been transferred to St. Christopher's.

He wondered how much of the truth Pembroke knew. And he wondered if, perhaps, Pirie knew something compromising about Pembroke that had compelled Pembroke to cover for him.

In any case, Thomas's disappearance had upset Peter, who then had tried to contact Emily, thereby unearthing events Pirie—and perhaps Pembroke—had sought to bury. Pirie might easily have killed Emily, driven from Basingstoke to Lipscombe and back in the space of two hours. Lamb was not yet certain how the killing of Will Blackwell fit this scenario, other than that Thomas might have said something to Blackwell about why he feared returning to Basingstoke. Again, Pirie had more than enough opportunity to drive to Quimby and kill Blackwell.

Now the threads of Pirie's elaborate deception were unraveling and he had gone on the run. But why hadn't he destroyed the incriminating photo of Thomas, or taken it with him?

He must speak again with Pembroke.

He also must find Gerald Pirie and discover with certainty the fate of Thomas Bennett.

TWENTY-ONE

—◆—

LAMB USED PIRIE'S HOME TELEPHONE TO CALL WALLACE AT THE
orphanage.

He described what he'd found in Pirie's night table and told Wallace
that he would await the arrival of the constables and the warrant at Pirie's
house, then return to the school with a constable who would take over
the job of waiting for Pirie. Wallace then would take charge of the search
of Pirie's house while Lamb went to Brookings to speak with Pembroke.

In slightly more than an hour, all was done and in place.

At Brookings, the venerable Hatton answered the door. "May I
help you, sir?"

"I'd like to speak with Lord Pembroke, please." The butler raised
his eyebrows slightly and gestured for Lamb to follow him into the
foyer. "If you'll just wait here a moment, sir," he said, then disappeared
into the bowels of the house.

Two minutes later, Leonard Parkinson appeared. "Chief Inspector," he said, offering his hand. "Very good to see you again. What can I do for you?"

"I'd like to speak with Lord Pembroke."

A cloud crossed Parkinson's round face. "Oh, dear," he said. "I'm afraid Lord Pembroke's in London. I'm sorry."

"When do you expect him to return?"

"Well, I'm afraid I don't know exactly."

"Do you know where I might reach him in London? It's rather important."

"I'm sorry, but I don't know that exactly, either."

"Can you get a message to him?"

"Yes—yes, of course. I expect he'll call sometime today. What should I tell him?"

"I have a question regarding Thomas Bennett's disappearance that I'd like to discuss with him."

Concern creased Parkinson's brow. "I don't mean to pry, Chief Inspector, but is there something that Lord Pembroke—or perhaps I—should know?"

"No," Lamb said. He left it at that.

"Yes—yes, I see," Parkinson said. "Official business; I understand. Well, I'll let Lord Pembroke know that you're trying to reach him as soon as I am able."

"Thank you."

As he departed Brookings, Lamb drove about two hundred meters up the main drive, until he was out of sight of the house. There, he pulled the Wolseley off the road, next to a small wood. He exited the car and began to move through the wood until he reached the lawn that fronted the main house. The house was about eighty meters away, to his right. He moved across the lawn until he reached the east side of the house. Between him and the house lay the fallow vegetable gardens. He saw no one. With the exception of Hatton and Parkinson, Brookings seemed deserted.

He moved along the east garden until he reached the high hedge that ran along the back lawn toward the cliffs and the sea. He followed the hedge, keeping to the side that was out of sight from the house, until he reckoned that he was near the place where the hedge opened onto the trail that led down the hill to Peter's cottage. He peered through the hedge and saw the opening on the opposite side.

He continued for another fifty or so meters until the hedge ended in a grassy area by the cliff edge. He walked to the edge and looked down at the sea surging and foaming among the rocks. The drop was at least thirty feet and nearly sheer. A pair of seabirds wheeled above, putting him in mind of dueling airplanes.

He crossed to the opposite hedge and walked along it until he reached the opening that gave onto the switchback trail to Peter's cottage. When he reached the bottom of the trail, he stopped and peered toward the cottage. He could see no sign of Peter. He moved to the front window but found it covered by the blackout curtains. He moved to the back and stopped at the corner in case Peter was in the rear yard. He was uncertain how he would communicate with Peter, even if he found him there. But he must try.

Peter was not there. He moved to the back door and again found it open. Inside the cottage, all appeared the same as it had on the first time he'd entered. He walked among the piles of papers, drawings, and files, lifting and sorting through them, hoping they contained something that would strike him as relevant. He looked beneath Peter's modest cot and through Peter's small dresser. He found only books, drawings, and dust.

He moved to the wall on which Peter had hung his collection of butterflies and other insects, the pinned-up corpses in neat rows. He stared at the papery veined wings of the butterflies, the fat venomous abdomens of the spiders, the needle-like stingers of the wasps.

The photograph of the tree caught his eye. It was off center, whereas before it had been perfectly centered between the butterflies and the spiders. Peter liked everything in its place. Even the smallest disruptions upset him. So Pembroke had said. He moved close to the photo and this time noticed that it possessed a vaguely arty quality, depicting the dead tree silhouetted against a stormy sky. He wondered if Peter had taken it. The photo seemed to Lamb an anomaly in the tiny, well-ordered cottage, not merely in its placement near the collection of insects but because the cottage contained no other photos. Peter drew and painted; he did not seem to take photographs. Lamb took the framed photograph from the wall and flipped it over, but found nothing attached to it.

He left the cottage and pulled shut the back door. When he turned to face the hill, he saw Peter standing at its crest, by the tree, clutching a sheet of paper in his right hand. Peter stood as if frozen, his eyes fixed on Lamb. Lamb remained still, worried that any move he made would cause Peter to run. They stood that way for several seconds, staring at each other.

"Peter," Lamb said finally.

Peter flinched, poised to run.

"I won't hurt you, Peter. I want to talk to you about Emily and Thomas." Lamb took a tentative step in Peter's direction. "It's all right, Peter. I won't hurt you. I promise." He took another step. "I want to help you, Peter. I know you're frightened. I can help you."

Peter took a backward step. Lamb froze. They stared at each other for another few seconds before Peter, still clutching the paper, turned and sprinted past the tree, and out of Lamb's sight.

"Peter!" Lamb said. He ran up the hill. He reached the crest nearly out of breath and stopped beneath the tree. In front of him lay a meadow, and on the other side of this meadow lay a wood. He caught a glimpse of Peter disappearing into the wood at a run, like a scared deer fleeing into a thicket. The boy moved with alarming speed. Lamb put a hand against the ancient, skeletal tree to steady himself. He looked at the sky through its naked branches and said "Damn."

He then noticed that Peter had dropped the paper by the base of the tree and bent to retrieve it. It was a sheet of sketching paper on which Peter had made a rough charcoal drawing of a dark oval, in the middle of which a spider with a fat abdomen had spun a symmetrical web. *Another bloody spider.* The drawing was not as detailed, as fine, as the other of Peter's drawings he'd found. Peter seemed to have rushed the sketch. Lamb flipped the paper over and found two words scrawled upon it in pencil.

tommss ded

He crossed the meadow to the wood into which Peter had run. He looked into the dense thicket of trees for some sign of Peter but could see nothing. He held up the drawing.

"I know Thomas is dead, Peter," he shouted. "But I don't know who killed him. Did Mr. Pirie kill him? Did Mr. Pirie hurt you, too? Did he hurt the other boys?"

Silence.

Lamb sensed that Peter was watching, *waiting*. But he also sensed that time was running out for them both.

—⁓—

Lamb stopped in at the nick, where he grabbed another wholly unsatisfying lunch of a cheese-and-pickle sandwich and a cup of weak tea. As compensation, he allowed himself to smoke two cigarettes in quick succession. The photo of Thomas haunted him and he wondered what sort of horrors might have transpired at The Resurrection Home for Boys.

He was readying to head back to Basingstoke, to check on the search of Pirie's house, when Harding entered his office.

"I just received a call from Constable Harris, in Quimby," the super said. "He has another body up there—a local man named Bradford. The body was found about an hour ago, in an old mill race." Harding shook his head. "The entire business is getting out of hand, Tom."

Lamb sat at his desk for a few seconds, frankly stunned. The killing indeed was getting out of hand; he'd never seen anything like it. Had Pirie slipped down from Basingstoke and killed Bradford too? But how, and why?

"I've got Larkin ready to go; he'll drive out there with you," Harding said. "I've also scared up three men to assist you and have called Winston-Sheed. Harris is standing by in Quimby."

"Yes—right," Lamb said. "Thank you, sir."

"What else can I do, Tom?" Harding asked.

"Wallace," Lamb said. "He's looking after the search of Pirie's house. I'll need him when he's finished there. The same with Rivers. He's taking statements in Lipscombe."

"Done."

"Also, Bradford has children—three children. The mother is dead."

"All right, leave it to me. I'll make the arrangements to see that they get to Castle Malwood, at least for the short term." Castle Malwood was a home in Minstead for children who had lost their parents to sudden tragedies. The war had created enough such children that Castle Malwood was becoming crowded.

Lamb looked at his desk; the crumbs from his sandwich were scattered on his blotter. For some reason, the mess offended him and he brushed the crumbs to the floor.

TWENTY-TWO

———w———

A CAR CONTAINING A TRIO OF CONSTABLES—ALL THAT HARDING could spare—followed Lamb and Larkin, who drove in Lamb's Wolseley. Harding promised that he would later send out a vehicle in which they could transport the body to the morgue.

They crossed the stone bridge in the middle of Quimby; Lamb pulled off the road and parked his Wolseley. Winston-Sheed had not yet arrived. The village seemed deserted. He figured that the news of Michael Bradford's death had made the rounds and that people had shuttered their doors, fearing another onslaught from the police. Lamb wondered where Bradford's children were and if anyone was looking after them. He would have to question Little Mike and his sisters. They might even have witnessed their father's death.

Lamb led the way up the path to the mill, where he, Larkin, and the constables found Harris standing by the crumbling fence that surrounded the mill yard. "The deceased is over here, sir," Harris said.

He led the small group around the rubbish-strewn main yard and down a short incline to the race. Bradford lay face-up in the race about ten yards from the place where the stream diverted into it; the shallow trickle from what still managed to make its way past the debris that clogged the race moved around his still body, carrying away, in a slender stream, the blood that seeped from the back of his head. A broken gin bottle lay at his feet and his eyes were open.

"Who found the body?"

"A Mrs. Lewis, sir," Harris said. "She lives just down the path, near the bridge. She came up to the mill to collect some of the wildflowers that grow along the bank and found the body." Harris gestured toward a spot slightly upstream that was alive with low, blue flowers. "She then called me."

"She saw nothing else?"

"She says not."

"Where are Bradford's children?"

"I don't know, sir," Harris said. "I haven't had a chance to look for them. Hiding somewhere, more as like. They have a hundred hiding places about."

"Find them. I'll need to speak to them, and we can't leave them unattended in any case."

"Yes, sir." Harris headed up the hill toward Bradford's cottage.

Lamb ordered the constables to go into the village and begin knocking on doors, taking statements. "Be persistent," he instructed them. "Don't allow them to shut you out. I've about had it with all the burrowing in around this damnable little place."

Lamb walked to a place a few yards above where Bradford's body lay and eased into the stone race. He walked to the body, sloshing through the inch-deep trickle, and squatted; given the blood coming from the back of Bradford's head, it appeared he'd either been struck a blow there or hit his head on the race as he fell. The gin bottle seemed to argue that he'd been drinking. In any case, Lamb couldn't move the body to look at it more closely until Winston-Sheed arrived.

He pulled himself out of the race and instructed Larkin to look around the race and mill yard for evidence. Then he walked down the lane to Mrs. Lewis's cottage.

She was a small, plump, gray-haired woman with a round face and fierce eyes. She showed Lamb into her neat sitting room and offered him tea, which he politely refused. Lamb concluded almost immediately that Mrs. Lewis's husband had died many years earlier. The mantel above the hearth contained three photos of a man who was perhaps twenty years younger than she now was; the photos constituted a small shrine to his memory.

She told Lamb the same story—of having found Bradford's body while picking flowers—that she'd told Harris. Suddenly coming upon Bradford's corpse hadn't seemed to shock her. She spoke as if she believed that Bradford was bound to have met an early, violent death.

"Not to speak ill of the dead, but Michael Bradford was a bad sort," she said. "I shouldn't think but his children will be better off now that he's dead. He was an execrable father."

Lamb nodded. "So you saw nothing else?" he asked.

Her fierce eyes flashed. "As I told the constable, no."

Lamb returned to the race to find Winston-Sheed finishing a cigarette and looking over the stream. Lamb moved next to him. A chill born of their disagreement over Winston-Sheed's having shot the seagulls lingered between them.

"Chief Inspector," Winston-Sheed said.

Lamb nodded. "Doctor."

"I'll get to him in a moment, as soon as I finish my fag." He took a long drag from his cigarette, then held up the smoldering butt pinched between his thumb and forefinger. "Horrible bloody little things when you think about it," he said, staring at the butt. He turned back toward the path and flicked the butt into the grass. Then he moved down into the race to examine Bradford as Lamb stood by.

A short while later, Larkin returned from his check of the mill to report that he'd found nothing useful. Lamb looked again into the race. The doctor held Bradford's head in his hands.

"The back of his head is bashed in; on first glance, I would say it's not the type of injury you'd expect to see if he merely fell in and struck his head," the doctor said. "It's possible that he was struck in the head and either was pushed or thrown into the race."

"Time of death?"

"Hard to tell yet, but I'd say at least twelve hours."

Lamb asked if he could lower himself into the race and examine Bradford.

"Please do," Winston-Sheed said. As Lamb examined Bradford's clothes and searched his pockets, a pair of crows flew across the stream from the opposite bank, cawing, and alighted in a tall oak tree about forty yards upstream.

"Welcome back," the doctor said, waving to them. Lamb thought the doctor's welcoming of the black birds strange, especially given that, only two days ago, he'd been shooting seagulls out of the sky willy-nilly.

Bradford's pockets contained nothing beyond a few pence.

Wallace appeared, trudging up the path with Rivers and a pair of uniformed constables who were carrying a stretcher. Wallace looked exhausted, Lamb thought. Rivers merely looked angry.

"We've brought the transport for the body," Wallace said.

"What happened to you?" Larkin asked when he saw Wallace.

"Fell off my bicycle."

"What did you find in Pirie's house?" Lamb asked Wallace.

"Sod all. No more photos—nothing that would connect him to anything like that. I left one of the constables in charge of finishing, but we got to most of it before I received Harding's call to come back down here."

Rivers peered into the race. "What's the story with Bradford, then?"

"His head's been bashed in," Lamb said. "I think he was killed and then dumped into the race."

"Did he kill Blackwell?"

"I don't see it," Lamb said. "I don't see what he would gain from killing him."

"Maybe he and Blackwell had a row and Bradford lost his head," Rivers said. He was fishing. Only a couple of days before, he'd been sure that George Abbott was the culprit, but now he was not as certain. He sensed that Lamb had run ahead of him in the inquiry and suspected that Lamb had decided to keep him in the dark.

"Yes, but then why go through all the rest of it—the pitchfork and the crucifix?" Lamb asked.

"Maybe he was smarter than you give him credit for," Rivers said.

Lamb let the remark pass. "All of this is connected in some way," he said, looking around the scene. "All that's happened in this bleeding little village, and in Lipscombe."

"How?" Rivers asked. He was determined to know what Lamb knew, to prod Lamb if he must. "I don't see it. And to be honest, I don't see why we haven't charged bloody Abbott with Blackwell's murder. We've more than enough evidence."

"But Abbott couldn't have killed Bradford," Wallace said.

"Bradford was a bleeding lush. He got drunk and fell into the race." Rivers gestured toward the gin bottle, then looked at Lamb. "You ask whether Bradford had motive to kill Blackwell, but who had motive to kill Bradford? He was nobody in this village. We're not seeing what's right before our bloody eyes. Instead, we're running after bloody retarded boys and ghouls."

Wallace glanced at Lamb, expecting him to smack Rivers down. But Lamb said nothing; he turned back toward the race and Michael Bradford's corpse.

Harris appeared, jogging down the trail from the abandoned cottage. He reached them puffing. "I found the children, sir," he said. "I coaxed them back to Bradford's cottage but couldn't get them farther. I promised them a sweet if they stayed put."

"Are they hurt?" Lamb asked.

"No."

"Do you have a sweet?"

Harris exhaled, regaining his breath. "I thought I'd leave that up to you, sir."

"Anyone have a sweet?" Lamb asked, looking around. "Gum—anything?"

No one spoke. Then Lamb remembered the tin of butterscotch in his jacket pocket. "I've got something," he said. He pulled the silvery tin of candy from his pocket and looked at it. "I got them hoping to give up the fags," he said, almost speaking to himself. "Every time I want a bloody fag I'm supposed to pop one of these in my mouth instead." He frowned. "The problem is, I keep forgetting."

Lamb sent Wallace into the village to scare up something for the Bradford children to eat. "Sandwiches—whatever you can find," Lamb said. "Harding is arranging for them to be sent to Castle Malwood."

He left Winston-Sheed and the two constables who'd arrived with Wallace to take care of the job of moving Bradford's body to the transport, and told Harris to go up the hill ahead of him with the butterscotch drops.

"Go inside and give them the sweets, as you promised, but say nothing about me," Lamb said. "I'll give you a few minutes to get them comfortable, and then I'll come in."

He gestured to Rivers to follow him up the path. They walked beside each other for a minute or so before Lamb spoke. It was time they discussed Eric Parker and the lingering enmity between them.

On that night twenty-two years earlier, Parker had been one of those who, with Lamb, Rivers, and five other men, had blackened his face in preparation for a quick raid on the German trenches that lay only two hundred meters distant. The mission was to be one of reconnaissance, to gain information for one of the many "pushes" that had marked the fighting along the Somme. But that day, too, a German machine gun had begun to spit at the British positions from a place near where their mission was to take them, killing two men, and Lamb had set himself the task of finding the gun that night and silencing it. Protective of Parker, Rivers had asked Lamb that Parker be spared the duty. But it had been Parker's turn to go and besides, Parker was good, reliable. He kept his head, showed more than the normal amount of courage, and followed orders.

And so, at two A.M., armed with wire cutters, knives, pistols, and a satchel of hand grenades, the eight men began to crawl on their bellies through the mud and coiled barbed wire toward the German positions. Four hours later, they had managed to map a good portion of a freshly dug extension to the main German trench that, so far as they knew, the British high command had no idea existed. Rivers looked at the sky; it would be light soon and he did not want to be caught in no man's land when the sun rose. He signaled to Lamb that it was time to go. But Lamb raised his hand; he wasn't yet ready. He'd seen the place where the Germans had set up the new machine gun, an MG-08. When the next push came, the thing would butcher the men who had the unlucky task of advancing on it. Rivers crawled next to him. "What's wrong?"

"I'm going after the MG."

"But it's not our responsibility. The bloody sun will be up soon."

"We have time."

"I'll go with you."

"No. Both of us can't go." One of them had to remain to command the others. "I'll take Parker."

Rivers grabbed Lamb's arm. "You won't."

"Take your bloody hand from my arm, Sergeant."

"He's too young."

"Would you rather one of the other men take the risk? Besides, you damn well know that he's the best of the lot."

The words infuriated Rivers. He thought he knew what Lamb was after—attention, promotion. Damn the consequences for Parker. Lamb could move the men under his command around as if they were nothing more than toy soldiers. Rivers believed that the men who faced the gun when the push came would have to take their chances, like the rest. But Eric was different; Eric would not have been there had it not been for him. They had been friends since they were lads, and Rivers had not been able to face going off to war without Eric. And so he had persuaded Eric to join the London Regiment with him, to do their duty, as he'd said, and to sign up. Short of mutiny, though, he could do nothing to stop Lamb.

Lamb and Parker slithered forward, each with a grenade. Lamb had gone first. He tossed his bomb into the place where the machine gun was located. There had been an explosion, followed by the sound of moaning coming from the German trench. Then rifle fire had begun to pepper them from somewhere to their left. The earth erupted in a tiny explosion a few feet from Lamb's face. Suddenly Parker was on his feet and Lamb was shouting at him to get down. He began to crawl toward Parker, intent on yanking him back to the ground. He didn't see Parker throw his grenade toward the place from where the rifle fire had come. Then Parker crumpled. Lamb reached him and saw his lifeless eyes and a trickle of blood coming from the corner of his mouth.

For his actions that night, Lamb had been awarded a Military Cross, which he kept in a box in his attic and hadn't looked at in more than twenty years. And Harry Rivers never had forgiven him.

Now, he and Rivers faced each other.

"I'm willing to consider your opinions on the inquiry," Lamb said evenly. "But if you ever challenge me in front of the other men like that again I'll have your arse. Do I make myself clear?"

Rivers glanced away, toward the stream. "Sir," he said. He thought of slugging Lamb but found to his surprise that he didn't quite have the heart for it. Besides, doing so would only land him in more trouble. They'd take his warrant card for striking a superior officer.

"I'm sorry about Eric Parker, Harry, bloody sorry," Lamb said. "You don't know how sorry. But I didn't kill him and neither did you."

Rivers continued to look toward the stream. "Convenient, that," he said. Even as he said it, he knew it to be unfair. Still, he wasn't able to let it go. Something in him wasn't.

"I've tried to be fair to you, Harry," Lamb said. "I don't insist that you like me. But I do insist that you recognize the fact that I outrank you and as such take on responsibilities for other men's lives, for their fates, that you are free of. And if you can't see your way to accepting that, then I'll have you sent out of here."

Rivers smiled sarcastically. "You'll use my cock-up in Warwickshire. You'd love that." He shrugged, as if he didn't care.

"I've no intention of using your mistakes against you. I've made mistakes, too, as you know. But I won't countenance your insubordination. You're a good detective, Harry. But you've got a bloody thorn in your arse and you enjoy it—enjoy the pain. But I'm finished wallowing in the pain, and the past. And that bloody MG had to go."

"And Eric with it," Rivers said. He turned away from Lamb and went down the hill.

—◊—

A few minutes later, Lamb entered Bradford's cottage; Mike and his sisters were sitting at the table sucking butterscotch drops. Their fingernails were black with encrusted dirt, their arms scabbed and hair tangled. They turned to Lamb, their eyes wide with surprise. The two girls froze; Mike shot from his chair in the direction of the back door but ran into Harris.

"Whoa, there, Mike," Harris said. "This is Inspector Lamb. You know him." Mike allowed Harris to lead him back to his seat at the table, but kept his eyes riveted on Lamb.

Lamb squatted next to Mike. "Hello, Mike," he said. "You remember me, don't you?" Mike nodded. Lamb turned to the girls, who were sitting across the table. "Hello, girls," he said. Neither spoke or moved. He smiled. "What are your names?"

The youngest, who was four, said "Natalie." She was the girl from whom Lamb had taken the stick on the night of Blackwell's murder.

"That's a very pretty name," Lamb said. He turned his attention to the older girl, who was six. "And how about you, love?" he asked. The look on her face made it appear as if she considered Lamb akin to something like a werewolf.

"Her name is Vera," Natalie offered.

"Vera?" Lamb said. "I have a girl named Vera, though she's older than you."

"What has happened to daddy?" Natalie asked. "Where is he?"

Lamb wondered how much the children knew or had seen. They seemed not to know that their father was dead. He decided that he must lie to them about Bradford's fate, so as not to upset them. If they knew their father was dead, they might not speak to him. There would be time later for someone to ease them toward the truth more gently.

"Your father is hurt and we are taking him to hospital," Lamb said. "And we are going to take you and your brother and sister to a nice place where you will be warm and safe and have plenty to eat."

None of the children spoke. Lamb wondered how they were squaring up what he was telling them in their childish minds.

"Is everyone all right?" he asked. "Is anyone hurt?" Natalie shook her head. The other two remained silent. "If you are hurt, you should tell me, so we can get you properly cared for."

"We're not hurt," Mike said.

"That's good," Lamb said. He smiled again. "Have any of you seen anyone around the cottage in the past day or so—maybe someone who was a stranger?"

Silence.

"How about you, Mike? Have you seen anyone?"

Mike shook his head.

"I want you all three to think back, please," Lamb said. "Did anyone visit your father in the past few days? Did you see your father talking to anyone?"

Silence again. Natalie eyed the tin of butterscotch drops, which Harris had left on the table. "Would you like another, Natalie?" Lamb asked. She nodded. He fished a drop from the tin and handed it to her. "Did you see your father talking to anyone in the past few days, love?" Lamb asked.

"No," she said. She rolled the candy in her mouth.

"How about you, Vera?"

Vera shook her head.

"Would you like another sweet?" Lamb asked Vera. She put her hands under her legs and shrugged.

"How about you, Mike? Would you like another?"

"Yes."

Lamb gave each of them another butterscotch. Vera examined hers for a couple of seconds, as if she found it suspicious, before popping it into her mouth.

"I know you all must be hungry and we won't take much more time here," Lamb said. "I've arranged for someone to bring you some food. Do you like sandwiches?"

"I like sandwiches," Natalie offered. Her small head bobbed; Lamb could tell that she had begun to swing her feet beneath the table.

"That's good," Lamb said. "But before we go, I must ask one more question." He turned to Mike. "Do you remember, Mike, that when I spoke with you before, you told me you had seen a tall man on Manscome Hill on the day Will Blackwell died?"

Mike nodded.

"That's good," Lamb repeated. "Now, I'm going to ask you another question, and I want you to know that you won't get into any trouble by telling me the truth. Do you understand?"

Another nod.

"Did you make that man up, Mike, or did you really see him?"

Mike hesitated. "I really saw him."

"You said the last time that the man was Peter Wilkins, Mike, though that was after I mentioned Peter's name. Are you still certain that the man you saw was Peter? Remember that only the truth will do. I promise you that, whatever happens, no harm will come to you from the police or your father or anyone else."

Mike nodded again.

"Can you tell me again how he was dressed?"

"Brown trousers and a brown hat."

"Anything else?"

"A white shirt."

The description matched what Mike had told Lamb the first time they'd spoken.

"Are you afraid of this man, Mike?"

"Yes."

"Was the man Peter, Mike?"

"No."

"Who was it, then?"

Mike hunched his shoulders, as if uncertain.

"About a year ago, a boy named Thomas Bennett ran away from Lord Pembroke's estate and came here to the hill," Lamb said. "Do you remember that?"

"Yes."

"Did you know about the boy hiding on the hill before Will Blackwell found him? Remember that no one can hurt you now and that you must tell me the truth."

"We gave him food," Natalie said.

Mike quickly turned toward Natalie, surprised that she'd spoken. Vera looked terrified.

Lamb smiled at Natalie. "That was very nice of you," he said.

"Yes, he were hungry."

"And did you see the boy with him—the mute boy, Peter?"

"Yes," Natalie said. "But daddy told us to stay away from the crazy boy. He were a witch, like old Will. Can I have another butterscotch?"

"Of course," Lamb said. He gave them each another butterscotch, then turned his attention back to Mike.

"I have one or two more important questions to ask you, Mike. You are doing very well and we're almost finished."

Mike sat stock still.

"I think you have seen things—know things—about which you haven't told me yet. Am I right about that?"

"Yes," Mike said quietly.

The fact that Pirie had not destroyed the photo of Thomas that Lamb had found in Pirie's bedside table continued to trouble Lamb. Why would a guilty Pirie run to avoid arrest but fail to dispose of the one piece of evidence that damned him? Lamb now tested the theory he'd slowly been developing about the killings.

"Did you see Will Blackwell on the day he died?" he asked Mike.

"Yes."

"Was he alive or dead when you saw him?"

"Dead. The crows were on him."

"Now, to the man you saw on the hill that day. Did you see this man before or after you found Will's body?"

"Before."

"How long before you found Will?"

"The sun were just topping the wood." Lamb realized that Mike didn't know how to tell time. If the sun still was just breaking over the trees, then the time must have been no later than an hour or so before noon.

"And was the man walking toward where Will was working?"

"Yes."

"But this man didn't see you because you were hiding and because he doesn't know you—doesn't know that you wander about the hill and see everything that goes on there?"

Mike nodded.

"Before you and I talked the last time, Mike, did your father know you had seen someone on the hill the day that Will Blackwell died, or did he find this out only when you told me?"

Mike hesitated.

"Mike?"

"He only found out when I told you."

"And did you then tell your father who the man really was—that it wasn't Peter?"

"Yes."

"Who was that man, Mike?"

Again, Mike hesitated.

Lamb moved close to him. "I promise you that you are in no trouble, Mike, and that you are safe."

Mike looked at his sisters, then at Lamb.

"It were Lord Pembroke," he said.

TWENTY-THREE

—∞—

LAMB, HARRIS, AND THE CHILDREN WALKED DOWN THE PATH to the village, past the place where Michael Bradford had been killed. Natalie took Lamb's hand. From the path, the children could not see their father's body in the race, where Winston-Sheed was finishing his work.

They found Harding waiting for them near Blackwell's cottage, along with Wallace and a woman Lamb didn't recognize. She was a young woman, not more than twenty-five or so. She wore white gloves on her hands.

"This is Miss Perkins from Castle Malwood," Harding said. "She'll take care of the children."

Mike was expressionless; the girls seemed confused. "I want to stay with the man," Natalie said. She squeezed Lamb's hand, breaking his heart.

Lamb squatted, faced her and took her hands in his. "There, now, love," he said. "Miss Perkins is a very nice lady. She's going to take you to a very nice place where there's a nice comfortable bed for you to sleep in. Does that sound good?"

Natalie nodded.

Lamb handed the tin of butterscotch to Natalie. "Now, you're a big girl," he said. "Can you be the guardian of these, please? Make sure your brother and sister get a few as well?"

"Yes." She clutched the tin.

Lamb put his hand gently on her head. "That's very good. I'm very proud of you."

Miss Perkins squatted next to Lamb. "Hello, Natalie," she said. She offered her hand to Natalie, who took it.

"Do you have the sandwiches?" Lamb asked Wallace.

Wallace handed Lamb three cheese sandwiches wrapped in waxy paper. Wallace smiled at the children. "Fresh from the pub," he said. "Cheese *and* pickle."

"How nice," Miss Perkins said. She took the sandwiches from Lamb. "You can eat them on the way," she told the children. Natalie smiled, but the other two seemed shocked into a kind of quiet submission. Miss Perkins guided Natalie and Vera toward a big black saloon. Mike hesitated; he looked back at Lamb. Lamb smiled at him.

"It's okay, Mike," he said. "You're safe."

Miss Perkins opened the back door of the car and gently herded the children into it. Once they were seated, she handed them the sandwiches. She turned to Lamb, Harding, Wallace, and Rivers. "Thank you, gentlemen," she said. "We'll take good care of them."

"I trust you will," Harding said.

"There are some formalities to attend to, obviously, but those can be handled later. Right now, I think it's best that we get the three of them settled."

"Let me know what you need and I'll provide it," Harding said.

Miss Perkins shook their hands and then got behind the wheel of the car. A few seconds later, the car crossed the stone bridge and left Quimby.

"A tough break," Wallace said as they watched the car leave.

"So it's another murder, then?" Harding asked, turning to Lamb. "Yes."

"And do you think the same man killed Blackwell?"

"I don't know," Lamb said. "The boy just admitted to me that he saw Lord Jeffrey Pembroke on the hill sometime before he came upon Blackwell's body."

"Pembroke?" Harding said. "But what does Pembroke have to do with any of it?"

"I'm not entirely sure yet. But his presence makes sense. As I said, I'm certain that the two boys—Peter and Thomas—figure in both killings. And then there's Pirie. All three of them put Pembroke in the picture. And Pembroke knew Blackwell and Emily Fordham, though I haven't established yet if he knew Bradford. But I think Bradford might have approached him."

Harding was silent for a moment. He looked at Lamb and said, "I don't have to tell you that we must move with delicacy where Pembroke is concerned."

"All due respect, sir, but why should we move with delicacy as regards Lord Pembroke?" Rivers interjected. Although Rivers spoke in a respectful tone, Lamb couldn't quite believe that Rivers now was openly challenging Harding. Apparently the talk Lamb had just had with Rivers hadn't penetrated him. Or he didn't bloody care. He seemed unable to be anything other than insubordinate. Even so, his question was one Lamb himself had intended to ask Harding in private.

Harding glared at Rivers. "I should think the reason is obvious," he said coldly.

"What if the boy, Peter, did it and Pembroke is covering for him?" Rivers asked, seemingly unaffected by Harding's obvious ire. But he refused to be left behind, kept in the dark. He had been sorting a few new theories of his own regarding the killings—theories that, he had to admit, were partly down to what Lamb had discovered—and believed the time had come to air them.

"The fact is, we don't know anything about the mute boy," Rivers continued. "We've only made bloody assumptions about him. He could very well have killed the old man, and the girl. Maybe the old man upset the boy in some way and so he bashed in the old man's head. Then Pembroke, the boy's guardian and protector, comes along and drives home the scythe and the pitchfork to shift blame from the boy because nobody is going to believe that a mute idiot would have known to have added the black magic touches."

Harding looked at Lamb. Despite himself—and Rivers's insubordination—he quietly believed the scenario a good one. It explained much. He'd left the delivery of Wallace's penalty up to Lamb. But *he* would give Rivers a bloody boot up the arse later. Still, for the moment, he had to consider what Rivers was saying.

"What do you think, Tom?" Harding asked, shifting the focus to Lamb.

"It's a good theory, but I'm wondering where Pirie fits in." He nodded toward the race. "And Bradford, and Emily Fordham."

"The boy could easily have killed the girl too," Rivers said. "She also upset him, though that time Pembroke wasn't around to neaten things up."

"And Bradford?" Lamb asked. He nodded at Rivers, remembering their talk of a half hour before. "Speak freely, Inspector," he said. Not that Rivers seemed to care.

"His son told him the story he just told you—that he saw Pembroke on the hill. And Bradford, being a stupid greedy lush, went to Pembroke and asked for a little something to keep his mouth shut. Except that Pembroke knows full well that a man like Bradford is incapable of keeping his mouth shut."

"So what, then?" Harding asked. "The bloody lord of the manor tromps over here and crushes the man's skull in?"

"No. He hires someone to do the job. He's got plenty of money."

"And Pirie?" Lamb asked.

"Maybe Pirie is exactly what he appears—a pervert who buggers little boys. If he is, and Pembroke found out about it, then it would have been in Pembroke's interest to keep it hushed up. Otherwise, Pembroke's little Bloomsbury experiment is ruined, shown to be a bloody fraud."

"Or Pembroke doesn't know about Pirie," Wallace said. "Or about Thomas."

"What's next?" Harding asked Lamb.

"I must speak again with Pembroke, obviously. But he's in London until at least tomorrow."

Rivers sneered. "How bloody convenient," he said.

—☞—

That night, Wallace walked through the darkness to Delilah's. He felt that he must see her again. Beyond that, he wasn't sure what he was doing, or why.

He found Delilah's house dark, the windows blacked out. He went to the door and rapped on it. He could sense no light or movement within. "Delilah," he shouted. He didn't care if anyone heard or saw him.

He waited for the sound of Delilah unlocking the bolt on the door. He heard someone passing on the sidewalk behind him and turned suddenly, expecting an attack. But the walker was a lone woman, her head covered in a kerchief. She glanced at Wallace, as if she thought him dangerous, and hurried on.

He turned to the door and rapped on it again. "Delilah!" He rattled the knob and, to his surprise, found the door unlocked. He stepped into the foyer. The house was dark except for the small lamp above the cabinet in which Delilah kept her whiskey.

Wallace went to the cabinet and found beneath the lamp a white envelope with his name on it. It contained another note. Wallace's heart dropped.

> *David,*
>   *I knew that when I asked you to stay away that you would not listen. You are too proud and valiant to listen. You are the most valiant man I have ever known. I'm sorry that I did not know you in another time and place, when I could have loved you.*
>   *I've gone away. I can't say where. Please do not try to find me.*

> *I am dreadfully sorry that I hurt you. I was a fool playing a foolish game. I wish you only the best, David. I hope you believe that. Please don't hate me.*
> *Delilah*

Wallace crumpled the note and tossed it onto the cabinet. He hoped she was safe, though he doubted it. He'd been stupid and reckless but regretted nothing. He was certain that she hadn't loved him—not really—though she might have thought that she had. She didn't love her husband either, and Wallace wondered if the poor bloody sod knew it, had always known it. And he wondered if Delilah's husband had loved her—if he'd been too bloody dense to see what he had right in the palm of his hand.

Please don't hate me.

He didn't hate her.

He started for home, his flat on the other side of Winchester.

On the way, he passed The Fallen Diva, which was darkened for the blackout, though he heard muted merriment coming from within. He badly wanted a drink; but he turned from the door of the pub and walked away. In that moment, he didn't care that he might disappoint himself if he entered the pub.

But he couldn't quite bring himself to disappoint Lamb.

—⁂—

Across the Channel, the engines of eighty German bombers came to life on an airfield near Cherbourg. They were on their way to deal a fatal blow to the Spitfire factory in Southampton. Among the pilots was Hermann Seitz, who firmly believed that he was about to die.

That night, too, Vera walked up Manscome Hill alone.

The hour was late, past midnight, but she hadn't been able to sleep. The news that another man had been killed in the village distressed her deeply. Though she hadn't known them, really, or their father, she had seen the Bradford children darting about the village. Once or twice she had tried to speak to them, but they'd always run from her, just as Peter always ran. She wondered whether it was wise to go out alone, given all that had occurred in the past few days—and, yet, strangely, she felt safe on the hill. She wondered if this, too, had something to do with the war—of how squaring yourself to the idea that the Germans might invade any day caused you to be brave in other ways.

As she trod the goat path, the dark outline of the wood that marked the border between Quimby and Brookings loomed on her left. Roughly a half mile to her right was the place where Will Blackwell had died, and beyond that the ancient footpath upon which, according to legend, a demon dog had appeared to him sixty years earlier. On the other side of the wood lay the ruins of the mill and its race, freshly stained with the blood of Michael Bradford. Farther still, beyond the mill and the village, was the spot upon which a deranged man had murdered an innocent milkmaid more than sixty years earlier. And in between and all around these places, life breathed.

She made it halfway to the crest before she began to tire and, feeling as if she now might sleep, turned for home and bed. But as she descended the hill, the dark figure of Arthur Lear suddenly appeared among the tall grasses and thistle in front of her. She could not mistake the stub hanging from his right shoulder.

At the same moment, Hermann Seitz maneuvered his Heinkel over the Solent, following the path of the German air armada heading for Southampton. The last time he'd crossed the British coast, he'd nearly died. Although a Spitfire had shot up his port wing, he'd been able to get his bomber back to Cherbourg in one piece, though badly damaged. The plane he now piloted was new, fresh from a factory in Hamburg. To Seitz, the thing handled like a busted-down lorry, turgid and recalcitrant, insufficiently broken in. Once again, fat Goering had sent them on a suicide mission, into the dark, without proper escort.

Seitz's last mission had left him feeling terrified of returning. But being terrified didn't get you excused from duty. Now, he literally began to quiver with fear as he turned the plane west, toward

Southampton. A minute later, the sky around him began to flash with the exploding shells of British anti-aircraft fire.

That morning, the RAF had reopened Cloverton airbase, which now sounded the signal to scramble. Two dozen pilots, Charles Graham among them, sprinted onto the patched airfield and climbed into their Spitfires. Emily's murder, and the murder of his unborn child, had quietly shocked Charles to his soul. As a consequence, a strange kind of lassitude had overcome him and he'd decided that he no longer cared if he lived or died, which, in the macabre, caustic, unrelenting actuality of life and war, made him lethal.

Vera stopped, her figure suffused in moonlight. Arthur's sudden appearance frightened her. Her first thought was that she'd been stupid to come up the hill alone—stupid to believe that the only thing she had to fear was the Germans.

"Have you come up here to meet him?" Arthur asked. "A little secret tryst, then? We used to have secret trysts, Vera. And you enjoyed them." His voice contained a hint of menace.

Vera told herself that she must be bold—that she must not show Arthur that she was frightened. She glanced at the path in front of her for something she might use to defend herself and saw the stub of an old oak branch lying about four feet away.

"Go home, Arthur," she said, calling up the most authoritative tone that she could muster. "Leave me alone."

"I don't take orders from you." He glanced toward the wood and said, in a high-pitched voice meant to be a parody of hers, "Peter! Oh, Peter! I'm ready. I've got my knickers down. Come bugger me!" He turned toward her and laughed wickedly.

He took a step toward her; his pinned-up sleeve swayed like a pendulum. Vera quickly moved toward the branch and picked it up. She held it up as if she meant to strike Arthur with it. "Stay away from me," she said. She heard in her voice the fear she felt in her heart.

Arthur moved another step closer. "Give me that!" he commanded.

"Stay back," Vera said.

"I said to give me that."

Peter watched them from behind an oak tree ten yards away, though neither of them knew it.

Arthur leapt toward Vera with alarming speed, reaching toward her with his lone arm. Instinctively, Vera closed her eyes and swung the branch.

A bomber exploded to Seitz's right and plummeted out of sight in a dozen pieces. "Fucking hell," yelled his navigator, whose name Seitz suddenly could not remember.

Then something rocked the rear half of the Heinkel, throwing Seitz toward Henning. *That* was the man's name—*Henning*. Seitz smelled something burning. He straightened in his seat and tried to bring the plane under control, but the machine fought him. He smacked the wheel and cursed it.

They were nearly over Southampton and the Spitfires from Cloverton were in among them now. "Get us the fuck out of here!" Henning yelled.

Seitz heeled the plane to the north, as he'd done the last time they'd flown above Southampton. And, just as last time, the Heinkel miraculously began to climb. Seitz put all of his strength into keeping the plane steadily moving upward, away from hell, which seemed to have swallowed them.

He told himself that he must stay focused on surviving. He remembered that the last time he'd turned east, away from Southampton and the ack-ack, then south for the Channel. And he remembered the bombs—he'd nearly forgotten to jettison them the last time. He heard the sound of the man in the roof turret fire his gun. Charles Graham, in his Spitfire, had fallen in behind the Heinkel. Seitz yanked at the wheel and the plane began to track back toward the southeast, in a wide turning arc that would take them directly over Quimby.

Graham fired a brief burst of his 20mm cannon at Seitz. The shells ripped into the tail of the plane and set it aflame.

"Shit!" Henning yelled.

Seitz remembered the bombs. They were at twelve thousand feet and over Quimby. "Release!" he yelled.

Vera felt the weight of the branch strike Arthur.

She opened her eyes to see him staggering backward, away from her, his face bleeding. He put his hand up to his face, as if he were trying to keep it from falling away from his head. He looked for an instant at the sky and said "Bloody hell." He was only three feet from her. Vera raised the branch, preparing to strike him again.

Peter watched.

Seitz shoved the plane east, hoping to make a circle and lose the British pilot who was trying to kill him. He did not know what else to do. But the ploy proved useless. Graham picked him up easily in the bright moon, just as Seitz was heading south again. He flew at the Heinkel from nearly broadside and fired his cannon. The shells ripped into the bomber's cockpit and blew Henning's head off; Henning's head landed in Seitz's lap. But Seitz also was dead; the big shells had ripped into the right side of his body just as he was beginning to say the Hail Mary. The bomber burst into flame.

The bombs from the Heinkel struck the ruins of the old grain mill in Quimby and fell among the decrepit mill houses, exploding with terrifying, deafening blasts, throwing tons of stone and mortar and rotted wood in every direction and shattering the windows of every building within a quarter mile. Three of the bombs hit Mills Run, sending up colossal plumes of water and mud. And some, too, burst in the wood by the old foot trail, felling and splitting trees. And a single bomb fell among George Abbott's ghostly sheep, vaporizing them in an instant and leaving a smoking crater in the meadow. The crows roosting in the dead sycamore took to the air, screaming.

Vera, Arthur, and Peter looked toward the place where the blasts had come from. For an instant, none of them understood what they'd just heard—knew what had occurred. Then the truth dawned on them. Vera dropped the branch. "My God," she said.

Arthur looked to the west, his mouth hanging open, almost stupidly. Peter remained crouched behind his tree. Throughout Quimby, people sat up in bed with a start, an instantaneous anxiety sweeping over them.

A small explosion lit the sky to the southwest for an instant—a flash only. The three looked toward the explosion and saw a burning plane falling, like a flaming comet, heading for the western edge of the village and the Lears' farm. The plane disappeared behind the wood by the mill and hit the ground, sending up a mushroom-shaped inferno of smoke and flame well above the tops of the trees.

"Father," Arthur said. He stumbled, then began to run across the meadow toward where the plane had fallen.

"My God!" Vera repeated. She saw Arthur moving away, down the hill, through the darkness.

TWENTY-FOUR

—ᨀ—

BY THE TIME VERA REACHED THE HIGH STREET, KNOTS OF PEOPLE
had begun to hurry along it, some in their pajamas and sleeping gowns,
toward the places where the explosions had occurred.

The western horizon was red from fire and the smell of smoke permeated the air. The sight of the plummeting plane spooled over and over
in her mind. It seemed to have been headed directly for the Lears' farm.

She reached the steps of the Parish office and began to turn the
crank of the siren for all she was worth. It started with a low whine but
quickly wound up to its full deafening wail. She cranked the siren for
a full minute, until she felt that her head might burst. Then she let the
handle go and ran up the steps to the office and the phone. She called
Southampton to report that the Germans had hit Quimby—that bombs
had fallen on the village.

"It's burning!" she shouted into the telephone.

"Assistance is on the way," the female voice on the line said. "Keep your head, my girl. People are depending on you. Good luck."

Vera strapped on the metal Great War helmet and set out in the direction of the chaos.

The mill was burning to the ground rapidly, the fire sweeping through the dry, rotted beams and timbers. A group of roughly twenty local men, and a few women, had gathered on the stone bridge over Mills Run by the time Vera reached it.

"I've called Southampton," she told them. "Help is coming."

Quimby had no fire engine; it depended on the one from Moresham. Vera had not thought to call Moresham. She hoped the woman in Southampton would.

The group decided they must let the mill burn, as it directly threatened no other inhabited buildings in the village. A large, stout man who was unfamiliar to Vera reported that an airplane had hit the Lear's farmhouse, plowed right into the bloody place; he didn't know if the plane was German or British; the house had gone up in a ball of flame; Lear and his boy had had no chance, the man said.

"I saw Arthur Lear on the High Street just a few minutes ago," Vera said, lying slightly.

"Are you certain it was him, miss?" the stout man asked.

"Yes," Vera said. "He was running toward the farm."

"We must do what we can to contain the fire until the truck from Moresham arrives," someone said. Another suggested they call the Hampshire police.

The group dispatched two men to go door to door in the village to ensure that no more casualties existed beyond those they knew of—Noel Lear—while the rest went toward the farm. On the way, Vera searched for some sign of Arthur. She expected to see him staggering toward them, his face still bleeding from the blow she'd struck him. Or he might have fallen somewhere, unconscious.

They reached the edge of the village, from where Vera saw the farmhouse burning furiously. Bits of burning wreckage lay strewn about the yard; the barn also was burning. The fire seemed to suck in all the available oxygen around them.

"Where is young Lear, then?" the stout man shouted to Vera.

Vera looked at the burning house, a feeling of disbelief and terror rising within her. She thought she knew now where Arthur was. But she looked at the man and shouted, "I don't know."

—m—

An hour later, Lamb and Marjorie arrived in Quimby in Lamb's Wolseley. Harding had called in to say that a German bomber had crashed into a farm near Quimby and that several other buildings were damaged. That's all he knew at the moment. He thought Lamb would want to know. "I'm sorry, Tom," he'd added.

Lamb had hung up the phone in the hallway by the kitchen and run upstairs to dress. Marjorie was sitting up in bed. He sat next to Marjorie and told her what Harding had told him. "Vera is all right," he said, as if he knew this definitively. He couldn't bring himself to say differently.

"I'm coming with you," Marjorie said. Before Lamb could answer, she was out of bed, headed for her closet.

They entered the village from the east, on the side opposite from where the bombs had fallen; Lamb parked the Wolseley by Blackwell's cottage and he and Marjorie fairly jogged toward the farm, holding hands, each of them keeping their worst fears to themselves. They soon found Vera working a bucket line that was having no success containing the fire in the farmhouse. The pump truck from Moresham had arrived, as had Harris and a cadre of Home Guard men and women from nearby villages and hamlets. The fires burned with such ferocity that Lamb felt as if they had entered hell as they approached the farm.

"Vera!" Marjorie yelled and ran to her. Lamb followed.

Marjorie gathered Vera into her arms; Vera's face was black from soot and smoke.

Vera didn't answer. She'd learned ten minutes earlier that someone had seen Arthur go into the fire after his father. In her mind, she saw him staggering down the path with his head bleeding—heading toward his death, his stubbed arm dangling. Since, she'd moved in a stupor of disbelief and conflicted emotion. Had Arthur gone into the house because she'd struck him such a violent blow in the head, ruining his bearings and better judgment? Or would he have run in after his beloved father regardless? Then again, he might have killed her had she not defended herself against him. As her mother held her, she began to cry—for Arthur and for herself.

—⁓—

The fires in Quimby did not burn themselves out until mid-morning the following day.

The mill burned to its stone foundation and became something beyond even a ruin. The bombs had turned the houses to rubble. Among the casualties was Natalie Bradford's sole toy, a rag doll she'd named Laura, after her dead mother. No one could find any trace of George Abbott's sheep, except for the crows, which discovered bits of them among the branches of the trees surrounding the meadow.

Marjorie and Lamb had stayed the night with Vera in her billet; they and the rest of the village finally had gone to bed in the early morning, with the fires still smoldering. Vera managed to scare up a pair of blankets for them. She tried to give her cot to her mother, but Marjorie wouldn't hear of it. Marjorie and Lamb slept on the narrow wooden floor in their clothes.

A couple of hours later, Lamb awakened with a sore neck and the feeling that he hadn't really slept. Daylight streamed in through the lone window of Vera's cramped billet. He found Vera and Marjorie sitting in the small back courtyard drinking tea and looking as he felt, emotionally and physically drained. Lamb hadn't even heard the kettle whistle as he slept. For their breakfast, Vera sliced what was left of the bread in her box and served it with marmalade, along with what was left of her egg ration for the month, which she fried.

Lamb and Marjorie stayed a while that morning to help with the cleanup effort. The sight of the blackened ruins of the Lear farm called up tears within Vera, but she stifled them. *Keep your head, my girl.*

She was genuinely sorry for Arthur. He had been troubled and violent and dealt a bad hand in life—and might, in the end, have killed her. But she could not bring herself to believe that he deserved to die in the way he had. And in thinking of Arthur, she thought of Peter, and wondered if she ever would see him again.

Lamb and Marjorie returned to Winchester at midday. Before they left, Lamb promised to return to Quimby later that evening with a loaf of bread and a half dozen eggs, to replenish Vera's empty larder. Once home, he and Marjorie went to bed, exhausted.

At a little before five P.M., the telephone in the hall jangled and Lamb rose from his slumber, still bleary, to answer it. It was Harding, who reported that Gerald Pirie had been found dead with a .22-caliber bullet in his brain, an apparent suicide.

"He was found floating facedown in a stream south of Basingstoke, off the main road to Winchester," Harding said. "The pistol was lying on the bank."

Lamb's first thought was to beg off. Vera's near miss in Quimby had frightened and drained him more than he had known. At the moment he didn't bloody care that Gerald Pirie was dead.

"Can Wallace or Rivers handle it?" he asked.

Harding didn't answer at first; Lamb understood that the superintendent was silently signaling his disapproval. "Are you certain Wallace is up to it?" Harding asked. The super had no intention of handing Rivers a plum after the detective inspector's public display of insubordination on the previous day.

"I'm certain of it," Lamb said. "I've spoken to him about his conduct. He understands that he has no choice but to straighten out. He's a good man at bottom. And he knows the case."

"Yes, but what about this bloody black eye and the rest of it? He's been up to something."

"He says he was beaten in a robbery and I believe him. Besides, a black eye isn't going to impede him."

Harding was silent again for a few seconds. More disapproval. "All right, Tom," he said finally.

Lamb rang off, put the kettle on the boil, and retrieved the day's post, which included a plain envelope addressed to him, with a return address in Lipscombe. The envelope contained two notes. The first, dated the previous day, was from Lilly Schmidt, the girl who had been Emily Fordham's best friend.

> *Chief Inspector Lamb,*
>   *The enclosed letter from Donald Fordham to Emily came in the post today. I believe it's his response to the last letter she sent him. I thought you should see it. I'm certain that Donald wouldn't mind under the circumstances.*
>   *Sincerely yours,*
>   *Lilly Schmidt*

Lamb unfolded the letter from Donald Fordham.

> *Emily,*
>   *I received your note of the fifteenth and was glad to receive it, though it worried me. Please, whatever you do, do not confide in P. He is not what he seems. I should have told you this before but didn't want to sully your experience at the estate. I know you loved it there, as I once did. Still and all, you must believe me that P. is no good.*
>   *I am worried about you and sorry that I cannot be there to comfort you. Please do not let any of this mess with the sketch and the photograph weigh too much on your mind. In the end, it is probably nothing. Please, please take care of yourself. I'm sorry that we must be so far apart.*
>   *I'm also sorry that this letter is so short but my time is limited tonight and I wanted to write some response to your last letter as soon as I could. I promise that I will send a longer letter soon.*
>   *Your loving brother,*
>   *Donald*

Lamb thought that "P" could be Pembroke, though it also could be Pirie, or even Peter. Donald likely had used "P" to get the letter past the censors, who might have stuck at any mention of Lord Jeffrey Pembroke, who was known to publicly hold a pacifist, dissenting view of the war with Germany. Lamb believed now that Pembroke definitely had been involved in the events of the past days, though he did not yet know how or how deeply. He did not know if Emily or Donald Fordham had known Pirie. Pirie might have killed Emily and Will Blackwell. He might even have killed Michael Bradford. In any case, Lamb also felt certain now that Peter knew something that he wasn't meant to know—something about Thomas Bennett—that he'd tried to communicate to Emily and might have communicated to Will Blackwell and now was trying to communicate to him.

Lamb saw no reason to awaken Marjorie. He gathered up the loaf and the eggs he'd promised Vera and put them into a brown paper sack with a pound note, then put the sack in the back seat of the Wolseley. He slid behind the wheel, lit a fag—he hadn't yet had a chance to buy a new tin of butterscotch drops—and pushed the starter. The car coughed and came to life on the first try.

He stopped first at the nick to gather the bits of paper evidence he'd collected and put them in a cardboard portfolio. These included the three "spider" drawings—the one he'd found in Blackwell's shed and the nearly identical one he'd found in Emily's wallet, along with the third drawing, of the spider and the black oval that Peter had left for him the day before; the small photographic portrait of Thomas Bennett; the letter from Donald Fordham; and the brief cryptic note he'd found in Will Blackwell's pocket: *in the nut*.

He hoped that he might sit down with the evidence later, when his head was clear, and sort through the entire bloody mess again.

He was in the incident room, about to leave the nick, when Rivers walked in, looking haggard and frustrated. They were alone in the room. Harding and the rest had gone home for the day or were clearing up the mess in Basingstoke. As punishment for Rivers's insubordination, Harding had put him on the phones that day, taking calls and tips, all of which had struck Rivers as useless and many of which clearly had come from loonies who wanted attention. Rivers had been in the loo when Lamb arrived and now was returning. He flinched when he noticed Lamb standing on the other side of the room.

"Lamb," he said.

"Harry."

"I didn't see you there."

"I didn't mean to startle you. I'm sorry."

Rivers went to his desk.

Lamb put on his hat. "Good night, then, Harry," he said. Rivers grunted a reply but did not look up from his desk.

Lamb was nearly out the door when Rivers said, "Lamb."

Lamb stopped and looked at Rivers. They were close now, only feet apart. Lamb recalled the many hours he and Rivers had spent huddled near each other in the damp, stinking trenches. Rivers turned to face Lamb, who expected to see something of the anger that he normally saw in Rivers's eyes. But Lamb saw only exhaustion, and perhaps a hint of the old anguish that Rivers had carried with him since the Somme.

"I heard what happened in Quimby," Rivers said. "Your daughter is all right, then?"

Lamb hadn't known that Rivers knew of Vera's posting in Quimby. "Yes, she's fine. Thanks for asking."

"Good," Rivers said. He nodded his head slightly. "That's good."

Lamb did not quite know what to say in response beyond "thank you." But Rivers spoke again before Lamb could. "I'm sorry to say that you've run ahead of me in this business and my response has been to act an arse," he said. "It won't happen again."

Lamb could not hide his surprise. He stood in silence and looked at Rivers for several seconds. He expected Rivers to add, "I'm sorry." But Rivers merely turned again to the papers on his desk.

"Thank you, Harry," Lamb said. Then he left.

TWENTY-FIVE

—⚏—

LAMB FOUND VERA SITTING IN THE SMALL YARD BEHIND HER BILLET, sipping tea. She also had slept into the afternoon and awakened only a few hours earlier.

"Relief," Lamb said, handing her the bread and the eggs. He said nothing about the pound note.

"Thanks, dad," she said. "I've eaten, though. Have you?"

He hadn't, but he'd already gobbled more than enough of her stores. "Yes."

"Tea?"

"I wouldn't turn it down."

She dragged a chair for him into the courtyard and they sat together for a time in the gathering twilight, not speaking. Then Lamb ventured a question. "How are you feeling?'

Vera shrugged. "All right."

He knew that Vera had known and liked Arthur Lear, but nothing more—though he recalled the day on which he'd met Lear and suspected that the boy had Vera in his sights.

"Was it hard?" he asked.

"Yes," she said. She tried to smile. Instead, she shook her head, as if in disbelief. "I thought the bloody Germans were invading."

A ripple of surprise shot through Lamb; he'd never heard Vera use "bloody," had no idea that she employed it. He'd always been reasonably good about not cursing in her presence. Then, too, she didn't belong to him anymore—not in the way she once had, when she'd been his Doodle Doo.

In the brief silence that followed, Vera thought of telling her father about Arthur—of telling him the entire story. She wanted to tell someone. But something stopped her; she believed that her father wasn't ready to hear the story yet. The story of her having had a lover—and of a man who had menaced her.

"Fancy a walk?" she asked. She wanted to move, to clear her head, not to sit and talk and keep secrets from her father.

Lamb stood. "I could use one. My head's still muddled."

They walked to the eastern edge of the village and back; Lamb smoked as they walked, lighting each fresh cigarette with the one he was finishing. He wondered about the Bradford children. By now, someone at Castle Malwood probably had told them that their father was dead. He wondered what would become of them and especially of Mike, who was old enough to understand, at least partially, the viciousness, cruelty, greed, and wretchedness that lay at the heart of his father's death and the other recent events in Quimby.

As they passed the place where the path that paralleled Lord Pembroke's wood snaked up the hill, Vera told her father the story of her encounters with Peter, the strange boy who so many in Quimby seemed to know *about*, but who nobody really seemed to *know*.

"He gave me two drawings," she said. "They're really quite beautiful, though one of them is also a bit disturbing." She did not know that her father considered Peter a potential key actor in the drama that had unfolded in Quimby and Basingstoke and even a possible suspect in the murders of Will Blackwell and Emily Fordham. She and Lamb had not discussed the case.

The fact that Peter had tried to communicate with Vera stunned Lamb. The boy seemed determined that *someone* receive and decipher his message. He immediately wondered if Peter saw Vera as a kind of substitute for Emily Fordham. Had he known that Peter was contacting Vera, he would have counseled her to avoid him as potentially dangerous. Now, though, he had to know what Peter had tried to tell Vera.

"Does the drawing you found disturbing contain a spider?" Lamb asked.

"Yes. How did you know?"

"He's been leaving drawings for me too. They all have spiders, though he's supposed to like butterflies. His guardian, Lord Pembroke, insists that Peter can neither read nor write, but I've come to believe that's not true. I think the boy is more sophisticated than most people realize. I also believe that he knows something about the killings and might himself even be in some danger. Either that, or he himself killed Will Blackwell and Emily Fordham."

Vera looked at her father in disbelief. She thought he sounded like Arthur Lear. "But he's harmless," she protested, defending Peter.

"He's volatile—he hates when his life is thrown into disorder. He apparently believed that Emily Fordham, the girl from Lipscombe, was in love with him. But she had moved on; she'd become pregnant by an RAF pilot from Cloverton airfield. If Peter had found this out somehow, it might have made him jealous."

"But why would he kill Mr. Blackwell?"

"I don't know—and I don't know that he did. But last summer, one of the orphan boys who was staying on Lord Pembroke's estate ran away. Blackwell found the boy on Manscome Hill and returned the boy to Brookings, which seemed to have upset the boy and, apparently, upset Peter."

"What do his drawings mean, then? What is he trying to say?"

"I haven't figured that out yet, though I do believe that they contain some sort of message directed at whoever finds them. Have you managed to speak to him?"

"I tried, but he always ran."

"This other drawing that he gave you—what is it of?"

"A blue butterfly. I came up the hill one day and sat in the grass, hoping to see Peter, and instead I saw exactly *that* butterfly—a blue butterfly with white and black bands at the edges of its wings. He must have seen me watching it, then sketched it. He left the drawing for me to find on the path, I'm sure of it. He wrote a kind of note beneath it, that I don't understand." She spelled the note out for Lamb: *tommss ded.*

Lamb recognized the weird train of letters. Peter had left exactly that message on his drawing of the spider sitting upon the dark oval that Lamb had found beneath the dead tree on the hill behind Peter's summerhouse.

"I think he's trying to say that Thomas is dead," Lamb said.

"But who is Thomas?"

"Thomas is the boy who ran away from Brookings last summer. We found very disturbing evidence connected with him in the home of the man who runs the orphanage in which the boys spend the rest of the year. I think that Thomas also is connected in some way to the killings of Blackwell and the girl from Lipscombe and perhaps even Michael Bradford."

"What kind of evidence?"

"Very disturbing photographs," Lamb said. "That's all I'll say."

"I'm no longer a little girl, dad," Vera said, openly exasperated at her father's unwillingness to speak to her as he would another adult.

Lamb hesitated. He looked at Vera. She was no longer a little girl, that was true—though she still was *his*. That wouldn't change; he couldn't bear that changing. Even so, he had no cause to treat her as a child.

"The photograph showed that the director of the orphanage was abusing Thomas sexually," he said. "Which means the director probably abused other boys as well. They were children, and his prisoners, and could do nothing about it."

Vera was silent for what seemed to Lamb a long time. He wondered what she was thinking. Had she known that adults raped children, conceived of such a grievous offense to God and everything natural and good in the world? Or was *he* the one who was hopelessly naïve?

"Did this man, the orphanage director, kill Thomas, then?" Vera said finally.

"It looks that way. Now the man himself is dead. He seems to have committed suicide. Shot himself in the head."

"That's terrible. So much death. It seems to have infected everything."

They walked for a few minutes in silence. Then Vera asked: "But what can it mean: 'Thomas is dead' written beneath the sketch of a blue butterfly? If you're right about Peter sending messages, then there has to be some significance in the way he joined the two, the drawing and the words."

Lamb stopped. "Hold on," he said. He lightly laid his right hand on Vera's shoulder. "Say that again, please, just as you just said it. The part about Thomas being dead."

"What—'Thomas is dead' beneath the sketch of a blue butterfly?"

"Bloody hell," Lamb said. He'd suddenly become so excited that he hadn't even realized he'd used "bloody" in Vera's presence. His mind was on something else entirely. A shiver ran up his spine. "I was there," he said. "*Right* bloody there."

"What are you talking about, Dad?"

Lamb wasn't yet certain he *was* correct. But light was flooding into corners that until that instant had been dark and hidden from his view. Vera's words had thrown open the curtains. He needed one more point of illumination: motive.

"Can you help me, Vera?"

"Of course." She hadn't the slightest idea what he was talking about.

"Let's get back to your billet and put the kettle on."

Ten minutes later, they were seated at the table in Vera's billet with their tea and the evidence from Lamb's cardboard portfolio spread upon it. He explained each piece to her—where he'd found it and what he believed its significance might be. And he explained for her his newfound belief of why Peter had written the strange message beneath the sketch of the blue butterfly he'd left for her to find. "All that's missing is motive," he said. "A reason for all the killing." For ten minutes, the two of them stared at the black spiders and the tiny, cryptic words, shifted them around the table as if they were puzzle pieces.

Vera picked up the drawing of the spider web spun across the black oval that Peter had dropped on the hill by the tree behind the summerhouse.

"Tell me again what you think this might be," she said.

"I don't know. A hole or void of some kind? I thought it might even represent a grave—perhaps Thomas's grave."

Vera stared at the drawing for several minutes, turning it in her hands and squinting at it. "I wonder if it's supposed to be a knot," she said finally. "The hole, I mean."

"A what?

"A knot—like a knot in a tree. They're oval-shaped, from where the branches have fallen off. I wonder if a spider has spun a web across a knot in a tree that Peter knows. Maybe the spider is real and not meant to represent something else. And maybe the hole also is real."

She laid the drawing next to the note Lamb had found in Will Blackwell's pocket: *in the nut.* "I wonder if that was what the old man was trying to say, too," she said. "Not 'nut,' but 'knot,' and he misspelled it."

Lamb recalled the photo of the tree on Peter's wall—how, on his last visit, he'd found it hanging crookedly on the wall, the only thing out of place in Peter's well-ordered cottage. And he remembered now that Peter had placed the photo between his exhibits of butterflies and spiders, as if between his ideas of safety and ruination. And he had dropped the drawing for Lamb beneath the tree. Lamb wondered how he could have been so dense. The boy had practically sketched him a bloody map.

"My God," he said.

"What is it?"

"I think you're right—I think you're absolutely right. The *tree*. It makes perfect sense. Whatever it is, he's hidden it in the bloody tree. And Thomas is beneath the blue butterfly."

Lamb thought he now knew what Peter had hidden in the tree, and the idea chilled him to the core.

"Which tree?" Vera asked. "And which butterfly?"

"I don't have time to explain," Lamb said. He clasped her shoulders, as if beholding her anew after a long and trying period of separation. "But you're right, Vera. You've done it. I have to go now, but when I see you again, I'll explain everything."

He stood and kissed her on the cheek. "First, though, I must use that official telephone of yours."

TWENTY-SIX

—⚭—

LAMB CALLED THE CONSTABULARY AND INSTRUCTED EVERS, THE
desk sergeant, to track down Wallace and Rivers and to tell them to
meet him as soon as they could at Brookings. They should not go
to the front door but should come around to the back of the house
and head toward the sea.

"There's a summerhouse back there, down a path in a break in the
hedge," Lamb said. "As soon as they can. Have you got that?"

"Right, guv."

Lamb reached Brookings in darkness. He drove slowly up the
drive before pulling off near the place where he had pulled off two
days earlier. He eased the Wolseley a bit deeper into the wood so that
it could not be seen from the drive.

He took a torch from the glove box, stuck it in his belt, and set
out along the same route he'd followed previously, past the east

side of the house and the vegetable gardens, down the hedge and along the cliff edge until he reached the path that led from the lawn to Peter's cottage. He relied on the moon to light his way until he reached the back of the summerhouse and was well out of sight from the main house. The night was warm and unusually muggy and Lamb perspired heavily. The cottage was deserted and dark.

At the top of the hill, the dead tree stood out against the moonlit sky, its long leafless branches reaching out like black, bony fingers. Lamb turned on the torch and headed up the path, the beam bouncing just ahead of him. He reached the base of the tree and played the light on the trunk. Its dry gray bark was scarred, pitted, peeling.

He walked around the tree, playing the torch along its trunk, until he found an oval knot of roughly a foot in diameter at just about the height of his chest. He played the light on the knot; it appeared hollow. He peered into the hole. A brown spider with an abdomen the size of a marble sat motionless at the precise center of a web it had spun across the opening. The mummified husks of a half dozen of its victims formed a dark clump just beneath it.

Lamb destroyed the web with a stick; the spider shot somewhere into the blackness of the hollowed trunk. He reached into the hole and found that he was able to get his entire hand into the opening before his knuckles scraped its innermost side. He moved his hand down, his fingers sinking into soft, coarse, slightly moist detritus a few inches below the knot's bottom rim. He winced, in part from what he feared his hand might land upon. He imagined, lurking within, a swarming, slithering horde of tiny monsters.

Moving his hand to the right, he touched something solid that seemed to be wrapped in cloth. He found that he could get his fingers around what felt like the spine of a book. He lifted it from the hole—the thing was heavy and nearly slipped from his fingers. As he pulled it free of the tree, he saw that it was indeed a book, wrapped in a stained and tattered white cotton pillowcase.

He placed the book on the ground at the base of the tree and carefully removed it from its covering. He played the torch on the leather-bound cover, which was trimmed in gold filigree. The book seemed to be a photo album or, perhaps, one of Peter's sketchbooks. He knelt on one knee and opened the book with his right hand, as he held the torch in his left.

The first page contained a photo of a younger Peter facing the camera, naked, his hands on his hips, standing in the same white cell-like room in which a naked, frightened Thomas stood in the photo he'd found in Pirie's night-table drawer. The photo was glued to the thick, sturdy page. Peter appeared to be no more than nine. Like Thomas's, his eyes brimmed with terror and confusion; like Thomas, he was a prisoner, humiliated, powerless, and afraid.

Lamb's heart flooded with revulsion and fear. The thought of what the book must contain sickened him.

He turned the page and found a photo of a boy he didn't know, posed in an identical fashion, utterly naked and facing the camera, an identical terror in his eyes. This boy also appeared to be about ten. He had dark hair and a small cut on his right cheek.

Lamb forced himself to turn the rest of the pages. They contained photos of nineteen boys, all posed in identical fashion. One of the pages was blank, though it contained a place in its center, spotted with dry glue, from which the photo had been removed. Lamb understood that the page had contained the photo of a naked Thomas he'd found in Pirie's room.

The final page contained a photo of a boy lying on a cot face-down in the frightening white room. He couldn't see the boy's face. But he clearly saw the smiling face of the naked man who sat atop the boy, straddling him, dominating and humiliating him.

It was Sir Jeffrey Pembroke.

Brimming with despair and rage, Lamb closed the book.

He heard the sound of movement behind him.

Then his world turned black.

He awakened in the meadow between the tree and the wood, his head throbbing.

Whoever had struck him had dragged him away from the tree. As he tried to stand, he realized that his wrists were tied behind his back and that his ankles also were bound, with a thin, sturdy rope. He felt the toe of a boot in his right side and heard Pembroke say "Sit up."

Lamb struggled to raise himself into a sitting position. Pembroke stood a few feet away, leveling a .22-caliber pistol at Lamb's face.

"You look ridiculous, Chief Inspector," he said. "Your torch gave you away, you know. I knew that Peter would never muck about down here with a torch. Not very intelligent of you, I must say."

"This is all a waste of time," Lamb said. "I know; Peter knows."

Pembroke smiled. "Yes, but neither of you will live through the night."

"You won't catch Peter. Had you been able to, you'd have done so by now."

"Oh, come now—you're not that dim, Lamb. I couldn't kill Peter without raising your suspicions. But once you are out of the way, I'll have a free hand."

"The others know." He was hoping to stall Pembroke as long as possible. "My men."

Pembroke sneered. "Know what, exactly?" he asked. "And based on what evidence? Peter stole the photo album from me—which, I'll admit, surprised me—and you found it, conveniently enough. I've been looking for it for nearly two weeks. Now it will disappear. Despite what your colleagues might say, I'm quite certain I can convince an inquest that I had nothing to do with any of this. Indeed, I'm in London at the moment with a rather expensive young woman who calls herself Crimson; she's ready to swear to it. The culprit was Peter, you see. Everyone knows that he's volatile and unpredictable. He killed Blackwell because he feared the old man was a witch and Emily because she rejected him. I'll testify that, after Peter sent Emily his strange little note, she came to me to say that she was frightened of what Peter might do to her. You then came snooping around here in search of Blackwell's and Emily's killer and so Peter panicked and killed you. You'll be found with some of his drawings in your pocket. Then Peter will hang himself—from guilt and fear, you see. He feared jail—feared being trapped and cut off from his beloved insects." He smiled. "I'll explain everything. After all, no one knows Peter better than I."

"You killed Thomas," Lamb said. "He resisted you by running away—his defiance frightened and surprised you because none of the others had defied you—and you killed him and Peter knows. Pirie helped you cover up what you'd done with his story about Thomas returning to the orphanage. Blackwell had no idea of the kind of hell he was returning Thomas to."

"A lovely tale, Lamb. But you haven't a scrap of evidence to back it up and you'll soon be dead in any case. As for Gerald Pirie, he shot himself after you found that horrid photo of Thomas in his night-table drawer and discovered that he'd faked the boy's transfer to cover his crimes."

"Donald Fordham knows the truth about you."

Pembroke laughed. "Donald Fordham dislikes me, but otherwise knows nothing. In any case, no one will take his word over mine."

Pembroke waved the pistol in front of Lamb's face. "I'm finished talking," he said. He pulled a small knife from his pocket and cut the ropes binding Lamb's ankles. "Stand up," he ordered.

Lamb got to his feet slowly. He looked for the photo album but didn't see it. Pembroke produced Lamb's torch and turned it on.

"What did you do with the album?" Lamb asked.

"Shut up and turn around." Pembroke pushed Lamb from behind. "Start walking toward the sea. Defy me and I'll kill you."

"Is that what you told Thomas and the rest of them?"

"I said to shut up," Pembroke said evenly.

He put the tip of the pistol's barrel against Lamb's head and said, "Walk. If you speak again, I'll put a bullet into the back of your head."

"Like you did Pirie's?"

Pembroke laughed. "I almost like you, Lamb. You're quite funny, really."

They made their way down the trail to Peter's summerhouse and then around it toward the cliffs. Lamb heard the surf pounding the rocks and smelled the sea. He decided that, if it came to it, he would die fighting; he would not allow Pembroke to push him to his death. He would have one opportunity and would have to pick his moment carefully. First, though, he must throw Pembroke off balance by rattling his poise, making him angry.

"Peter won't listen to you any longer," Lamb said. "He knows what you've done."

Pembroke said nothing. The cliff edge loomed less than ten feet ahead.

"You molested him, like you did the others, believing that he could never reveal your secret. You tired of him eventually, but there were so many others—a steady supply of them. But you never worried about Peter. He was like a loyal dog. But then you killed Thomas and something changed in Peter. *He* also defied you."

"I told you to shut up, Lamb."

"You said that Peter stealing your photo album surprised you, but that hardly describes what you actually felt. It shocked you. In his sudden and unexpected defiance you saw your entire rotting façade crumbling and began to panic. You knew that he might have hidden the album anywhere on the estate. Then you discovered that he'd contacted Emily. So you had to act. But the entire thing has spun out of your control. You control nothing now. Peter is no longer your faithful dog."

Pembroke pushed Lamb violently, causing Lamb to stumble and fall. Lamb managed to twist his body so that he struck the ground on his left shoulder. The rope bit into his wrists.

But Pembroke had pushed Lamb with such force that it caused him also to stumble forward. Lamb saw Pembroke fall to one knee and drop the pistol. Here was his chance.

He scrambled to his knees as Pembroke reached for the pistol. Lamb hurled himself at Pembroke's doubled-over figure; his face hit Pembroke's back and they fell together. Lamb rolled over Pembroke, the ropes biting again into his chafed wrists.

Pembroke pushed Lamb away, then crawled like a spider toward the pistol. He retrieved it as Lamb rolled onto his back. Pembroke got to his feet and stood over Lamb, breathing hard. "Get up," he ordered. He pointed the pistol at Lamb's face.

Lamb got to his feet. He'd had his opportunity and failed. He searched the ground for something he might use as a weapon but could see nothing in the darkness; he fought a rising sense of panic.

"Move," Pembroke said.

Lamb turned slowly toward the cliffs.

"I said move, goddamn you!" Pembroke barked.

Lamb moved to the cliff edge, his back to Pembroke. Below, the foamy surf broke on the rocks and the small beach. He became mildly dizzy and felt his bowels threatening to give way. He felt Pembroke shove something into the right pocket of his jacket. *Peter's drawings.* He heard Pembroke's labored breathing and told himself that his only chance now was to hurl himself again at Pembroke, no matter the consequence.

"Turn around," Pembroke said.

Lamb did as Pembroke ordered. Pembroke stood before him, smiling in triumph. "It's time for you to go away forever, Chief Inspector."

Lamb was on the verge of launching himself at Pembroke, when he caught sight of someone to his left moving quickly through the darkness straight at Pembroke. The figure hit Pembroke a savage blow, knocking him to the ground and sending the pistol spinning from his hand. He saw the figure land atop Pembroke and heard Pembroke yell in pain; he saw the pistol lying only a few feet from him in the grass at the cliff edge. He kicked it over the edge and then turned toward the struggling men just as Pembroke struck the other man. The man yelped and fell away, his long arms and legs flailing.

It was Peter.

Pembroke hefted himself to his feet, facing Peter. Peter stood, slightly crouched.

"It's all right, Peter," Pembroke said in a low voice. "You've made a mistake, haven't you?" He gestured toward Lamb. "You thought I was him and that he was threatening me. He is the one you must fear. He wants to put you in jail for the rest of your life. He believes that you killed Emily and your friend, Will Blackwell. He told me so."

Peter looked at Lamb.

"It's not true, Peter," Lamb said. "You know the truth. You know what he's done. You tried to tell me—and to tell my daughter, Vera, the girl from Quimby. You tried to tell us with your drawings and the photo of the tree and now I know. Thomas is dead beneath the blue butterfly."

Pembroke took a step toward Peter. "He's lying, Peter; he's trying to trick you." He held out his hand to Peter. "You know me. I've always cared for you, given you everything you ever needed."

Peter tensed, as if readying to run.

"He killed Thomas, Peter," Lamb said. "He killed Emily and Will and Mike Bradford's father. You know he did. You *saw* him kill Will. You've done a brave thing in standing up to him. He'll never be able to hurt you or anyone else again. I promise you."

"He wants to put you in jail forever," Pembroke said. "He hates you and wants to hurt you."

Peter glanced at Lamb again, and in that instant Pembroke lunged at Peter, though Peter was quick enough to leap aside. Peter turned toward Pembroke, whose back was to the sea. "Come to me, Peter," Pembroke said, gesturing with his hand. "You and I belong together."

Peter blinked and made a hesitant move in Pembroke's direction.

"He'll kill you, Peter!" Lamb yelled.

Pembroke smiled. "You belong to me, Peter. You always have."

The sound of Harry Rivers's voice calling Lamb's name, barely audible, came from the cliff path. A quintet of torch beams danced down the path like far-off fireflies.

"Come here, Peter!" Pembroke hissed. "Now!"

Peter took another step in Pembroke's direction.

"That's right," Pembroke said.

In the next instant, Peter thrust out his long arms; his hands struck Pembroke's chest, sending Pembroke stumbling backwards, onto his heels. For a second, the top half of Pembroke's body hovered in the space above the crashing surf below. His eyes filled with shock. "No," he cried in disbelief. Then he fell away and disappeared.

Peter stood at the cliff edge and stared down at Lord Jeffrey Pembroke's shattered body lying on the little beach.

He then looked at Lamb, startled.

"It's all right," Lamb said. "Let's step back from the cliff now."

Lamb glanced down at Pembroke's body, which lay like a discarded rag on the sandy spit, a dark stream of blood trickling from his head toward the surf. He had to step back as vertigo threatened to overwhelm him.

Rivers, Wallace, Sergeant Cashen, and two uniformed constables, the beams of their torches bouncing before them, appeared from the direction of Peter's cottage. "Lamb!" Rivers shouted.

"Here!" Lamb said. He looked at Peter, expecting him to run. Instead, Peter abruptly sat on the ground, crossed his legs, and closed his eyes.

The detectives, Cashen, and the constables arrived, panting. Rivers played his torch on Lamb. "Are you hurt?" he asked.

"He's tied my hands."

Rivers pulled a folding knife from the pocket of his jacket and cut the rope binding Lamb's wrists. "What happened?" he asked.

Lamb touched his stinging wrists and grimaced. "Pembroke was going to kill me—push me from the edge." He nodded at Peter. "Peter saved me. There was a struggle and Pembroke fell."

Rivers moved to the cliff edge and looked down.

"He did it—all of it," Lamb said. "I found the evidence in a tree behind Peter's cottage—more photos, like the ones we found in Pirie's drawer. Dozens of them. Peter stole the album and hid it. Pembroke knocked me cold as I was looking at it. I don't know what he did with the damned thing. He probably destroyed it."

"I know," Peter said. He sat cross-legged in the grass, his eyes still closed.

Lamb turned to Peter. "What do you know, Peter?" he asked.

"I know."

"Where the photos are?"

Peter opened his eyes. "I know."

"Will you take us to them?"

Peter stood. He nodded, wrung his hands.

Lamb turned his attention briefly to Cashen and the constables. "Get up to the house and call Harding," he instructed Cashen. "We'll need a sling of some kind and some ropes and ladders and at least a half dozen more people to retrieve the body. We've got to get it before the tide takes it. If anyone at the house tries to impede you, arrest them on my authority."

"Right," Cashen said. He and the constables retreated up the cliff path toward the main house.

"You two stay with me," Lamb said to Rivers and Wallace. He looked at Wallace and smiled. Relief was flooding him and he realized how happy he was to see Wallace and Rivers. "Ready to get your trousers dirty, David?" he asked.

"As dirty as it takes," Wallace said.

"Good."

He turned back to Peter. "May we go now, Peter?"

Peter abruptly stood and began to walk in the direction of the cottage. Lamb, Rivers, and Wallace followed him past the house, up the hill and past the scarred tree, into the meadow just beyond it, and thence into the dark wood on the other side. They moved along a narrow path that led into the heart of the wood. Peter walked just ahead of them, a singular purpose in his stride. He seemed to know every rut, protruding root, hole, and fallen branch in the trail. They moved for perhaps fifty meters before Peter turned off the trail to the right and stopped in front of the fallen trunk of a red cedar. Rivers played his torch on the trunk. It lay half buried in the detritus of the forest floor and was spotted with a white fungus that grew from it like ears.

"Is it under the tree?" Lamb asked Peter.

Peter nodded. "I saw him."

"You saw him bury the book beneath the tree?"

"I saw him." He stood as if at attention and wrung his hands again.

"Help me lift it," Lamb said to Rivers. They bent together and lifted the trunk near its center. Pieces of the dead tree came apart in their hands. Rivers shone his torch on the loam beneath the trunk. It was mounded slightly, like a small, freshly covered grave.

Lamb knelt next to the mound and began to dig into it with his hands. He moved away a foot of the rich, dark soil before he saw the dirtied pillowcase. He dug around the edges of the album and lifted it out.

Lamb stood and handed the album to Rivers. He turned to Peter, who continued standing by them like a sentry.

"Now, Peter," Lamb said. "I saw the drawing you left for me and the one you gave my daughter, Vera, in Quimby. I know that Thomas is buried beneath the blue butterfly in Lord Pembroke's garden."

TWENTY-SEVEN

—m—

THEY LIFTED PEMBROKE'S SHATTERED BODY FROM THE BEACH
below the cliffs and, on the following day, dug up the round stone
terrace in his Alice-in-Wonderland garden and the beautiful blue
mosaic butterfly at its center. Beneath it they found the decayed
remains of Thomas Bennett wrapped in a dirty white sheet.

That same day, Lamb sat with Peter at the drawing table in Peter's
cottage and attempted to tease from him the story of how he had come
to steal Pembroke's photo album. Peter scribbled a few drawings and
words on paper but did not speak, and Lamb had found himself unable
to fully decipher what Peter was trying to say, though he believed he
understood the story's rough outline.

Then he thought of Vera.

He fetched her and brought her with him to the cottage. A change
came over Peter almost immediately. He smiled when he saw Vera.
Lamb again thought of Emily Fordham—how she must have sat with

271

Peter, talking with him, paying him attention. Peter began to sketch furiously for Vera and spoke to her with a coherence and fluency that Lamb had not believed he possessed.

"Did the planes hurt you?" Peter asked.

"No," Vera said.

"The boy hurt you."

Vera reddened slightly and looked at her father, who couldn't help but register surprise at what Peter had said. *Which boy? Arthur? And how had he hurt Vera? Or was Peter mistaken?* But now was not the time in which to seek an answer to those questions from Vera. He would ask later. And he hoped that she would tell him.

"No," Vera said. "I'm all right, Peter."

Over the next two hours, Peter told Vera and Lamb, in a matter-of-fact fashion, a tale of horror, abuse, humiliation, and fear. He managed to get across to them that Emily Fordham had taken the photo of the tree and given it to him as a present. When he finished, Peter smiled at Vera. Lamb wondered how well Peter understood the connection between his stealing of Pembroke's photo album and the killings that followed it—that his standing up to Pembroke had led to Pembroke's murder spree. He moved next to Peter and said, quietly, "Nothing is your fault. Do you understand that, Peter?"

Although Peter nodded, Lamb wasn't certain he understood.

Later in the day, Lamb related the story to Harding, Wallace, Rivers, and Larkin.

When Peter had first come to Brookings, Pembroke had molested and photographed him, as he did the others. Pembroke had told Pirie that he admired Peter's talent and believed it needed nurturing and so Pirie had agreed to let Pembroke take possession of Peter. At the time, it was possible that Pirie did not know of Pembroke's perversions, though he eventually did learn of them, Lamb said.

Even after Pembroke tired of Peter, he continued to force Peter to look at his book of photographs each time he added to it.

"He controlled Peter in that way," Lamb said, adding that Pembroke had kept the album in plain view on a shelf in his library. "Pembroke also kept a photo album for public consumption that contained head shots of all the boys who had visited Brookings, along with photos of their visits, some of which were taken last summer, innocently enough, by Emily Fordham. Peter knew about that album also and took from it the photo of Thomas he sent to Emily.

"When Thomas ran away, Peter suspected that Pembroke had hurt him in some way. Then Blackwell found Thomas on Manscome Hill and handed him back to Pembroke, who killed the boy to keep him quiet. On the night following Thomas's return to Brookings, Peter watched the main house, certain that Pembroke would *do* something; he knew Pembroke as well as Pembroke knew him—a fact that Pembroke, in his narcissism and arrogance, didn't fathom. And sure enough, Peter saw Pembroke bury Thomas in the butterfly garden. A few days later, workers came and built the terrace and the tile mosaic of the blue butterfly over Thomas's grave. Pembroke told everyone else connected with Brookings that Thomas had gone back to the orphanage, a lie that Pirie agreed to help him keep, apparently for the basest of motives: money. Also, Pembroke obviously had removed the photograph of Thomas standing naked in front of the sheet from the album *before* Peter stole the album. My only guess is that Pembroke must have decided sometime earlier, perhaps last summer, after he killed Thomas, that he might need to use the photo to throw suspicion on Pirie, which, of course, he eventually did.

"For nearly a year, Peter said nothing about what he knew. He feared Pembroke. But then, when the boys failed to return this year, something in him changed and he decided upon the idea of stealing Pembroke's album and writing to Emily about his concerns. He felt he must do something; felt morally responsible, if you will. He told Blackwell about the album and where he'd hidden it and Blackwell made a note to himself about the location, which we found in his pocket. Peter intended to show the album to Emily, but she never contacted him. Instead, she took her concerns to Pembroke, whom she trusted. That mistake proved to be fatal. Although Emily might never have known of the existence of Pembroke's photo album, Pembroke believed he could take no chances with her. Peter obviously was trying very hard to communicate with her, and he worried that Peter might eventually get his message across. He had to kill everyone who knew—or might come to know—of the photos, including, eventually, Peter himself. But as he told me, he could not kill Peter outright without casting suspicion on himself. He counted on Peter staying quiet thanks to his fear of strangers, and he was mostly right in that. Peter refused to speak to me or to Vera, though he did leave us the drawings as a kind of substitute. In the end, though, Peter finally found the courage within himself to act when he saw Pembroke and me by the cliff. Pembroke intended to hang Peter and make it appear that Peter had committed suicide out of guilt for committing the other killings and fear that he would spend the rest of his life in jail. Although Pirie conspired with Pembroke in covering up Thomas's death, once we began to get close, Pembroke decided that Pirie also had to go."

Lamb had checked Pirie's and Pembroke's bank accounts and discovered that Pembroke had paid Pirie nearly ten thousand pounds over the past three years. "After he spoke to me, Mike Bradford told his father—probably under the threat of violence—that the man he'd actually seen on the hill shortly before Blackwell's murder was Pembroke and not Peter, as Mike had told me. Stupidly, Bradford attempted to blackmail Pembroke and so Pembroke killed him too. I believe that he and Pembroke met at the mill yard after dark to discuss the matter and that Pembroke brought along a bottle of gin, waited for Bradford to become drunk, then killed him and shoved his body into the race." Lamb paused, then said, "Bradford would probably still be alive had I not managed to get his son to tell me that he'd seen a man on Manscome Hill on the day Blackwell was killed.

"I also put Peter's life in danger by showing the drawings he left for me to Pembroke, who realized that Peter was becoming more aggressive in trying to communicate with Emily and with me than he'd known or imagined."

"How did Pembroke know that the boy had told Blackwell about the photos?" Harding asked.

"He might not have known for certain that Peter had confided in Blackwell, but he knew that Peter communicated with Blackwell—that he felt comfortable with Blackwell—and therefore could take no chances. He might also have been worried that Thomas had said something to Blackwell about the abuse, which is why, I believe, he gave Blackwell the one hundred seventy-five pounds. He hoped that Blackwell would take the money and keep his mouth shut, which Blackwell did. But after Peter stole the photo album, Pembroke decided that Blackwell had to be silenced for good and all. So he killed him in a way that he hoped would lead us down the wrong path."

"And the altar and slaughtered chicken?"

"Something Pembroke added after killing Blackwell, for good measure," Lamb said. "Peter obviously was watching Pembroke more closely then Pembroke knew. And so after Pembroke left the slaughtered chicken in the shed, Peter entered the shed and left the drawing of the spider and the bird by the altar. Of Lord Jeffrey Pembroke and Will Blackwell."

Harding shook his head. "Mad," he said.

—m—

Two days later, Lamb stood atop Manscome Hill looking over the valley in which Quimby nestled. *The Valley of Death*, he thought.

He'd returned *Myths and Legends of the Supernatural in Hampshire* to Harris, told Harris to thank his wife again for loaning him the book, and thanked Harris for his work. "All's well that ends well, as they say, sir," Harris had said, rising on his toes a bit with his hands behind his back. Lamb thought that Harris might one day rise to a high rank in the police services—that is, if the war didn't take him.

He'd thought of looking in on Vera, but decided not to trouble her while she was on duty. He and Marjorie would surprise her on Saturday with a bottle of wine and a beef sausage and a loaf of decent white bread. Maybe then the three of them would discuss "the boy"—Arthur Lear. But that would be Vera's choice.

He descended the hill to the village, passing the bomb crater in Abbott's meadow, where the sheep had grazed. As he walked beneath the ancient, barren-branched sycamore by the bridge over Mills Run, the crows that roosted in the tree set up a racket. Lamb looked up at them. They were well fed, their plumage shiny.

"You lot go to hell," he said.

He looked forward to an easy afternoon. He'd buy a racing form and maybe place a bet on one of the following day's races at Paulsgrove. He'd still yet to buy a new tin of butterscotch. He took the cigarette he was smoking and dropped it into the moist mud of the path and willed himself not to light another.

At that moment, more than a hundred German bombers were forming up over Calais preparing to fly up the Thames estuary for the first daylight raid on London. Hermann Seitz's remains lay among the ash of the Lears' farmhouse, along with those of Arthur and Noel Lear.

—⁂—

When Lamb reached Will Blackwell's cottage, he found Rivers leaning against his Wolseley, waiting for him.

"Harding wants us in Portsmouth," Rivers said. "The head of a freight warehouse down there called this morning to report the theft of a hundred cases of overcoats meant for frontline troops. American-made. Someone stole them right off the bloody boat in the night."

"How did you know I was here?" he asked Rivers.

"Guessed."

Lamb smiled slightly. "Well, you were right then, weren't you?"

Rivers lifted his chin. "I suppose so," he said.

ACKNOWLEDGMENTS

—ᴍᴍ—

I COULDN'T HAVE WRITTEN THIS BOOK WITHOUT THE ASSISTANCE and guidance of many people, chief among them my beautiful and loving wife, Cindy, who has supported me without complaint or qualification in everything, and my generous best friend of many decades, Bryan Denson, the first person who ever told me that my wanting to be a writer wasn't a stupid idea. For their help along the way, I also owe a debt of gratitude to: Maria Archangelo, Avi Azrieli, Lloyd Batzler, Carrie Brown, John Gregory Brown, Elizabeth Eck, Mark Hertsgaard, the late David Kelly, Michael Kelly, Paul Milton, Jean Moon, Dave Stewart, Karen Webster, and Ken Weiss.